G000141853

$14
CASH
ONLY

LAST HORSE STANDING

ALSO BY MIKE KEENAN

The Horses Too Are Gone

Wild Horses Don't Swim

In Search of A Wild Brumby

LAST HORSE STANDING

MIKE KEENAN

BANTAM
SYDNEY AUCKLAND TORONTO NEW YORK LONDON

Author's note: Some names have been changed to protect the privacy of individuals.

LAST HORSE STANDING
A BANTAM BOOK

First published in Australia and New Zealand in 2006
by Bantam

Copyright © Michael Keenan, 2006

All rights reserved. No part of this publication may be reproduced, stored in a retrieval system, transmitted in any form or by any means, electronic, mechanical, photocopying, recording or otherwise, without the prior written permission of the publisher.

National Library of Australia
Cataloguing-in-Publication Entry

Keenan, Michael, 1943–.
    Last horse standing.

    ISBN 978 1 86325 579 0.

    ISBN 1 86325 579 6.

    1. Wilderness survival – Western Australia – Kimberley –
    Biography. 2. Droving – Western Australia – Kimberley –
    Biography. 3. Cattle trade – Western Australia – Kimberley
    – Biography. 4. Kimberley (W.A.) – Biography. I. Title.

919.414

Transworld Publishers,
a division of Random House Australia Pty Ltd
Level 3, 100 Pacific Highway, North Sydney, NSW 2060
http://www.randomhouse.com.au

Random House New Zealand Limited
18 Poland Road, Glenfield, Auckland

Transworld Publishers,
a division of The Random House Group Ltd
61–63 Uxbridge Road, Ealing, London W5 5SA

Random House Inc
1745 Broadway, New York, New York 10036

Typeset by Midland Typesetters, Australia
Printed and bound by The SOS Print + Media Group

10

I wish to dedicate *Last Horse Standing* to Peter Wann, his wife Ngaire and their two daughters Jenna and Kayla.

CONTENTS

SUMMARY OF REPORTS IN *THE WEST AUSTRALIAN*, MARCH 1971

An intense tropical rain depression crossed the west Kimberley coast on 22 March. The Fitzroy River had a sudden and spectacular rise, recording thirty-seven feet at Fitzroy Crossing one day later. All roads in the district were cut and the river village was caught with little food. The airstrip was closed and a further five inches of rain fell on 24 March.

On 26 March the bureau of meteorology at Perth issued a warning that Cyclone Mavis had formed, was 300 miles wide and, due to high sea temperatures (80°F), it would probably intensify to a category two or three. The cyclone moved off the coast and appeared to be heading away from the main-

land, but on 27 March it suddenly altered course and struck the coast at Hamelin Pool, a long way south for a tropical cyclone. On 29 March some of the heaviest rain in memory fell across large areas of Western Australia, washing away rail lines and bridges. A day later heavy stock losses were reported and food was airdropped to stranded motorists. At Shark Bay, boats broke their moorings and a major sea swell damaged the town.

In the archives of the Perth Weather Bureau, Cyclone Mavis is described as one of the longest-running cyclones in Western Australian history.

Overview of the West Kimberley coast and adjacent inland region.

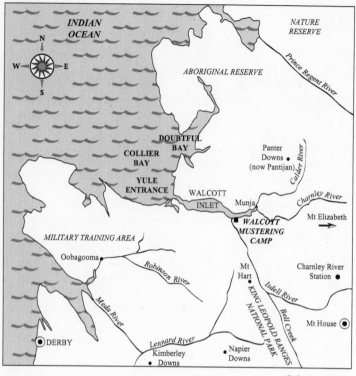

Scale: 1 cm to 15 km

Route taken by Jack Camp in 1971, from Oobagooma to Panter Downs.

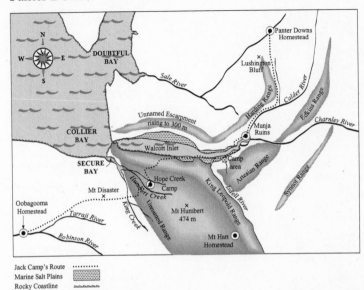

Jack Camp's Route ....
Marine Salt Plains ▦▦▦
Rocky Coastline ⌒⌒⌒

The eastern tip of Walcott Inlet from Mt Talbot to the old Munja Reserve.

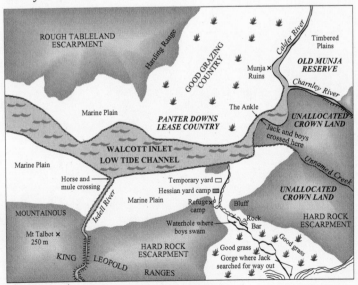

Mangrove bank ⌒⌒⌒
Vertical drop to water ⊔⊔⊔⊔⊔

FOREWORD

I FIRST HEARD about Jack Camp's amazing story at Beagle Bay in October 2002. Nearly everyone who visits Broome for a holiday gets to hear about the Catholic church at Beagle Bay, built by priests from the German Palatine Order in 1918. This exquisitely beautiful church has no equal in out-back Australia. Under the guidance of the priests, Aborigines made the mud bricks for the new church and collected the tens of thousands of seashells used in its decoration. They were from the language groups of the Jabirryabirr, Nyulnyul and, to the north, the Bardi people. My first connection to this story was Bardi man, Otto Dibley. Although not in the traditional land of his people, Otto settled in Beagle Bay before he died in the late 1980s.

Otto's name tumbled out from desultory conversation with a local Elder. My wife and I had visited the church, Sal had taken some photos and we were about to drive the 130 kilometres back to Broome. I have never been shy to talk to strangers and over a mug of tea from a thermos I asked the

Elder if his people worked the surrounding country with cattle. He was seated on the ground, leaning against the trunk of a tree. The only shop was nearby and the local people loved to sit around and yarn. The Elder had been talking to a couple of women while he waited for his wife who was in the store. Despite his age, he was handsome with long grey hair and a slightly Malay appearance.

He didn't answer me directly. When he launched straight into the past I knew the cattle days were long gone. He told us he was reared at the mission and later got a job as a deckhand on the *Watt Leggit*, a lugger that operated out of Derby carrying supplies to remote settlements on the west Kimberley coast and returning with lepers destined for the leprosarium. Leprosy is a disease obscure in Australian frontier history and I asked him where the worst affected area was.

'The Munja community at Walcott Inlet,' he replied. 'The police patrols brought in the sick and locked them up in a big compound, to await the lugger.'

I mentioned having heard Walcott Inlet had spectacular scenery and that I was hoping to go there some day soon.

His eyes narrowed – to him, I was just another tourist who knew nothing about the dark decades of the Kimberleys, that part of the history either lost or destroyed. Walcott Inlet had been the meeting place for the tribes. Now there was no one there, not a living soul.

'In my time,' he said, 'Walcott was the destination for the sick. The women there had no young, and crocodiles took more men there than anywhere else on the coast. I suppose we blackfellas would call it the land of the devil devil,' he shrugged and smiled. 'It's nonsense I know, but it became that sort of place. I had a good friend called Otto Dibley. He's gone now, but he had this story about a white man and his boys caught in a willy willy at Walcott. Otto left them before the big storm to get more supplies, they were branding cattle. He got caught too and for a month battled flooded rivers, no food, and when he got to a place called Oobagooma a white lady gave him food and spare horses to rescue those white people. But a white man pulled a gun on him and stopped him. Otto never made it back.'

Curious, I asked what happened to the white man and his boys. The Elder shook his head and seemed irritated he couldn't relate the conclusion of the story.

'I expect the eagles cleaned up their bones,' he said at last. 'Otto returned home after a brief stint at the killin works and never left the peninsula again.' He paused and looked towards his wife, who was approaching with a hessian bag of groceries. 'We got our own station up and running, not far from here. Otto could lasso and throw anything. No white man could near match him.'

The story had a touch of the real Australian frontier about it that intrigued me. The incident would have to have taken place in the 1960s or '70s, I calculated. But I wasn't surprised – so many parts of Australia were still frontier territory even so late in the twentieth century. My own experience in Queensland in the drought of '94 (told in *The Horses Too Are Gone*) comes to mind.

Broome and Derby had become an annual holiday destination for me. So when I returned in 2003 I made a few enquiries also in Derby. Most people over fifty vaguely recalled a story about a stockman lost after a cyclone. One Aboriginal Elder knew a little more than most.

'Yeah, that was Jack Camp,' he said. 'He cleaned up the country where no one else could. They called him a wet season man.'

When I tossed in Otto Dibley's name I detected a slight reticence. Over more than one hundred years the Aboriginal people of the west Kimberley have learned to think long and hard before speaking frankly with a white stranger.

'He was from One Arm Point, just north of here near Cape Leveque. Became a fighter in the show tents.'

I pressed for more, asking whether it was true Otto had been forced to turn back at the point of a gun when he rode out to rescue his white employer and friend.

The Elder looked at the ground for a while. There was no way of knowing what was going through his mind. He could have been struggling to recall anything, but my old sixth sense told me he knew it all. It all came down to who was still alive and old extended friendships.

'Otto had a son called Ralph. They both went out with Jack Camp. I haven't seen or heard of Ralph for a long time.' He looked up at me, his eyes screwed against the sun. 'Haven't been east of Derby for twenty years either and when I go to the town I stay with my own people. Perhaps Camp and those boys did make it out. I don't know.'

In 2004 I pursued the story again. I was too late too meet Jack Camp – he died in 2000 at Kununurra – but one of his sons lived at Wyndham. George had suffered a tragic horse fall in the late 1970s and complications had overwhelmed him. Over a cup of tea he could yarn along like anyone else, but he readily admitted that he had lost much of his memory. He had gone to Walcott Inlet with his dad in 1971, he told me. There was a great flood, he recalled. Cattle and horses were sucked down in blue mud and they ate rotten meat.

One year older than George, Peter Camp was Jack's oldest son. He owned Charnley River Station off the Gibb River road and I went out there to see him. He was proud of his father as a rugged bushman and I felt that Peter attributed his own success in life to his father's training. He was out riding alongside Jack when other boys were starting school. Right from the beginning, however, I sensed his uneasiness about how this story might be presented. My own family has had some dramatic ups and downs on the land in the past thirty years, making me very sympathetic to the need of families to retain a sense of dignity, irrespective of events outside human control, and I assured him that I would deal with his father's story honestly and with respect. But he remained cautious and there was no further contact.

But just who was Jack Camp? From many sources I managed to put together a picture of this reticent bush man.

At forty-four, Jack Camp had experienced more than his share of misfortune. In the late 1950s his father acquired Robinson River station: in the Northern Territory, not far from the Queensland border. He put Jack on to manage it and the intention was for Jack to own the property, but busy men in the outback sometimes don't get around to attending to legal documents. Jack's father died suddenly and the whole estate was registered in Queensland. The looming death duties were bad enough, then a few months later Jack's mother died. She was the sole beneficiary of the estate. The second probate on the family's assets almost wiped out the whole pastoral enterprise. Robinson River had to be sold.

Undaunted, Jack walked his station horse plant from the Gulf to the west Kimberley, to take up a position on Ooba-gooma, then owned by Dr Lawson Holman. First selected in 1887, it was abandoned to the Crown in 1935. Striated by numerous streams and intersecting divides, it was once described as a nightmare station to manage. After the Second World War more optimists arrived to try their hand, but soon departed. It was a wilderness deemed never to be tamed. Encouraged by a buoyant cattle market, Dr Holman acquired the station in 1959. He was the flying doctor for the west Kimberley region and on his rare days off loved going out from Derby to see how the men were getting on. A notable bush character, he became something of a legend in his own lifetime. On one occasion he stood his ground, facing a full-on charge from a huge wild bull, coolly waiting and squeezing the trigger when the animal was within ten yards.

Some staunch men pitted their wits against this land, but all were defeated by nature's extremes. Holman grew more and more frustrated with the station's inability to produce profits and offered Jack Camp a fifty per cent share of the profits to reverse the trend in the ledger. But even the inde-fatigable Jack Camp was powerless against seasonal extremes, reluctant staff and rapacious cattle ticks. The whole industry was in transition. Aboriginal stockmen had always been the backbone of the industry and when they were granted equal pay in 1968 many of the stations floundered, unable to meet the new wage regime and remain viable. In 1968 Dr Holman sold Oobagooma and the new owner installed his own manager from another property. His name was Hilton Walker.

Oobagooma had been Jack Camp's home for four years. To be uprooted again was another bitter disappointment. His horse plant was his sole asset and without a word uttered to anyone outside the family, Jack walked his horses out to Humbert Creek. In the shadow of the King Leopolds, Humbert Creek was a piece of no man's territory. It lay within the boundary of Oobagooma, but so isolated by ranges, rivers and distance, it was never a proposition to muster.

Slowly an association developed between Jack and Walker. No lover of the rugged tropical bush, Walker was more adept in an office wielding authority than taking charge of mustering camps. He could use a man like Jack Camp and did. Both he and Jack had personal ambitions: each hoped to one day acquire a station of his own. Walker wasn't employed on just a salary, for few men would endure the privations and loneliness on the remote, hard-to-manage stations. Good operators demanded a share of the profits as an incentive so he had a stake in the business. It was all about deals. There were plenty of cattle and the prices at the meatworks were good. Anyone who could pull off a big muster got enough out of it to put down a deposit on a cattle station. Tough stockmen like Jack Camp saw an opportunity and would ride to hell and back to get that deposit. Walker knew Jack could round up the cleanskins in the far-flung pockets of unoccupied lease country bordering the King Leopold Ranges. So in March 1971 Hilton Walker and Jack Camp made a mob-splitting deal. Jack would get the cattle and Walker would provide the legal access. Utterly different in both temperament and nature, they were not good friends.

There was one more survivor to talk to. A lifelong resident of Derby, Sylvia Wann, told me where to find her nephew Peter Wann. She had been like a second mother to Peter and recalled the anxiety: 'It was the talk of the district. People feared the worst.'

Peter Wann worked for Rio Tinto at Karratha, about 1000 kilometres south of his home town of Derby. He was a little man with a beard and bright blue eyes. Spontaneous warmth emanated from him from the first handshake. He worked twelve-hour shifts in the mine and on his days off put the same effort into his fishing forays among the Dampier Islands. 'I've said for thirty years this story should have been written!' Peter exclaimed when I first posed the possibility of a book. 'I've never had time. If I'm not workin, I'm fishin.'

Peter was so enthusiastic I suggested that I should tell the story in his voice, and Peter readily agreed to tell me as much as he could remember of the mustering trip with Jack Camp, his sons, and Otto and Ralph Dibley that went so horribly wrong. To refresh and stimulate his memory I suggested a helicopter flight from Derby to the area concerned. Peter was quite ecstatic about the prospect of going back after so long. The terrible memories had faded like a childhood nightmare and, secure in the knowledge he would never have to endure such privation again, he said he would love to see the country once more.

So in order to write this book I have drawn upon Peter Wann's recollections, which at the time of writing were thirty-four years old. In most cases, it was impossible for Peter to recall exact conversations for me after so long. However, some Peter did indeed recall word for word. Where it proved necessary, dialogue is based on my knowledge of the people involved, the complexities of the issues, the scene at the time and the impending dangers or problems.

In addition, sometimes a paucity of detail in Peter's memory of certain places and events made it necessary for me to imaginatively fill the gaps, but in each case I worked within the rigid sequence of events related to me by Peter. With authenticity at the core of my mission, I made three separate trips into the wilds of the west Kimberley to thoroughly research the detail of this story.

A writer must examine his or her conscience when pursuing a story that some of those still living may wish to be left alone, buried in lost memories. But in a troubled world, it is my belief that every piece of inspiration should be recorded. Every day, somewhere on the globe someone will be facing a crisis – whether it be manmade, like war, or caused by the unpredictability of Mother Nature's tsunamis, cyclones, floods, droughts and other catastrophes, it is the way individuals deal with it that may inspire others to tackle adversity with courage and dignity. That's why I've persisted with this nearly forgotten story of human struggle against the fury of nature.

Routes taken by 19th and 20th century explorers in the Prince Regent and Walcott Inlet region

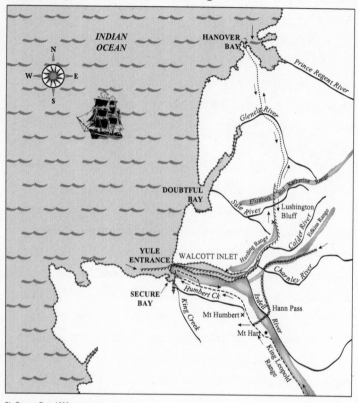

Sir George Grey 1838 ....

Alexander Forrest 1879 --------

Frank Hann 1898 ×××××××××××

Frederick Brockman 1901 ⁄⁄⁄⁄⁄⁄⁄⁄

PROLOGUE

THE FIRST
EUROPEANS

*(A brief historical account of the region where this
story takes place)*

WALCOTT INLET AND the associated river valleys is a unique
area in the Kimberley region. It's hot, inaccessible and uninhabited. The area within the story comprises four major
streams: the Isdell, Charnley, Calder and Sale. Only the Sale
River doesn't flow into Walcott Inlet. The whole drainage
basin is approximately 20,000 square kilometres.

In the dry season a few Aboriginal people from Derby
visit Pantijan (formerly Panter Downs Station) and many stay
for a few weeks to hunt and fish along the Sale River. A
couple of rugged tour operators also manage to negotiate the
water-gouged track from Mount Elizabeth Station to the old
Munja ruin.

A mere eighty-five years ago, the region provided thousands of Aboriginal people with a healthy, vibrant lifestyle.
Following their rapid demise there was a brief period of
frontier settlement, lasting thirty years.

The first recorded exploration was by Sir George Grey in

1838, slightly to the north of the Walcott drainage basin. He was instructed by the British Government to explore the country south of the Prince Regent River. The original proposal submitted by George Grey himself was to explore tropical Western Australia. Grey had served with the British Army in Ireland and was appalled at the poverty there. He wrote to the Colonial Office and the Royal Geographical Society, advocating the merits of creating a colony in Western Australia's tropical north. Grey was related to Lord Glenelg who had considerable influence in the British Parliament.

After chartering a schooner in Cape Town, South Africa, Grey's first attempt at exploration nearly ended in disaster. Upon anchoring in Hanover Bay about seventy-five miles north of Walcott Inlet, a reconnaissance party headed by Grey became lost and ran out of water. It was in December, possibly the worst month to walk anywhere in the Kimberleys. As he returned to the schooner, Grey was caught in a tidal outflow and had to be rescued by rowing boat. Now appreciating the enormity of the task he had set himself and his men, Grey sent the schooner to Timor under the command of Lieutenant Lushington to buy twenty-six pack ponies. Grey himself remained behind with most of the expedition party to undertake further reconnaissance and try to acclimatise to the exhausting humidity and high temperatures.

Impatient to set off, Grey left a couple of days after Lushington's return, on 29 January 1838. While Lushington had been in Timor, the Kimberley wet had arrived and swamped the landscape. The rivers were in flood and Grey was forced to search for trails in the rugged tableland country.

In every direction the expedition was faced with impassable ravines, sweeping, endless lines of cliff and steep, boulder-strewn slopes. Several ponies were lost just in the first week and the men were forced to carry much of the gear in stifling humidity and heat. The expedition ground to a halt when Grey rode ahead with two companions to search for a trail. They were surrounded by hostile tribesmen and Grey was speared.

Stubborn and mindful of the mission the British Government had entrusted him with, Grey struggled on for two days before collapsing from exhaustion. The spear had penetrated deeply into his hip and he lay immovable in a tent for two weeks.

But Grey lost none of his enthusiasm for the area. While recovering from the spear wound, he wrote, 'I have traversed large portions of Australia, but have seen no land, no scenery to equal it. I could not but feel we were in a land singularly favoured by nature.'

The expedition pushed south and, although there is no written record, Grey may have reached the Sale River. A prominent bluff attached to the northern end of the Harding Range, south of the Sale River, was named Lushington Bluff by Grey, after his deputy. Grey's diary and general records indicate the expedition got no further than the Glenelg River, but Lushington Bluff cannot be seen from that far north. Grey had become very ill and may not have recorded much after the spear injury. Finally returning to Perth, Grey reported to the Colonial Secretary that the country was suitable for mass immigration from Britain. He had never seen the Kimberley in the dry season and had no accurate concept of the land and the climate.

There appears to be no further reference to the region until 1865, when a private explorer, Duncan McRae, led a foot party east from Collier Bay to the area now known as Pantijan. They trekked inland for thirty-eight miles. According to a newspaper of the time, the *Enquirer*, McRae reported that 200,000 acres was suitable for agriculture. In the same year McRae discovered Walcott Inlet, referring to it as the Walcott River, a 'fine navigable river eighty miles south of Camden Harbour'. Although there's no direct reference, a Walcott was captain of the cutter engaged by McRae.

The next attempt to explore the region was undertaken by Alexander Forrest in 1879. The expedition was sanctioned and financed by Sir H. G. Ord, Governor of Western Australia. Forrest lacked nothing in terms of experienced men and provisions, yet the expedition nearly perished just south of Walcott Inlet. A member of the expedition wrote in his diary: 'For the past ten days we were battered about, making road bridges and passes through some of the roughest country horses ever travelled. Several horses were lost and half the party became ill.'

Forrest was forced into a humiliating retreat from the King Leopold Range (as he named the range), by the constant harassment from warriors of the Umiida tribe, a shortage of water and the unbroken cliff lines. (For an account of Forrest's bitter struggle to try and cross the Leopolds, see Appendix 1.)

Towards the turn of the century the whole of the tableland country north of the King Leopold Range had earned a

formidable reputation among the pioneers on
watersheds. They simply referred to it as 'ove
unexplored and occupied by hostile tribes. The most intrepid
pioneer explorer in Western Australia was Frank Hann. In
August 1898 Hann crossed the King Leopolds about one
hundred miles east of Walcott Inlet in search of cattle country. Delighted with the grazing land he saw along the Adcock
River he hastened to Derby to apply for a lease. He knew
other pastoralists were also dreaming about land over the
range and, fearful someone might apply for a lease ahead of
him, he opted to look for a short cut to Derby. With his
horses, mules and little band of loyal Aborigines, he planned
to cross the Edkins Range to the east of Walcott Inlet and
search for a route over the King Leopolds where no one had
yet crossed. A superb bushman (and with Aboriginal help),
Hann doesn't appear to have had any great difficulty in crossing the range about thirty miles south of the inlet, not far
from the present day Mount Hart homestead. He called it
Hann Pass and today it is marked on all maps.

Frank Hann had conquered the mountain barrier which
had frustrated explorers and pioneers for decades. Only the
far western arm of the King Leopolds, a distance of approximately sixty-nine miles from Hann Pass to Secure Bay,
remained impenetrable. By this time Walcott Inlet had
already been explored by boats passing through the tricky
Yule Entrance.

In 1901 Fredereck Brockman and naturalist Dr F. M.
House sailed into Walcott Inlet and discovered the Calder
River at the far eastern end of the inlet. They trekked northeast

along the river, crossed the Harding Range into the Sale River watershed and went as far north as the Glenelg River. Dr House noted the presence of unique Aboriginal art in the area. These paintings became known as the Bradshaw figures. It appears this modest expedition was the first to overlap Sir George Grey's 1838 expedition.

The first white man to attempt to settle on the Walcott shores was Jack Eastman just after World War I. There was no known track out to the south and eighty years on there still isn't. The Artesian Range, although low and insignificant when observed from the air, is impassible. Eastman arrived with his provisions by boat and purchased a mob of cattle from Nulla Nulla Station near Wyndham, delivered by drover Billy Hay. Both men were soon to die. Hay was speared on the Durack River in 1925 and Eastman was taken by a crocodile. After Eastman's death, the pastoral lease lapsed.

By the 1920s, the coastal tribes had widespread contact with foreigners. The pearl fleets needed Aboriginal deckhands and blackbirding along the coast was not uncommon. Leprosy spread from these swashbuckling fleets and by the late 1920s the disease was endemic in the Aboriginal population of the west Kimberley. At Walcott Inlet the government established a ration station and a receiving depot for leprosy victims. It was called Munja, the Aboriginal word for 'Meeting place of the tribes'. In 1927 Harold Reid was made manager and a homestead and outbuildings were erected.

The only contact between Munja and the outside world was the lugger from the Port George Mission, which anchored off Munja once a month in the dry season, June to

December, to collect the peanuts the Aborigines grew under Reid's supervision, as well as any leprosy cases bound for Derby for medical treatment. In those days, cyclones and weather extremes of any sort could not be forecast, which meant that the lugger remained at Port George throughout the wet season, January to May.

In 1933, the writer Ion Idriess rode out from Derby with a mounted police patrol. They left Derby on the tail of the wet season, when there was plenty of surface water and ample fresh grass for the saddle horses and the pack mules. The mounted police track to Walcott Inlet was the same one that the packhorse mailmen used. They passed over Hann Pass on the King Leopolds, rode southwest for thirty miles to cross the Precipice Range and then sixty-two miles straight north to the headwaters of the Charnley River. With no route possible down the Charnley they crossed the Edkins Range and followed the Calder to Munja. Idriess concluded it was one of the most isolated locations in Australia. Fifty-four years after explorer Alexander Forrest, no one yet had found a way into Walcott Inlet from the south.

In his book *Over the Range*, Idriess devoted a whole chapter to Walcott Inlet. He recorded it to be the best agricultural land he saw during the patrol, which trekked as far north as the Prince Edward River in the northern Kimberley. The Munja community was almost self-sufficient with an abundant water supply from a nearby wetland. The Aborigines grew vegetables, bananas, passionfruit, pineapples, mangoes and African beans.

Idriess also made special reference to the Walcott mud,

describing how it could engulf unwary horses and cattle, slowly crushing their ribs. When Jack Camp arrived at Walcott Inlet, nearly forty years later, he might have become a rich man if it were not for that clinging, sucking mud.

ONE

OOBAGOOMA

Peter Wann's story, as told to Mike

IT WAS LATE February, 1971. The mail plane, operating out of Derby, had been my passage to freedom.

I left school at fourteen. Too early, in hindsight, for I was only the size of an apprentice jockey and in the hard frontier culture of the Kimberley the size of a man and survival went hand in hand. The unrelenting heat, the isolation and the scarcity of white women to soften the excesses of white stockmen had all contributed to an ugly macho culture. Taking a job as a jackaroo on a cattle station in the Halls Creek district I had endured every form of humiliation from stockwhip thrashing to being forced to ride wild mickeys (bulls) while the ringers jeered from the top rails. If you were small, you were a target for every stockman's boot.

There's always a few mongrel horses in the stock camps and I soon learnt to handle them. Each station had a contingent of racehorses to compete at the annual Halls Creek race meeting, and being so small I was the obvious choice for track work rider. Being perched high on the racehorses in a tiny saddle gave me a great sense of balance and in 1970 I competed in the Mount House rodeo. To my surprise – and probably everyone else's, too – I made the grand final. Wearing the standard cowboy chaps for the event was compulsory. After a frantic search and calls from the loudspeaker, I did find them, but it caused more stress than the wild bull that finally threw me.

A particularly severe stockwhip lashing at Halls Creek was the final straw. The rawhide bit so deep the scars on my lower leg are still there after thirty-four years. I managed to sneak a letter to the mailman, who only visited the station once a week, which eventually reached my father in Derby. Dad (Ron Wann) made contact with the station and demanded I be taken to Halls Creek where he would collect me on his next truck run. Dad had a truck delivery business and arranging for me to be billeted for a week or two was no problem.

The manager of the station basically refused, telling Dad that no one was going into Halls Creek for some weeks and it was too far for a special trip in a 4WD truck. It was bordering on slavery, as jackaroo wages were a pittance at the time. I was a useful pair of hands and the cattle industry had entered a boom period. There was a scramble to get cattle to the meatworks. Booms never lasted and no one knew it better than the cattlemen. Dad wasn't going to get me away without a fight so he presented the case to the Child Welfare Department. An authorisation was dispatched via the pilot of the mail plane and I was finally re-united with my family.

Other than a brief period at boarding school, Derby was

all I knew before becoming a jackaroo. Out on a peninsula, the town is almost besieged by the giant Kimberley tides. When the tide's out, the grey silt plains stretch to the horizon and if the out tide synchronises with a summertime noon, the town bakes. The streets are empty. No one moves, except those in air-conditioned shops or offices. Then the tide rolls in, flooding the silt plains and carrying with it a breeze. The breeze gently stirs the leaves in trees, birds come alive and people once again venture onto the streets. A new town emerges, on the edge of the sea. For a few hours Derby takes on the appearance of a town on an island, with saltwater lapping the outer streets on either side.

For me, it was the perfect environment to be reared in. I had an insatiable passion for fishing. The mangrove-jacks rode with the inflowing tide and me and my mates knew exactly where to wait, casting from homemade rods. When we grew tired of tramping through the mangroves I produced a billycart and we took off for the Fitzroy River. All the camping gear and fishing tackle went into the billycart and we hotfooted it down the dusty road for twenty-five miles, spending two or three nights on the river. The tropical bush of northwestern Australia had become my second home.

But February 1971 in Derby was not a happy time. My mother and father separated. Whatever house I stayed in, I missed the company of the other. More so in the old house where mum now lived alone. My friends still tucked away at school and I was lonely and at a loose end. Where was I headed? School days were long gone; I moved in a man's world, but with no career. After a month back in my home town it began to weigh on me heavily so when he heard a business acquaintance needed a young stockman, Dad seized the opportunity.

'Jack Camp's looking for a horseman,' Dad told me one night. 'He's got a contract mustering job on Oobagooma and wants an extra hand who can ride. Quick job, he said. Be gone about a month. Said you can have the job.' He paused and looked through the window at the receding tide. Only a dirt road lay between the house and high tide level. 'Reckon you should go. Some say Jack's the best wild cattleman northern Australia's ever seen. Big call to say that, but it's the opinion of several big station owners. Up in the rough country some don't muster the far flung corners. It don't pay em. By the time they finance long-winded mustering camps and long haulage to the works, there's nothing in it. But they'll cut a deal with blokes like Jack Camp. So go out with him and learn all you can. Get along with him okay and he might take you on for a year or two. Not many can handle the wild cattle. Learn the tricks of the trade and you might end up with a station of your own one day. Out here in the Kimberley good cattlemen can build an empire, starting from nothing. Not many places in the world you can do that.'

I met Jack Camp in Derby's main street. Dad had said it was best if I went alone – he didn't wish to look like a teacher handing over a pupil. Jack was seated under a boab tree, quietly smoking. He was medium height, his brown hair tinged with premature grey, and when he stood up to shake hands with me the bow in both legs was evident. He smiled and sat down again on the weathered wooden seat. The main street was a popular meeting place for members of the Aboriginal community and the council had provided seats under some of the shady boabs.

'Your dad says you ride okay?' Jack queried, fixing me with unflinching blue eyes.

'Good enough, I suppose. When do you want me?'

Over the coming months I was to find answers came grudgingly from Jack Camp. Especially if it was time to roll another cigarette. First he would lick his bottom lip and stick the paper on it. Then he would shake a measure of tobacco into his palm and use the heel of his other palm to grind it. Satisfied it would spread evenly, he would tip the ingredients onto the paper, roll it neatly then reach for a match before putting the cigarette into his mouth.

'We'll fly up to Oobagooma in the morning,' Jack said, after taking the first draw. The Log Cabin smoke drifted my way. It was a pleasant aroma and I felt for my own packet of cigarettes.

'I've had to charter the flight,' Jack went on. 'Expensive, but the rivers are running bankers. No other way in.' He went silent, just sitting and looking at me, as though preparing me for what he said next. 'I'm taking my two young boys, Peter and George.'

With an effort I tried to show no surprise. Last time I'd seen them they were little boys in the primary school playground. That was only two years ago.

'I'm sure they'll love it,' I said, not knowing what else to say.

'They're good little riders,' Jack added. 'And so light their mounts never seem to tire. Mind you, their mother's not wrapped in the idea – missing school. But the best education they can get is what I teach them about handling cattle. They can always catch up on the schoolwork.'

Some Aboriginal women and their children emerged from a store across the street. Two multi-coloured dogs rose from slumber and trotted along as the families headed away. Jack Camp had a faraway look, as though I wasn't there.

'I was wondering, Jack,' I said at last, Dad having instructed me to enquire, 'what my wage will be.'

Jack Camp always spoke quietly. 'I'll look after you,' he said, and suddenly re-focused on the purpose of our meeting. 'I've got saddles. You bring two changes of clothes and two towels. Rolled up, towels make good pillows. Toothbrush, too, and a comb. Don't worry about soap, I've got plenty. I like a clean camp.'

Just then two men drew up in a car and Jack told me he would pick me up about an hour after sunrise the next morning. We shook hands and I got up and left.

The chartered plane was a four-seater Cessna. The middle-aged pilot said the mist was lifting and motioned us all to climb aboard. He seemed unconcerned about Jack Camp nursing his son George on his lap. The combined weight of Jack, me and the boys must have been little more than two average-sized men.

In the summer, the tepid waters of King Sound exuded a saltwater mist in the early morning, when the slightly cooler air slipped off the coastal ranges to the north. A thin blanket of grey fog lay over the sound and adjacent coastal plain for about an hour after sunrise, then a hot sun dispersed it almost as fast as an open window releases steam from a bathroom. I gazed down on a wilderness of broad sweeping rivers, savanna woodland and, as we neared Oobagooma, the stark skeletal spines of ancient granite ranges.

The landing strip at Oobagooma had not been used since the last dry and it had been raked by tropical storms. The pilot dropped the flaps and throttled back. Only near the point of touchdown did he see the washout hidden in the scattered cane grass. He throttled sharply and adjusted the flap. It got the plane over the ditch, but we landed with excessive speed and it took all the braking skills of the experienced pilot to stop the aircraft crashing into the timber at the end of the runway. Little did I know that it was the first of many narrow escapes.

The pilot taxied back to the washout, where a man waited by a high wheel based Toyota Landcruiser. Hilton Walker's welcoming smile died on his lips when the pilot jumped from the Cessna and lambasted him for not maintaining the landing strip. Emergencies could crop up at any time and a neglected runway was a recipe for a disaster. Walker just shrugged and apologised. He seemed an affable man and the issue was dropped. Sturdy in frame, he was about the same age and height as Jack, but much more robust looking. Walker had an arresting black moustache, short black hair and pressed khaki clothes.

The homestead was about 200 yards from the landing strip. It was a historic stone building and uniquely constructed in an area where timber and corrugated iron were the only materials used for most structures. Leichhardt pine had been used for the frame and large flat stones had been embedded into an ant-bed sludge. It was built to last – and to survive the dry-season fires, which periodically ravaged the landscape. It's not clear who built it or when. What is known is that the whole settlement went perilously close to being razed during the Bunuba uprising. The uprising was sparked in 1894 when 'Pigeon', a police tracker, shot dead Constable Richardson at Lillimooloora Station, about seventy-five miles to the southeast of Oobagooma. The local Umiida and Unggarranga people joined the resistance and speared the Oobagooma saddle horses. They gave the black stationhands a stark choice: join the resistance or be speared. A hurriedly dispatched police patrol from Derby confronted eighty painted warriors not far from the homestead. The warriors, many fluent in English by this time, vowed to kill all the whites and the black stationhands and burn the whole settlement. Western Australia was still a British colony and the mounted police troopers were well trained and disciplined. There was a code of battle ethics against tribesmen bearing spears which didn't apply when locally recruited posses took the law into their own hands. Careful not to ride into spear range, the troopers fired warning shots, and only when the warriors refused to yield were some of them wounded. There was no loss of life.

In the early 1940s, Oobagooma was once again the frontline. The headquarters for Australia's defence in Darwin considered Japanese invasion of the west Kimberley almost inevitable due to the region's relative proximity to occupied Timor. The Third Australian Guerilla Warfare Group was based there from November 1942. But the only shot fired in dire defence was by Officer Merv Stanton. He observed one of his corporals having a swim in a billabong near the homestead. Aware of the presence of saltwater crocodiles in the wet season, he strolled down from the tent lines to warn his corporal of the risk. He arrived just in time to see the snout of a large crocodile surface behind the unsuspecting soldier. Knowing the speed at which they can attack, Stanton didn't waste a second. He slammed his .303 rifle butt into his shoulder and fired directly over the terrified man's head. The corporal thought the bullet was intended for him and lost his false teeth. Stanton later wrote that, despite the sixteen-foot crocodile floating belly up only yards away, the corporal repeatedly dived, scraping the bottom with his hands until he recovered his false teeth.

At the homestead I was introduced to Hilton Walker's young wife. She was a pretty young woman with blonde hair. My uncle, Allan Wann, had a deli bar and small grocery shop next to the picture theatre in Derby. He knew everybody in the district. When I told him I was going out to Oobagooma he said not to count on Hilton for any help in the bush, that the brazen manager from the Territory had enticed a beautiful young woman to live with him on one of Australia's most inaccessible stations, so he wouldn't be leaving the homestead for any length of time.

'But what's than got to do with Jack Camp?' I asked.

Uncle Allan used to come around to my Dad's place for a beer after shutting the shop. 'I'm working for Jack, not Mr Walker.'

'Jack had a bad trot. He bought a secondhand road train and started carting cattle for a few stations others wouldn't truck for. He didn't get paid by a couple of big operators and the bank closed.' Allan hesitated, choosing his words. 'Jack'll be runnin on a shoestring. That's why he's taking those young kids out of school. None of my business, I know, but it worries me a bit.'

'Oh come on, Allan!' Dad exclaimed. 'Fantastic experience for Peter. Couldn't be taught by a better master.'

'I understand all that,' Allan retorted gently. 'It's just there'll be no support. Walker don't stack up somehow and I can't put my finger on why. Nice enough bloke to meet, I know.'

I recalled my uncle's remarks when the pilot reprimanded Walker over the ditch on the runway. It unnerved me, until I met his young wife. She welcomed us, offered us each a soft drink and showed us where we would be sleeping. Adult yarning held little interest and heading outside we met Ralph Dibley.

Ralph was Otto Dibley's son, about twenty and solidly built. The Bardi men were noted for their prowess. Otto had been a heavyweight fighter in the travelling show tents. Very tall and super strong, shoeing horses was about as easy for Otto as beating eggs. Ralph took us over the bare, hard-trod ground to meet his father. There was no garden fence around the homestead, and with the stockyards close by, the whole settlement had a bleak, frontier aspect.

Otto clinched the last nail on Paw Paw the mule and straightened. He had a scar above one eye and one on the side of his mouth. Sweat trickled down his chest over the initiation scars, and under the hot sun his black skin glistened with vitality. He had already shod two horses, which had been released into a yard, and had the two pack mules to go. He looked quizzically at the two young Camp boys, stifling a smile.

'Looks like Jack made up his mind to feed you two to the gators after all,' he growled, then erupted into laughter, like a rumble from a bull. 'But you're both too tiny for an alligator to be bothered.'

'Nearly as tall as him, I am,' Peter Camp snapped defiantly, jerking his head at me. 'Anyway, Dad said you're big enough to wrestle em and open their jaws. We got nothing to fear.'

'Shit, where are we goin?' I asked.

'Walcott Inlet, up near Munja, only old Munja is on the other side,' Otto said. Sober faced, he treated the boys as equals when imparting information. 'Me and Jack was out there last year. Them cattle in hundreds on the Crown land side of the Charnley, all unbranded and no one own em, so we swim some of em over. Now we goin out to get em and walk em through this place to the meatworks.'

Otto and Ralph had been a part of Jack Camp's team for the past two years. They had ridden the two mules out from Derby, swimming rivers. At Oobagooma they waited for Jack to fly in with the boys and a few supplies. They spoke of the horses as theirs as much as Jack's, who treated them as his equals, which was still rare in the post-war Kimberley. They would have done anything for Jack Camp and they joked with his sons as though it was a blood bond.

'You gonna jump on one?' Otto tempted Peter Camp. Peter was already leaning against a stockyard rail looking at the horses. He had a quiet, watchful disposition. He didn't speak much and only when an answer was expected. The luxury of childhood had never been bestowed on either Peter or George, for their father catapulted them into manhood almost from the cradle. There was no such thing as recreation or idle days, life was a journey of achievement and anything which digressed from that was superfluous.

'Where are the saddles?' Peter asked.

Otto motioned to a corrugated iron shed and little George followed his older brother. I hesitated; there were only two horses, and Ralph seized the opportunity.

'Pigs, they down there,' he declared, pointing towards the Robinson River some forty-five yards away. 'Heard em early. You come and we get one for the charcoal.'

Ralph didn't have to twist my arm. It was still quite early. The plane had landed before nine o'clock and I'd only been in the house a few minutes. I loved pig hunting and expected Ralph to produce a gun. Instead he emerged from the nearby quarters carrying two spears. At One Arm Point where Ralph grew up, men still used spears to gather fish. Every boy was taught to make them. The Aborigines in Derby had given spears away decades ago and I'd never seen a spear thrown.

Ralph leading, we made our way down to the river. He soon found the nest. Young pigs darted in all directions, most above sucker size. They didn't go far. The thick dry cane grass provided good cover and they squatted in twos and threes, terrified. The sow ran to begin with, as though trying to guide her babies, then she turned and with a high-pitched squeal charged Ralph. His spear caught her between the neck and the shoulder and the weight of the shaft flipped her onto her side. Her screams were ear piercing and the porkers scattered in panic, with Ralph in pursuit. He left me to deal with the sow. By the time I had put the sow out of its misery Ralph returned with one of the porkers. He retrieved his spear from the sow and wiped the blood from both spears with a handful of grass.

Otto was delighted. He tossed a few bits of wood into a heap and from a handful of leaves lit a fire. He asked Ralph to collect a few chunky bits of wood, about forearm size, to make a bed of coals. Peter and George were still saddling up. The pig hunt had only lasted about twenty minutes.

The porker was placed on some fresh green gum leaves and Otto waved his shirt to keep the flies off. The fire seemed to fan another tier of heat into the rapidly warming day and when enough wood had been added to the fire Otto dropped his shirt over the pig and joined his son and me in the shade of a boab tree. Flies began to swarm onto the shirt and when the big blowies arrived Otto walked over to a gum and broke off more leaves, but the flies were inexorable.

An hour passed before Otto was satisfied with the coals. Using a shovel he made a charcoal bed, placed the pig and shovelled hot coals on top. Then it was back to the shade and desultory talking. When the pig was finally cooked, Otto used the shovel again to lift the hairless carcass back onto the pile of leaves. The flies backed off, not liking hot flesh. It was time to eat and bush knives were drawn from scabbards. Another two Aboriginal men joined the impromptu feast. They were wet season maintenance men employed by Walker.

I enjoyed the hunt, but I was too exited about the adventure ahead to focus on food.

Feeling the homestead might be much cooler, I wandered over and sat down in a spare chair. Mrs Walker was ironing in a corner and Jack and Hilton were seated at the table, their tea mugs empty. The pilot had gone. I suddenly realised that I hadn't taken much notice of the plane taking off and banking towards Derby. It was at the height of the pig chase. Now it struck me. There was no way out. I was committed.

'Where are the boys?' Jack asked, looking relieved to see a new face.

'They went for a ride.'

'Young Peter don't feel the heat. Never did,' Jack said, leaning back against the wooden frame of the chair. 'Been a slight change of plans,' his voice measured and quiet. 'A few weeks ago Hilton chartered a Cessna out of Derby and had a fly all over the run.' He paused and butted his cigarette into the ashtray. 'How many you reckon, Hilton, running on the Humbert Creek plains?'

'I counted 300 and would have missed a lot,' Hilton replied, visibly excited at the prospect. 'That's the beauty of this place, son,' he added, looking at me. It's so big and the country's so wild, cattle just show up and there is no telling where they came from.'

'They're running on Oobagooma,' Jack put in. 'So you might as well get em before someone else does.'

He half-turned in the chair to look at me. I got the feeling that addressing me gave him an excuse to play his hand in front of Hilton. Jack definitely wanted to make a few things clear.

'But these cattle at Humbert Creek leave me out on a bit of a limb with the mob at Walcott. Hilton and I were going to take a split down the middle. My job was to go out and get em, bring in here and put em on some good grass until the meatworks opened in early May. Hilton's side of the bargain was the grass and use of the yards. Before going into the meatworks they have to be branded, de-horned and, if you want the good money, you have to castrate the bulls. It was pretty straight forward. But now we got two separate mobs to deal with.'

'I don't see a problem Jack,' Hilton said, a little irritated. 'Walk the lot to Derby after the clean up and split the cheque. It's so simple.'

There was a brief silence while Jack rolled another cigarette. 'Those cattle of mine at Walcott,' he began, 'are on Crown land with no complications about ownership. But this other mob.' He raised his eyebrows and looked askance at Hilton. 'I think they've wandered west from other leases. I crossed the Humbert a year ago and saw very few cattle. Most might be cleanskins, but some will carry brands. I don't want to be any part of em when it comes to handover time at the meatworks. I know they turn a blind eye to brands unless a leaseholder turns up with a complaint, but I'm a contract musterer and my name is everything.'

Hilton Walker sighed and bunched his fists on the table.

'Do it your way then. Bring them all in here and split the mob. Goin to be hard to know what's what. They'll be short-horn base with a splash of this and that. The cattle don't vary much up in the ranges.'

'I'll brand all the calves and weaners at Walcott,' Jack said evenly. 'Then it's only a matter of locking them up overnight in the yards here and the mothers will hang back for em. The bulls and heifers I'll bang-tail while we're drivin em along from the Isdell to the Humbert Creek. It won't be perfect, but near enough.'

Hilton frowned. 'Goin to be one hellava job roping those calves out there on the salt flats, in this heat. You got hessian?'

'Rolls of it in the truck,' Jack said with a grin. To Hilton it was a horror prospect. To Jack, a challenge; a victory over nature. Such was the irrevocable difference between the two men.

'Righto,' Hilton said, thin lipped and unhappy. 'There's some cold beer in the fridge. I think we'll all have one while my lovely girl fixes a bit of lunch.'

TWO

MY FIRST DAYS
WITH JACK CAMP

AT DAYLIGHT NEXT morning two vehicles headed east. Jack Camp was the pathfinder in his 6WD Austin ex-army truck. It had enough clearance to straddle small boulders. Hilton Walker followed in his 4WD Toyota, also with abundant clearance. The boys travelled with their father and I sat in the 4WD cabin with Hilton. It was so slow and rough that Otto and Ralph, who rode on the two mules each leading a horse, spent half the time waiting in the shade of a stringybark for us to catch up. These two horses belonged to Oobagooma. Jack kept his own horses on the Humbert Creek. He told me it was a huge valley at the foot of the King Leopolds and that's where we were headed. When I asked about the horse poison, the notorious walkabout plant that grows throughout this area, he said they only ate it when there was little else. I'd never seen walkabout. It didn't grow in the semi-arid country of Halls Creek.

We loaded the Austin the afternoon before – bundles of hessian for making a temporary holding yard, pickets to support the hessian, stock saddles and packsaddles, spare clothing, a tarpaulin to sleep under, Jack's cattle brand and dehorners, ropes and some food. The tucker looked monotonous, I must say – onions, potatoes, flour, rice, sugar, salt and tea. No luxuries, except maybe treacle. There wasn't much in the back of the Toyota. Hilton had loaded his swag, saddle, a box of supplies, four jerrycans of diesel – which were fastened to the front steel rail – and a big, useless bull terrier.

By mid-afternoon, tropical storms had swept in from the coast and we came to a sudden halt at the King Creek, running a banker. Otto had already hobbled out the mules and two horses. Raindrops the size of bullets pounded the windscreen. Hilton didn't get out. I took his lead and sat there too. I thought we'd sit and wait for the squall to pass. But not so with Jack and Otto about. With Ralph's help they slung a tarp between the two vehicles and pegged it out. They'd done it a few times before. It took only minutes and when Hilton and I got out we remained dry. The rain made such a din on the tarp, you had to yell to be heard. Jack got a fire going from wood he kept behind his seat. Soon two billies were in the flames and two battered quart pots waited beside, one full of tea leaves and the other, sugar. Jack lit a smoke and sat down on his swag. He could have been in his living room back in Derby, he looked so comfortable.

The storm passed and the sun came out. It seemed to be the signal for the bush turkeys to poke around. They had no fear of us. The Aboriginal people had been gone from the land for more than twenty years, so to the turkeys we were just another mammal, displacing lizards and insects they could eat. They crept to the edge of the shelter and shook themselves, but were always watchful, never coming within reach.

It wasn't long before we had more visitors. Jack had prepared a damper and placed it in a camp oven to cook. The pleasant odour was too much for the nearby bush goannas. We boys had the job of chasing them away with sticks. Ralph wanted to knock one on the head and cook him up on the coals, but Jack said we might all end up with diarrhoea and we didn't have the time for urgent sprints to a bush or rock. I don't think that was the reason at all. Jack carried an air of dignity about him. He didn't want it getting around Derby that goanna was main-course tucker on his musters.

Any prospect of crossing the King next day was wiped out when more storms struck after midnight and the creek rose even higher. We all slept under the tarp, close by each other in our swags. I don't think Jack slept much, though. Whenever I woke and looked out at the sheet lightning I saw the faint orange glow of Jack's cigarette. He was up before dawn, boiling the billy and making another damper. Laced with treacle, Jack's dampers fresh out of the oven were delicious.

We sat out another stormy day, chasing away the goannas and tempted to grab a turkey for the pot. Otto lit his own fire under a rock overhang and I think he and Ralph ate well. I wanted to go over to the other fire, knowing baked bush turkey might have been on the menu, but I didn't want to get Jack offside. He talked to me a lot, even shared some of his doubts, particularly when Walker wasn't about. Walker only left the cover of the tarp to give his bull terrier a walk. It had to be kept on the chain to stop it chasing the turkeys. Jack liked the turkeys. There were a few words over the dog and it went on the chain. Jack was boss.

The weather cleared the next night and the King began to drop. Jack cooked three dampers before dawn, gave Otto one and sent him and Ralph off at daybreak. The mules had no trouble driving through the fast flowing creek and the horses willingly followed. Otto was to ride to the Humbert River and track down Jack's saddle horses. When the King dropped another half-metre the plan was to get Hilton's Toyota across. Jack decided to leave the Austin behind. The storms had saturated the floodplains and two ranges had to be crossed before the Humbert Creek valley. Jack said his old truck would sink to the axle on those vast floodplains. By comparison the Toyota was light and, given a few hours of sunlight, should find enough traction without bogging. We transferred all the gear.

It was about noon before Walker was game to ease his vehicle into the water. High snorkels were not fitted in the early days of 4WDs and the exhaust was going to go underwater. If sucked up to the manifold, water can be devastating. The trick was to accelerate and blow the water back. To throw in a shade more horsepower, Jack and the three boys tossed their boots into the back and pushed. Minutes before, Jack had waded through the hip-deep water to check for submerged boulders.

The submerged exhaust churned the water like a propeller, but with the little truck tilting and jumping like a stranded whale, they made it over. Jack Camp had a big wide smile when he was pleased. At forty-four he could still look like a boy. There was a disarming spontaneity about the man, as though he'd never quite grown up and never would. He loved the whole pantomime and he infected those around him with his enthusiasm. Even Walker seemed to be enjoying the adventure, despite knowing that if the vehicle had come to a stop and water entered the diesel engine, it would have to be abandoned.

The two young boys and I crammed into the back and Jack rode with Walker in the cabin. For the next twenty-five miles, Jack directed Hilton. How he did it seemed something of a miracle. Few men ever rode this country. No white men knew it, except one. My dad said if someone was looking for Jack Camp the answer never altered: 'Out mustering'. But you can't muster cattle alone.

The country we entered was like nothing I had ever seen. It made you feel small, vulnerable, as though plans of any sort were plain ridiculous. It was no longer undulating with outcrops of limestone, where the boabs clung, looking like old alcoholics, stomachs all spread and the skin tight and drained of colour. The mountains here sprang straight out of the wide floodplains. No foothills, just straight up and there were those boulder screes from top to bottom, rock as black as the night, making the ranges look like they were bruised. Water from the storms still trickled down the fissures and precariously clinging trees sprouted wherever water flowed, green thin lines on the deep black.

Driving east, skirting the boggy flats and rocking gently over countless streams, we crossed two ranges running parallel. From the floodplain they loomed like an inexorable barrier, but Jack knew all the passes. The buttress of some mountain would fall away as Hilton drove on and then a gap appeared, a smooth surfaced saddle covered in new season spear grass. The second pass overlooked the Humbert river valley. Beyond rose the cliffs of the King Leopolds. The Humbert was a wide, breathtaking valley, wedged between ranges of the same height.

It was a gentle decline into the valley and the Humbert presented no crossing problems. It was a wide, stony water-course with expanses of shallow water. Once again Jack waded ahead of the vehicle, directing Hilton. To the north an almost treeless hill rose out of the plain. It was Jack's marker to the Humbert yards, which were on the other side. Rocky streams with upland catchments in the main range still carried fast-moving flows, forcing Hilton into a perilous traverse on the slopes of the solitary hill. In the twilight the long shadows were filling the valley and no one wanted to make camp in the spinifex.

Off the hill and back onto the floodplain, Hilton had to thread his way through scattered woollybutt and bloodwood, with blue grass threatening to smother the vehicle. This was the tall variety, endemic to the higher rainfall areas on rich soils held together by a covering of gibber rock, ranging in size from emu eggs to the size of a football. The truck lurched and jolted every yard of the way. Poor old Hilton must have been thinking about his profit margins as we crawled along, pushing the thick grass down with the bullbar.

A mob of shorthorns, only their raised tails and heads above the grass, ran into a group and warily watched our advance. A bull stood above them all, the dying sun catching the sleekness of his hide, and the slanting rays shone on his sweeping horns. It must have been a welcome sight to the two men in the cabin. In 1971 the Derby meatworks were paying one hundred dollars a head for all adult cattle. That's the equivalent of $1000 a head these days. A man with no resources, but brave and skilful in the bush, could become rich within the space of a few weeks. It was better than digging for gold in Victoria in the 1860s.

Our new camp was on Hope Creek, a small tributary of the Humbert. With no possibility of accidentally starting a bushfire Otto had a big fire going, which guided Hilton for the final 500 yards. We caught glimpses of the huge flames through the woollybutts, enough to conjure up images of billy tea and damper, and the boys said they would kick up a fuss if their dad didn't produce the corned beef. I didn't think they would have to say anything. Jack was in a great mood.

Ralph killed and cooked a water goanna, and the odour from ashes scraped away from the big fire aroused mixed sensations, depending on your cultural upbringing. Ralph always had a cheeky grin, his black cowboy hat more for look than for sun protection.

'Don't think we'll share with you,' Jack said dryly, pulling his swag out of the back. 'Okay boys, get yer swags and find a patch. Rake up the leaves with your hands and burn em, keep them roo ticks at bay.'

Otto unloaded the supply boxes. 'Sorry about the big hot fire, Jack. It got dark quick and thought them big flames might help yer find the camp.'

'It did. She'll soon burn down. The storms have cooled things down a bit. Reckon we'll be placing the billy about four in the morning to get warm. Horses okay?'

'Them out on the plain between the two creeks. Your bay mare, she run up to Paw Paw and I just drop me throwin rope over her head.' Otto grinned, a big wide smile and the fire-light catching the yellow in his teeth. 'That easy, Jack.'

Jack laughed. 'Be good if it was like that all the way, hey Otto.'

Hilton tied the bull terrier to the trunk of a bloodwood. Jack turned and stared at it, then said, 'if you don't want the ticks to eat it alive you'll have to get that shovel I tossed in and drop red coals all around that tree. Burn the ground and they'll stay out.'

Hilton said nothing. He and Jack trying to get on made me think of a steel gate holding up a wobbly wooden one.

'See many cattle?' Jack asked Otto. He'd dropped his swag only a few metres from the fire and rolled a cigarette. It was so dark the glow cast from the flames was better than a kerosene lamp. We had no lamps. They made you sit up and yarn, Jack said.

Otto threw a handful of tea leaves into a billy that had seen a thousand fires. 'Cattle everywhere, Jack,' he said. 'We get this bunch in three days.'

'Did yer ever meet Bunch-em-up?' Jack mused. 'Black fella from Mount Hart.'

'Rode with him.' Otto smiled. 'Old Felix Edgar could do nothing without him. It was never run the horses in: bunch-em-up he'd say. It was the only whitefella word he knew.'

Next morning we ate damper by the fire and watched the faint red rim in the east slowly emerge into dawn and a trace of daylight. Peter and George were eager to get aboard their horses. Most kids of their age don't like pre-dawn rises, but not those two. They were talking between themselves, ribbing each other, saying the other's horse would buck. 'No, mine never bucked,' I'd hear one say.

Jack grabbed a bridle and saddle from the harness pile and motioned for me to follow. We pushed through the blue grass to a large square yard, big enough to hold 500 head of cattle. Otto and Ralph had already caught their mounts for the day and were leading them to the creek for a drink. The two boys had run ahead, carrying a bridle each.

There were about twenty horses milling around in the yard. When the two stockmen had run them in the evening before, the yard was fence to fence grass. Now the grass was trampled and there was a pungent smell of manure and urine. They would have been thirsty. The plan was to get our mounts for the day and release the rest. Jack cornered a grey gelding nearly racehorse size and bridled him.

'He's a quiet fella,' Jack commented as we walked through the sliprail opening, Jack leading the horse. 'He can get along a bit, but I want you to save his energy. We poke the cattle along, never rush em or drive em hard.' He threw the saddle on, clinched it and nodded for me to mount. 'Trot first, then canter, all in a big circle. Never mind the grass. They're used to it.'

I mounted, expecting to have to go for the grip on the saddle pommel the second my left boot touched the iron.

That's how it was at Halls Creek. A horse not ridden for months bucked. You either rode your arse off for up to three minutes or got thrown. But this bloke didn't even tuck his tail. He just walked off. I did what Jack asked and when I saw him fetch a bridle to catch his horse, I knew the test was over.

Peter Camp rode a smart looking chestnut horse and George a bay gelding. Both horses were about average size, fourteen hands. Little George sat the saddle like an over-grown flea. Peter led out and the woollybutts closed behind them. Jack had instructed Peter to ride north towards the main range then swing east, riding parallel with Hope Creek. About five miles out he was to pick up the creek again, and sweeping from one side of the valley to the other, hunt every little mob they saw towards the camp. They were to ride quietly, no calling out or whip cracks. Meanwhile Otto and his son were to muster up the cattle within a couple of miles of the camp. The outlying mobs would run into Otto's mob. Jack, Hilton and I were to ride downstream, towards Secure Bay. Jack expected a big mob to be put together by smoko time.

I asked Jack what my fella's name was. I really liked him. He and I were going to get along well.

'They don't have names. Too many horses pass through my hands to bother with names. They're just work horses.'

Hilton had saddled his own horse, led in by Otto. The other one looked all confused and was going to stay with us. It didn't know the bush horses. When Jack dropped the sliprail they bolted. The bull terrier had been let off the chain and was sniffing around. It looked better suited to a park.

I asked Hilton what he called it. He didn't answer for a while. Something didn't fit; it looked like his stirrup leather. There was sweat on his brow and he was trying to make a hole in the leather with a pen knife. I don't think Hilton rode much.

'His name's Boof,' he replied at last. 'He's going to get lost in this bloody grass.'

'I'd leave the bugger here,' Jack said, sitting his horse and looking disdainfully at Hilton's feverish fingers working with the knife.

'He'll yap all the time. Spook the cattle.'

'That's all we need,' mumbled Jack.

The dog was a serious liability within an hour. There was plenty of water and it was used to heat, but the country was covered in small round stones, the remnants of an ancient sea bed. The dog became footsore. I wondered how long the horses would manage without shoes until I asked Jack. He said just walking and short days in the saddle, there wouldn't be a problem. Their hooves were tough, they were mountain horses.

Jack could contain his frustration no longer. 'The job's hard enough without a stupid house dog in tow. Tie it to a bloody tree and we'll drive out after lunch.'

'He'll fret and die in the heat,' Hilton retorted, colouring around the neck with indignation at the description of his dog. 'I'll carry him.'

'The horse won't have that on,' Jack growled in disbelief. 'You'll have to go back. We'll ride down to the salt swamps and collect what we can.'

The two men parted and I rode along with Jack. As soon

as we were out of earshot, Jack opened up. 'Station manager, what a bloody joke,' he grumbled. 'He's got no idea. But he'll learn a thing or two out here with me.' He began to roll a cigarette, deftly holding the reins and rolling tobacco instantaneously. 'The blackfellas do all his musterin in the dry. I guess if there was some justice in this world they'd have a place of their own. I want land again. I want my family out of Derby.' He took a long draw and looked at me hard, a glint in his eye. 'This mob out at Walcott is big enough for a deposit on a station. I got my eye on one. The only thing between me and that place is the Isdell. We gotta swim the Isdell with the whole bloody mob. No other way out coming south. I've poked up every waterway, hoping a gorge might cut right through. Dead-ends, everyone of em and the range itself,' he took another puff and shook his head. 'You don't walk when on foot. You jump, straddle and climb. Break the leg of a mountain horse in half a mile.'

I asked him how we were going to get over. I'd been looking up at the range, fascinated by such bold cliffs. Out at Halls Creek I saw cliffs on occasion, but up here on the far arm of the King Leopolds they went on and on, the ultimate barrier to the north.

'There's a passage,' Jack replied. 'It's good goin too, even get that truck a long way in. Just a pity it's on the wrong side of the Isdell.'

We rode northwest for about an hour. Sometimes the cattle ran, others squared up and stood watching us. They grazed at this early hour and some had bits of blue grass in their mouth. Quiet cattle carry on eating when horsemen ride by, but not these. The ones that had seen man before were no more comfortable that those that hadn't. The colours ran from red shorthorn to the inbred brindle and white. In some you could still see the remnant genes of the Santa Gertrudis. The Santa bulls never made it in the rough Kimberley country, wiped out by ferals. These cattle were fat, as though they had busted out of a feedlot. Jack said the big blue grass was the fattening grass of the coastal plains. One horse stride above the floodplain and you were back in the spear grass. The shit grass, Jack called it.

The ranges on either side seem to close in on us, forming a gap only a half-mile wide. You could hear something, a sound like a chopper almost out of hearing range, pulsating, but never coming on. I mentioned it to Jack and he chuckled.

'That's the tide. You put your ear to the ground like the Indians used to and you'll always hear it, except at tide change. For just five minutes, dead low or gorge fill high, there's nothing.'

We rode onto what looked like a land reef, a narrow strip of raised ground under boulders and scattered cane grass as high as the horse's heads. Ahead stretched a wall of mangroves.

'Welcome to Secure Bay,' Jack said. 'We won't get to see it. You gotta ride through those mangroves for a mile and then out onto a salt plain. Tidal creeks cut through the mangroves and when the tide runs out the sun bakes em dry, making a hard crust. You'd think no water had been up those creeks for months. Proper trap it is. You can be out on the salt plain for just a couple of hours and when yer turn back you might be faced with swimming ten dirty creeks. A croc or two moving along as well. Just keep it mind because at Walcott we're goin to be on the edge all the time.' Jack reined in and dismounted. 'Suggest you take a pee here. This is as far as we go. Going back we'll have the cattle. We won't get a breather, not for a second, until we run em into Otto's mob.'

While Jack rolled a cigarette I led Bluey towards a stand of paperbarks. I had named my horse Bluey without telling Jack. He might have thought it wasn't my right, but my bloke had to have a name. I got halfway over, pushing through the cane grass, when Jack stopped me.

'You goin to that waterhole?'

I told Jack I saw water there. Looked like a big pool of freshwater. I was thirsty and thought my horse might drink too.

'I'll teach yer now. You gotta treat every waterhole with suspicion in this country.' The cigarette smoke rose above the grass. It was so still and hot it seemed to hang there, marking where Jack stood. Then he followed me over and we tethered the horses to a bauhinia. It was a short walk to the waterhole.

'For a start, take no notice of the size of the hole. Big crocs have been known to claim piddly holes for their home. It's about territory. Most of the time they're not hungry, but step into their hole and you're a gonna.'

The hole was about thirty yards long and half that wide. On either side the paperbarks towered above it, their roots in the water. Most of the water was under shade. In the heat it looked cool and inviting. On the tidal side we stood on open sandstone, near the edge. Jack dropped to one knee to scan the rock, smooth and clean like a cement footpath.

'This is where it's hard,' he said. 'The bugger could drag himself over this rock and disturb nothing. There're a few twigs and the odd leaf here, but they could have come off them paperbarks yesterday or the day before. The croc might have moved in the day before that. Let's work down the sides, but don't go near the edge.'

I followed Jack into the paperbarks. Pandanus palms were thick when we got into the permanent shade and tropical vines caught our hats. The mosquitoes were bad and all I could think about was getting out.

'If there's drag marks I'll spot em through here,' Jack murmured.

It took about ten minutes to work around the perimeter of the hole. We saw nothing and Jack remarked the water was nice and clean.

'I'd say this hole's right,' he said at last, when we were back out on the sandstone. 'Unfortunately there's always some risk. Further upstream there'll be little fresh holes from the rain.'

But my thirst and the cool clear water was too much. I was always going to take a calculated risk, I decided. We both drank from ground level, went back for the horses and led them over. They drank without hesitation.

'Remember too,' Jack remarked, 'if the horse won't drink or won't lead up to the water, it's a bad sign. Given the drift of the wind's towards em, they can smell a croc.'

We mounted and Jack explained how we were going to drive the cattle. Hope Creek would be our centre line. Where water was semi-permanent you could see the pale green leaves of the paperbarks, up to ninety feet high. In between, those

Kimberley creeks were nothing but dry rocky beds, wet only after rain. The tall rivergums with white trunks grew near or in these long sections. Not thick, like a line you could follow. Just enough of them to mark the watercourse as you rode along. Jack rode one side of the creek and I the other. We couldn't see each other, but knew where each other was by our voices. 'Whoop there! Whoop there!' Some lifted their tails and bolted upstream. Others stood their ground, curious, until you got close enough to see right into their eyes. Then one would snort, up shot the tails and the bunch trotted briskly away, swallowed by the blue grass. If a mob angled away from the general line of the watercourse you had to angle away too, at a fast canter. They only had to hear the horse rushing through the grass to swing back. They didn't know they were heading for a trap and their instincts were to travel up or down the watercourses. The ground was rough underneath, but Jack was right, the horses walked it every day and sailed over the scattered stone when a canter was needed.

Cattle tire quickly and soon we had a mob walking ahead, mostly out of sight. There was plenty of noise now, cows calling up their big babies, making sure they walked right behind. Most of the calves had been dropped months before back in the spring and many were already half the size of mum. As the mob grew and the sun climbed, the heat coming back at you off the rock, some of the bulls would drop back and start looking for the rider. At Halls Creek we called these the break-away scrubbers. The mickeys you could flick with the whip and they'd charge back into the mob. Jack said he wanted no loud cracks, it can stampede semi-wild cattle. I just let my whip roll out behind, same as a cast for barramundi, and with the jerk of my wrist let it sail past Bluey's head and make the cracking lash bite on their rumps. There was a tiny report, like a Tom Thumb cracker. Bluey didn't flinch. Jack had whip trained all his horses and his boys could crack a whip before they could write.

When tailing wild cattle you dread the big bad rogue showing up. They're the dangerous ones. If they come at you, the only difference between them and rhinoceros is weight. The rhino will kill you. With the big scrubber it's the luck of the horn thrust. They make no bones about their intentions either.

When a big one dropped back and was running all alone I got a good look at him. He was a rogue all right. He had a wall eye and one ear had been slit down the centre in a fight. Just the colour sent a shiver through me and onto the saddle: charcoal all over the top and rust coloured underneath and on the legs. It was the horns which would have made him a prize beast in Spain. They were so wide no factory-made cattle crush would have accommodated him. He was running with his head high and swinging back to see where I was with his good eye. Another sign of trouble was his tail, curled so tight between his legs you could miss it and think a dingo got a bite in just after birth. This bloke wasn't worth it. Desperately I looked for Jack, I'd seen his hat floating above the grass a minute before. I wanted to yell: 'Let him go, hey?' But if he didn't sanction it I'd have to make a stand.

The bull broke to escape and avoided the front-on charge. He crashed over old logs and fallen branches bordering the

creek and charged through some water with such force the
sound of the hollow splash would have alerted Jack.

I gave Bluey full rein and tacked onto the same precarious
path, jumping the logs and leaping into the shallow stream.
Bluey quickly gathered in the bull and in a rush of blood
I thought I might throw him. That's what we did at Halls
Creek. We'd toss them and when they regained their legs
more often than not they would flee back to the mob. But
I had never seen the men toss one this big. I guess I wanted to
show Jack I could do it – I forgot he wasn't there anyway.
I reached down and got the tail, the bull felt my hand and
whipped sideways, throwing me clean out of the saddle.
I rolled like a racing bike rider flung on a corner, the thick
grass saving my bones and when I sprang to my feet the bull
was locking his hindquarters to turn, like a campdraft horse.
He was about to charge and Bluey was out of sight. I sprinted
for a bauhinia thirty yards away. I'd done it before in big yards
holding wild cattle. You reached the rails, you were safe, but
I'd never bolted for a tree before. The bull had started to
charge when I took my first stride. I wasn't going to make it.
Where would the horns take me? It was terrifying. I was
vaguely aware of a crashing sound from where I'd come from,
but stretching to get the last inch from each stride I couldn't
look. There was a sharp crack which echoed through the scattered timber, but I didn't stop. I saw a lateral branch about
three metres above ground, jumped for it, caught it and let my
legs catapult over so that my head was nearer to the ground
than my feet. Upside down, I looked back. Jack was there, like
an apparition. He sat his bay mare like a statue. He took aim

again. The first shot had taken the bull in the shoulder, collapsing his charge. The second killed him.

'They said you could run,' Jack said dryly. 'That old bull was in top gear and struggling to pull the ground on yer.' Then the mirth on his face faded and he lifted the flap of his saddlebag to return the revolver. I didn't know he had one. 'But he'd have got you just the same. Don't ever do that again. Good horses are too valuable for the risk of a fatal goring. We're not here on a rodeo.'

I opened my mouth to explain and thought better of it. I knew I was smiling and turned my head so Jack couldn't see. I don't think he meant it. It was just the way it came across. No horse was expendable, but little buggers like me, we just kept coming from the same place.

Over the next three days we rode out to bring in the scattered mobs. I rode with Jack, and Peter and George worked as a pair. Peter had been camp mustering with his father since he was seven and when it came to handling cattle, he was as good as any man. The procedure was simple. We rode out early before the heat. Otto and Ralph tailed the big mob. They let them spread over a couple of thousand acres and kept a watch out for wandering groups. The cattle settled quickly, accepting the horsemen. Most of them were born in the valley and had no wish to be anywhere else.

During this period Hilton had volunteered to be camp cook. Jack suggested the first thing he could turn into a stew was his dog. Hilton retorted by challenging Jack to eat it and was forced to eat his own words when Jack offered to shoot it and skin it. He said he'd eaten far worse. The dog had opened a worrying divide between the two men. Jack was a no nonsense man. There was no place for useless trivia in his life. He didn't even name his horses, yet he put more effort into their stock training than most would.

While Hilton cooked we ate a bit better. He opened up some of his tins – mushrooms, baby carrots, peas and some herbs. With the damper he mixed a weak solution of powdered milk and dropped in some cinnamon. It puffed up like an oversize scone and, laced with apricot jam from a tin, it was about as good as it gets.

When the evening meal was over a bottle of rum would come out of Hilton's tuckerbox. On the night of the first day's mustering Hilton didn't offer Otto any rum. He asked only Jack for his pannikin – as far as Hilton was concerned only he and Jack would have a shot. When no one else was offered any, Jack got up and walked over to Otto, who lay full length on the ground with his head on the soft underbelly of his saddle. Jack didn't say anything. He simply leant down and tipped his rum into Otto's pannikin. To me, it was deeply moving. A bond between a white man and a black man was rare in the Kimberley at the time. But you have to appreciate that Jack Camp was a Territory Gulf man. Same continent, different loyalties. When Jack sat down again Hilton passed him the bottle and Jack nodded at me. 'You got yer initiation to-day little fella. Hand me yer mug.' Then he passed the bottle back to Hilton.

Hilton said nothing. He dropped his nip in a single gulp and poured another. The cooking fire had died down, leaving all of us in shadow. Ralph had gone fishing. Jack had offered the fishing line from his saddlebag to Ralph when Ralph turned his nose up at whitefella tucker. The black bream were in every waterhole and a piece of meat stuck on the hook was all it took.

We sat there in silence. The barking owls put up a racket nearby and the unsettling call of a curlew seemed louder than it normally was. I saw Otto take the rum. After the tent fights a man would want a rum and you wouldn't take it like tea either. When I looked at him again I was sure he was asleep. I was leaning against my saddle between Jack and Otto. The kids were asleep. It had been a huge day for a ten and eleven year old. I thought what might have happened had George been me and the bull dropped back. He was just a kid. I had found a way to tactfully put it to Jack when we unsaddled late morning. 'They know what to do, my boys, I taught them.'

Tension hung in the air like the smoke and I wasn't surprised when Jack got up. He said he wanted to check the horses. Apart from Hilton's two geldings and the mules, they hadn't been hobbled for months. Ralph hadn't come back. He would have lit a little fire before casting out, ready for the fish. It was a clear starry night and you could see the outline of the ranges.

The second shot of rum had affected Hilton. Cold sober he didn't speak to me much. I rode with Jack and we got along well. Maybe Hilton thought I could tip the balance.

'I want to take these cattle straight back to the station,' he said to me when Jack's foot fall could no longer be heard. Otto had started to snore. 'We got about 500 and they're fat.

They're worth fifty grand. I can put a deposit down on that place up on the Lennard that's on the market.'

I had drunk my rum by this stage. I was tired and my head was floating a little. Jack had given me a good nip.

'Perhaps you and Jack after the same place,' I said, and gave Hilton a big grin. 'You two are destined to lock horns at every turn.'

Hilton still had his hat on, his face shaded from the firelight. When he stretched his arm to the rum bottle his hat shifted and the firelight caught his face, a bit like a torch about to run down and the light's gone all yellow. It was then I wished I hadn't said it. I carried that stone face into my memory for a long time and I wanted Jack to have the place of his dreams. His boys didn't belong in a town. None of the family did.

It all came to a head on the fourth night, the night before we were to go to Walcott Inlet. Hilton had prepared another good meal and we were spread out around the fire. Hilton always lay back into his swag. He rolled and buckled it each morning, something about king brown snakes loving beds left on the ground, he murmured one morning. I heard it said at Halls Creek too. I didn't think it was a problem. You just flipped the blanket before dark and hunted it if there was one in there. But Hilton was careful – and increasingly anxious. That night he produced the rum again and gave Jack the bottle. Otto and I got our nips and lay back into the saddles. A good meal and a rum. Life wasn't bad in those evenings. Hilton had his good points and we knew it every night on Hope Creek.

Hilton come straight out with it. 'Jack,' he said. 'What about driving this mob to Oobagooma? We got them, they're ready to go. When we get there I'll get some station boys to tail them and we'll come straight back out. I'll wait this side of the Isdell with the supplies while you round up your lot. No need to build a yard and brand. Mob them up and push them over the river. At Oobagooma we can keep the mobs separate.'

When he stopped speaking there was an uneasy silence. A curlew gave a shrill whistle somewhere up the creek and some ash in the fire broke off, causing a spark of flame to leap up and then die. There was just the faint outline of Jack's form, the glow of his cigarette marking where his mouth was. Otto moved a little and you could hear the dry leaves under his backside.

'The truth is we probably won't get back here this season, Hilton,' Jack said at last. 'It's the time of the year for the big storms. The horses will be footsore by the time we reach the station. Take a near month to come right. I got a chance now and I'm in no mood to miss it.' The glow of his cigarette brightened and you could smell the tobacco above everything else. The tension and the smell made me fiddle for my own packet. I only had a few left.

'You'll be in there for days, Jack. One or two days to build the yard. One little mob each day. I think it'll take ten days and in the meantime anything could happen with the weather. We'll end up with nothing.'

Jack didn't respond for nearly a minute. I watched as the red point of his cigarette was raised to where his mouth would be and then lowered to knee level.

'Reckon the boys are asleep, Peter?'

I was lying against my saddle on the opposite side of the fire, now a dying amber of coals. I got up and walked softly over to the huddles in the dark, careful not to step on them.

'They are,' I whispered and flopped down again. I was tired and saddle-sore.

When Jack began his tone had an icy edge to it.

'Hilton, I came out here with one job in mind – the mob at Walcott Inlet, and it's a dangerous gamble. We ride with the coffin lid open. If it's not a horse goin arse over head, it's a rogue bull eyein yer off or a croc waitin in a waterhole. I don't want to have to do this again. If I can pull off this job I can get myself a station. You see, Hilton, I'm riding out to Walcott for my family.'

'Well, that's okay, but why not rope and brand at Ooba-gooma? Just work on numbers.'

'Once the cattle walk onto Oobagooma and my brand's not on the young ones, I've got no legal claim.'

'You don't trust me,' retorted Hilton.

'In my life I've found no reason to trust anyone, except my wife and kids. And all those different brands we've seen these past few days, I don't want to be mixed up in it. With my mob I want it clean and straight. What I don't want is a random split out of the one big mob. They got Starlight on one bull, one brand. That's all it takes.'

'I'll wait six days.' Hilton growled, ignoring Jack's piece of good sense.

The coals had gone out. With no moon it was a dark night and a little eerie listening to two men engaged in a heated argument.

'I'll take Ralph with me then. The roping and brandin's goin to be tough.'

'Don't you dump me,' warned Walker.

'I don't intend to. You're threatening to dump me and take my man.'

'I'll go out alone.'

'You won't make it out on yer own, Hilton, and you know it.'

There was a brief silence while Hilton groped in the dark for the rum bottle. A horse snorted somewhere nearby and you could hear the clink of the hobble chains. In Jack's corner all I could see was the cigarette glow. Hilton found the rum and I heard the liquid hit the bottom of the pannikin.

'Good luck to you, Jack,' he said, a sardonic twist in his tone. 'I'll help you all I can. We're all goin to need the angels' blessing.'

THREE

THE CROSSING

THE DINGOES WERE drawn by the smell of cooking. On the second morning it began with one, on the next, two or three more joined in, till by the final morning a whole pack howled from a nearby escarpment. I always woke the same, wanting to shut my ears to it, as though the mournful sound was a crack-of-dawn reminder of where we were headed. Fully awake, I thought no more of it. They never went for long, slinking away to lie up somewhere for the day.

As usual, Jack was standing over a little fire scraping hot ash onto a damper. Hilton was emptying one of the jerrycans into the truck tank. Otto's and Ralph's swags were already rolled up and I heard Otto cough – a deep throated rumble – somewhere out in the gloom. They were gathering the horses. The boys hadn't moved – they slept right through the burst of howling.

Jack made the tea while he waited on the damper. I heard an empty jerrycan clang as Hilton tossed it back on board. It struck another empty one. The low-gear work chewed up the fuel. Hilton tightened a strap to secure the fuel cans and joined Jack by the fire.

'I don't want to be tailing these cattle for long,' I heard Hilton grumble.

'I need eight days,' Jack replied. 'Two days to get in there with the stuff. One day to get the hessian up. Four days branding and one day to swim the river and walk over the range. I need low tide to be early morning on the eighth day to make it here in one day.'

Hilton didn't say any more and I made an appearance.

'Big day coming up, Peter,' Jack said to me cheerfully. 'Sleep all right?'

I said I had and poured myself a mug of tea. Hilton remained quiet and the light started to come quickly. I heard Otto cough again. He and Ralph were coming back. I could hear horses snorting and as I peered through the gloom I saw a couple of them.

Otto knelt down and poured tea for himself and Ralph. When he straightened, I could see there was a troubled look on his face. He and Ralph had been talking while they brought the horses in.

'We could do with Ralph, Jack,' he said. 'Brandin them weaners in a curtain yard's gonna be hard.' He looked at the two boys, not long awake and yawning. The big black man had more creases on his face than a charred boab when he wasn't happy.

'No, Hilton can't be left on his own,' Jack said flatly, then an idea seemed to strike him and he looked straight at Hilton. 'You could join us. No hard work. Just be the camp cook.'

'I'm not swimmin any crocodile river, Jack,' Hilton replied, forcing a hoarse chuckle. 'You got a missus like mine you don't take those risks.'

'I got a good one too,' Jack retorted.

Otto laughed, his big battered face suddenly transformed. 'My woman all right too.'

Jack flipped the damper out of the ashes with a stick and with his bush knife cut it into several sections. On a tin plate he'd sliced up some corned beef. There were no invitations in the bush. The tucker was on the table and everyone helped themselves.

'Right, that settles it,' Jack said. 'We gotta saddle up in a minute and get going. Hilton and Ralph stay together when we split.'

It wasn't satisfactory. Young, skilled and very strong, Ralph would be sorely missed when the bronco work began. But what else could Jack do? He couldn't abandon Walker. In the bush the man had limitations, we all knew that.

It was little wonder the explorer Alexander Forrest never saw the gap in the range he was looking for. You could be 300 yards from the opening and still miss it. From the floodplain the range rose more than 1000 feet, most of it a sheer cliff. A narrow gorge cut right through but, because it zigzagged, no break in the cliff rim could be seen from the plain.

In the gorge, Jack walked ahead of the truck, directing Hilton. It was steep but otherwise good going on soil already dry after four hot sunny days. The rest of us rode. Otto led Jack's bay mare and the two mules followed, snatching mouthfuls of the succulent herbs not found on the floodplains.

Eventually we ascended out of the gorge onto a pass. To the east the surface was a tangle of jagged rock. Below and facing north was a deep, boulder-strewn ravine running right back down to what appeared to be nearly sea level. We still couldn't see Walcott Inlet. An imposing sandstone mesa blocked our view straight ahead and away to the right and east the range continued to rise. Jack said it was only five miles to the saltplain. It was the end of the road for the truck. We tied the horses and mules up to one of the many bloodwoods and helped unload. Otto and Ralph grabbed the packsaddles and took them to the mules. Jack and I struggled over with the heavy gear. A thick, weighty saddle blanket went on first. The mules would have to swim twice, Jack said. There was no hope of ferrying all the stuff in one go. The first to go would be the packs, crammed full with supplies, spare clothes and sundry gear. The boys kept bringing other items and Jack started putting some of it aside for the next trip. The camp oven alone was nearly twenty pounds. Jack put it aside and scratched his head, 'We've gotta have the bloody thing. If we cook all the meat in the ash we'll get sick. You can't cook it right through without it looking like a charred up sausage. Good dampers come out of a camp oven too.'

Time was precious but the changeover didn't take long. Jack had brought a tide chart with him from Derby and the next high tide was two hours away. He said we could be on the river mouth two hours before the following low.

There was another brief standoff before we split up.

I think Hilton hated the prospect of sitting down for eight days. It was clear he wasn't going to do any tailing of the cattle and, unable to do much on his own, Ralph would probably spend the time fishing.

'They always say a bird in the hand is better than two in the bush,' Hilton said to Jack through the window of the truck. He had no intention of shaking hands with Jack or waving farewell.

'It was a skinny bird,' Jack shot back. 'Even though most are cleanskins you'll have to give the leaseholder a split of the spoils.' Jack led his mare over towards Hilton. 'I'm doing you a favour, Hilton,' he went on. 'A three-way split on this mob wouldn't have done much for any of us.'

Before Ralph got into the vehicle beside Hilton there was a sad little minute or two. Otto put his arm over Ralph's shoulder and they walked away into the bloodwoods and wattle. Jack said he thought Otto only had the one son. He wasn't sure. They worked together and were nearly inseparable.

The packmules walked unled. They were sensible mules and had done a lot of pack work. Jacko followed Jack's brown mare, Paw Paw dutifully fell in behind, and tailing close behind were the boys. The horse Ralph had been riding was now a spare and was left loose to follow. Otto and I rode at the rear. It was all downhill and reasonable going for horses. On the steeper sections we traversed from one side to the other. On either side of the rock spinifex and wattle, the ground gave way to impenetrable rock; a buttress of quartz-topped sandstone. Boulders as big as cars had tumbled from higher up, perhaps hundreds of years ago, and hit a chock to remained fixed for another few hundred years. Time here was measured in millennia. Some of the packs scraped hard against the boulders as the mules stepped around them, looking for secure footing. At the bottom we entered a narrow valley, heavy with blue grass on the flats – and in the deeply shaded areas, protected on the southern aspect, I saw my first patch of rainforest. Trees tangled overhead in a bind of branches and underneath, vines clung to every trunk. Lateral vines, the connecting threads as thick as a little finger, ran from tree to tree like lattice work. It was hot and steamy and you could feel the pulsating of the tide. We skirted a long waterhole lined with paperbarks and then came onto another with a wide shelf of sandstone on the upper end. The water was shallow and clear and you could hear the water running at the other end. A couple of kingfishers fluttered up into the paperbarks and some brolgas circled and one squawked loudly, as though it gave the orders to the others. They had heard us before we saw them and when they rose off the sandstone you heard the flap of wings, like someone shaking a blanket. Jack said where the brolgas waded there was no salty and we could dismount, take a pee and let the horses drink.

Jack checked his watch. He didn't wear it on his wrist. It was in his pocket with a tiny chain attached to his belt. To read the time he had to pull off a rubber band and remove it from a plastic freezer bag. It was about one o'clock, he said, then he carefully put it back in its waterproofing. He said we'd have some damper and treacle, but there was no time for a billy boil. It was like taking alcoholics to a bar and saying they couldn't have a beer. He drank some water, spat some of it out and rolled a cigarette. For me, it was too hot to smoke. Otto had smoked all the way down and dropped a butt onto the sandstone.

Soon we mounted up again and it wasn't long before the horses were sloshing through water, fetlock deep. It was a wetland. Magpie geese rose with an indignant cackle, flew for 300 yards and outstretched their wings to glide back onto the water. A jabiru flew overhead, the rise and fall of its wings so slow you wondered how it stayed up, and higher again circled a pair of sea eagles. Jack told us that in the wet a great spring flowed all along the base of the Leopolds in this area and at high tide the salt and fresh water met in all the creeks. We had entered the mangroves and some of the creeks still had salt water from the noon high tide. The horses didn't like those creeks and shied away. But they had to be crossed and the bay mare always obeyed Jack. When she went over, the others followed.

It was creepy in the mangroves. The trees grew so close and the dark green foliage was so dense the sun didn't make it through, making it a dank gloomy place – unnerving when you knew what might lurk in the deeper channels. The spiny grass came up to the horses' shins and several times the grass rippled ominously in a straight line, as though a torpedo flew at ground level. That's how fast the creatures – whatever they were – moved. Goannas, Otto said, adding that it was nesting time for the salties. It was a good thing, he commented, that the salties had been shot out because they fiercely protected their nests and where we rode now was perfect habitat for them. It was strange how you could ride from such a scenic landscape teaming with birdlife to a place that felt so alien in a matter of a few horse strides. The more we headed towards the saltplain the more aware we were of the tidal regime. When we first saw the salt water we were riding near the upper limit of the tide and most of the water had already gone. We crossed three salt creeks little more than a fetlock deep, but as we moved out onto the plain you could hear the run in the water a couple of minutes before the first horse reached the edge of the channel. The flow out to the inlet made me think of a burst water main in town. There was no hope of crossing there, so we rode back up to the shallow arms, the heat all the more intense for it came back at you off the hard-crusted surface. When you rode over it, the salt was hard to see. It appeared as a light grey soil, all cracked like shattered glass on the bare patches, but more than half of it under a harsh marine reed. When you stared ahead into the glare of the sun it all shimmered white and you began to wonder if you were riding towards the edge of hell. The inlet itself we still hadn't seen. There was a line of mangroves about two miles to the north and Otto told me they marked the main channel. He said at low tide Walcott Inlet was just a miserable strip of water spreading out from the distant line of mangroves.

The swing back towards the range was only for about a mile. Little channels, just a few feet wide, fanned out from the main and the horses reluctantly stepped into the mud to cross them. There was no water left and in an hour the mud would bake dry. Jack angled back to be on course again and soon nothing but saltplain lay between us and the river mouth. If

Jack got ahead a bit and the mules trekked close on the mare's heels they seemed to float above the ground and Jack's form and the animals became distorted. Closer to Otto and me, the two boys rode on the edge of this extraordinary optical illusion caused by the heat. There were two big hats and stick figures between the hats and saddle – with George you didn't see much more than a hat. If it wasn't for the saddle that horse might have wondered if he was carrying anything. It was above 120° Fahrenheit and I wondered what degree of heat was too hot, when human beings withered and perished.

Otto rode up alongside of me. Since the lunch break he'd stayed behind, last one on the trail. 'Don't like it when it get this bad in March,' he mumbled, more out of his chest than throat. 'Heat like this suck in storms – them big ones the whites call cyclones. We call em willy willies.'

'Think that might happen?' I asked. I felt so lightheaded I don't think any prediction possible on the face of the earth would have scared me at that moment.

Otto shrugged. 'No sign of it. But the weather will change. The air goes real thin in bad heat and all that damp air, way out in the Timor,' he jerked his chin sideways in the direction of the coast, 'blows up into them storms. Them bigfella storms.'

About two hours after the last rest, Jack called another halt and dismounted. He told us all to stay on; it was no place for a rest. He had two waterbags, one fitted to each mule; harness waterbags with thick protective leather on one side. Jack unstrapped one and walked along, starting with Peter. I took notice of where we were, for in the last hour I hadn't seemed to think or see. Just registering Otto's voice beside me when he talked about the storms. Jack must have seen me trying to look through the glare. Your eyes screwed half shut, instinctively. We all should have had sunglasses, but no one contemplated such luxuries in those days.

'Across the inlet is the Harding Range,' he said to me. 'In the soft light before sunset they look magnificent.' Then he pointed east. 'Out there is the Edkins Range and to the south-east the Artesian Range. We're hemmed in by rock. On still days this would be the hottest coastal basin in Australia. But by the time we make camp it won't be too bad.'

It was about four o'clock when we reached the river. We teth-ered the horses in the mangrove shade and took a long drink from the waterbags. Otto lit a fire and placed the billy. The heat dropped off a little and it was good to walk a bit and stretch. Before we did though, we dropped the packs off the mules. The horses and mules were tired and one or two whin-nied when they saw the waterbag being passed around. You felt uneasy drinking and them not. We all felt it. But there was no water to spare.

The river scene wasn't great. It was nearly 200 yards to the mangroves on the other side and the tide fall still had a way to go. The wet mud looked dreadful. I envisaged the horses dropping to their bellies in it, but obviously they didn't. Jack had done it all before, several times.

The fire had to be lit out in the sun on the bare saltpan. In the mangroves the reeds ran over the ground like a mat, spongy to walk on, and inflammable once the sun dried it out after each receding tide. It wasn't comfortable to sit on either, but that's where we waited; anything to be out of the sun. Jack said the king tides swept over the saltplains. One was due in a week's time with the full moon. He took out his watch again and said the out tide had a little more than an hour to run. We would load the packmules fifteen minutes before dead low and be ready. The animals hated the mud, he said. We would wait for the flow to stop – that five minutes of no movement before the tide turned – and go for it. The inflow would begin before we made the east bank. The first wave to pose any threat would be five minutes after tide turn. We would all be okay, he said. Jack clearly wanted to imbrue confidence, make it feel like a game. The salties, he added, had all been shot out.

Legislation to protect the crocodiles had passed through the western Australian parliament the year before, but it would take years for the numbers to increase significantly, from what some claimed had been a near-extinction crisis. It was in the backwaters where the professional shooters didn't go that we had to watch out. Just the same, after a mug from the billy Jack did go for a walk, looking for the telltale slide marks. Peter went with him. His energy was inexhaustible and his regard for his father fell little short of hero worship.

When you're looking forward to something, time drags. Alternately, with a sense of foreboding, time moves fast. Jack lay down on that coarse mud grass, had a sleep – went right off I think – then next thing I hear: 'It's time. Give me yer tobacco rolls and I'll seal em in a freezer bag.' He eased one of the plastic bags out of his nearside saddlebag and took our tobacco. The little bag had a zipper opening. He sealed it, then rolled it tight and pushed it down hard in the saddlebag, joking that dry tobacco was more important than dry gunpowder.

He and Otto packed the mules and we all mounted, rode through the narrow belt of mangroves and waited on the edge of the mud side by side. Otto had put a halter on Jacko and Paw Paw and had Jacko on a lead rope. Paw Paw apparently followed Jacko everywhere, no matter how unappealing the going was. Just in case typical mule stubbornness emerged, Jack carried an extra lead rope.

We sat our mounts in silence. There seemed to be no life out here. The main channel of Walcott Inlet was a mere thirty yards to our left, an expanse of water stretching more than a half-mile at low tide. The Isdell channel was still 150 yards wide, a long swim in clothes and boots. I wanted to take my shirt off and tie the arms around my waist but Jack said there were too many marine nasties and on no account was I to take it off. As we watched the water, it went still: a dead calm descending on the whole waterway.

Otto didn't wait for Jack's urging. He ran the coin in his spurs down the ribs of his horse, a solid bay about sixteen hands. The mud was firmer than it looked and only the hooves squelched out of sight. Jack had his whip at the ready to crack it sharply whenever Jacko hesitated and the lead rope in Otto's hand went taut. The big mule plunged forward and Paw Paw went with him. Next went the boys, using their tightly coiled stockwhips to get their mounts started. Jack and I were the last to leave the bank.

The two mules and the horses had swum tidal rivers before. When Jack managed Oobagooma he said mustering the coastal side of the station would have been impossible if he hadn't frequently swum the tidal streams. His horses had become quite used to it, but none the less hated the mud and the salt water. Once committed, all that was in their minds was to get it over with. Near the water they sank further into the mud and they took headlong bounds until the water was too deep and all of a sudden they were swimming, only their heads still in the afternoon sun. They swam vigorously, sucking the hot air in urgent gasps. The boys had been taught what to do at the age of seven. They slid out of the saddles on the near side and seized the pommel of the saddle in their right hand. Their left hands paddled and they made sure their bodies floated as close to the surface as possible. Horses used their legs like pistons when they swam and if a rider's legs were to sink there would be bruising or even worse, the whole body might be dragged down.

'Hold tight,' gasped Jack, he and his mare swimming close behind. He never took his eye off George.

For me it was another initiation. I had never swum with a horse before, but it was common sense. When I felt them begin to swim I slid off and clung to the front of the saddle flap. For small boys the pommel was okay, but anybody bigger might inadvertently push his mount deeper into the water.

The water was tepid and the colour of it made you feel the Isdell was a big sewer channel. None of us, man or beast wanted to be in it a second longer than necessary. The harsh breathing of the horses injected even more of a sense of urgency. A tide change too soon would be disastrous. It was impossible to judge distance – three minutes' hard swimming could seem like eternity. Otto swam without any help from his horse. He was just too big and would have hampered it. Instead he swam breaststroke. The mules powered through the water and at the halfway mark were fifteen yards in front. Otto had dropped the lead rope on Jacko once the mule began to swim. The packs buoyed them up, their backs and rumps above the water. It gave them an advantage over the horses.

'Tide swing!' Otto was the first to feel the tug in the current. With water filling his mouth I couldn't be positive that's what he yelled, but at least it was better than 'Croc comin!' I couldn't feel any drag, just a little wave that lifted us all like floating bottles, then soon after came a bigger one. Then we heard it – a muffled roar. Where we were swimming would be thirty-five feet deeper in just six hours. It's a monster flood, twice a day, the Kimberley tide. I couldn't swim any faster and Bluey was powering like an engine at full throttle. Ahead I saw the mules and the packs rise out of the water. They'd touched bottom. Bluey had seen them too. All the horses had, and the knowledge that their ordeal was nearly over helped them find a bit more kick. In no time we were out of the water and floundering through the mud. Another couple of minutes and we'd all made it to the mangroves on the eastern side.

No one spoke. I grabbed the trunk of a mangrove and heaved, trying to get air back into my lungs. Big Otto lay on the reeds, his knees drawn up. Jack was on all fours. The boys hadn't got winded and I saw Peter go up onto the saltplain to grab Jacko and tie him up. Jacko was always hungry and looking for a pick. The older mule, Paw Paw, had pushed through the mangrove belt and lay down on his tummy with his legs underneath. He was just tired, not winded like the horses who drew in air with quick pants, flanks rising and falling in stress-charged urgency. They made no effort to leave the narrow band of mangroves until they'd caught their breath, then they became restless and began to wander, the dragging reins catching their legs.

'They're thirsty,' Jack mumbled, his voice still hoarse from breathlessness. 'We'll mount and get going. Head straight for the camp.'

We saw scattered mobs of cattle all the way to Jack's old camp. They didn't turn and bolt like most of the Humbert Valley cattle did. These cattle had been handled, yet not a single beast I saw carried a brand. All of them were in fat condition too. The range on this side − the north side − was barren and inhospitable. The tiny pockets of jungle were locked away in deep, inaccessible gorges. The rest was rock under wattle and spinifex. Here and there, the dark green of solitary boabs could be spotted against the rock which seemed almost blood red in the lowering sun. But savanna glens lay trapped between the saltplain and the rock, so sharply defined you wouldn't have been surprised to see a fence as though some farmer had put down pasture improvement. On the narrow flats in these glens grew the tall blue grass. Jack was right about the blue grass. If the flats on the tiny freshwater streams grew nothing but cane grass, the cattle wouldn't have made it through one winter. The Walcott herd was confined by land and water but well-fed. It was Jack's holding paddock. A clever bit of planning, I thought.

Jack's old camp was on a raised plain. It was only a few feet above the saltplain, but not even the king tides pushed up this high and the ground was at last soil, not that cracked, salt-crusted claypan we had ridden across. Cane grass grew to stirrup iron height. Cattle tracks ran through it everywhere and patches of grass had been eaten right down to the ground. When young and growing, the grass could be sweet enough.

A low ridge half a mile long blocked our view of the inlet. A short way ahead of us, directly opposite the sun, rose a steep bluff. The sun lit up the exposed rock, not vermilion like most of the range, but black with traces of pale quartz. A patch of laurel underneath hinted at a jungle pocket. Behind us and almost shutting out the sun as I looked, was a steep ridge studded with boulders and shattered rock. Between the camp and the ridge was a flowing spring, Jack said, ideal for the horses. As we unsaddled I could hear the evening breeze stir the leaves in the biggest boab I have ever seen. It was the marker of Jack's camp.

'Good spot, isn't it,' Jack said, the saddle already off his mare. There was excitement in his voice. 'This old giant throws out a nice bit of shade.'

Before putting the hobbles on we led our horses over to the spring, close to where the ridge petered out onto the salt-plain. Issuing from the range, a narrow stream fed into the spring, forming a large pool. Otto already had his own big bay and Jack's mare drinking when the boys and I walked our horses towards the stream.

'Keep away from that big pool,' he warned. 'Good place for a gator.'

Everyone had their own names for crocodiles. To Jack they were salties or crocs, Otto called them gators and my dad just called them crocs.

The mules and the spare horse had gone ahead and were drinking like bushfire suction pumps. Bluey was so eager, I had to run beside him for the last fifty yards. It was lovely clear water with the green cane grass right to the edge. You could kneel down, drink and stay clean. One of the boys pulled his boots and socks off and waded in, his horse going with him. Otto shook his head.

'You get away with that today,' he said grimly. 'But if there's one of them gators in that there pool, tomorra he be waitin. They smell em good through the water and they wait. That's how they get all their tucker.'

We let the horses have a long drink and when they backed off, they pawed the ground, slicing little strips of grass right out of the soil. Otto said the intense heat and the saddle blanket all damp with sweat affected their skin and they needed to have a good roll on the fresh grass. It would have been better if they could swim, he said, but the horses and the two mules were gator-savvy and knew the fine line between safety and becoming gator tucker. Those that didn't learn at Oobagooma soon parted company with the herd.

It was great to see the horses rolling and kicking their legs in the air. The big mules knelt down and rolled too. It had been a long, thirsty day for them. I saw George stroking his brown gelding down the neck and Peter had his pocket knife out, cleaning around the frog area of his chestnut's hooves. I suddenly thought of the horse poison plant and asked Otto about it.

'Plenty of it here,' he said. 'It like damp place, near the rocks.' He pointed to a small grey-leafed bush on the other side of the stream, growing among the rocks. The ridge rose sharply from the other side.

'Plenty feed,' Otto went on. 'Horses not eat much. Might eat none of it. But if the feed fall away, they eat it and get bad sickness. Go down quick. Except them mules. It don't affect them.' He paused, looking around with an expression of distrust, as though the land welcomed no one. By the camp-fire I had already heard him say nothing good happened at Munja. Jack's Walcott camp was only about seven miles from the Munja ruins.

'I hope we get them cattle quick and leave. Leprosy skeletons all up in the caves about here. Them old blokes will tell yer.'

When the rolling was over and the last horse stood up and shook off grains of soil and bits of dry twigs blown off the fan palms, we hobbled them out. The mules we let be. Otto said they had just about lived with Jack and him over the past three years. They wouldn't wander far. The horses, however, were not far from their home and the herd. Given the chance and a low tide, we could wake in the morning and find ourselves all alone if not for the hobbles. If the horses left, even Jacko might reconsider his loyalties, and if he left, Paw Paw would be right behind.

The night came in so quick the flames of Jack's fire guided us back to camp, each carrying a bridle and any scattered wood we saw in the grass. While we were away with the horses Jack had snapped off some foliage from a nearby river-gum, broken it all into short pieces and laid them on the ground, having first trampled the cane grass with the weight of the packs. For the next few days the leaves would be our tablecloth and already the aroma of damper cooking in the camp oven filled the air. The camp oven was near the fire, the corned beef under an old tea towel and potatoes and onions in the hot coals. There was a bottle of mustard, salt and pepper – and a spray can of insect repellant. That I hadn't seen before, and when I commented Jack said it was to put on when we went to the swag. Keep the mosquitoes away until we got to sleep. We put our saddles into position, depending on whether you wanted an armchair or a headrest, and waited for dinner. I felt relaxed for the first time since we'd left Ooba-gooma. We'd swum the river and everything was going to plan. Life at Walcott Inlet was going to be good fun, I thought, leaning into my saddle and listening to the dry sticks crackle in the flame and sniffing the smell of campfire smoke. We had our tobacco back. It was the first item unpacked, Jack said, smiling at the power of his own addiction.

Jack was able to relax and lean back into his saddle too. He rolled a cigarette and for awhile there was silence. The boys had fallen asleep. It was small wonder.

'There's a salty-free hole less than half a mile from here,

Peter,' Jack said, the shadow from the flames dancing over his whole form with the tiny red glow in the centre. 'You and the boys can bathe there every day. The less you smell the better, helps with the mozzies and the flies. Between us and that bluff is a mangrove saltwater creek. It's a deep channel. The salties use it. Be wary any time you go near it.'

'Must be damp here after rain, Jack,' I commented. It felt like we were on a floodplain, even though the ground fell away slightly on either side.

'It's more than that. If it rains we'll move over to the ridge. I got a spot there too. Its disadvantage is the stream. You gotta walk through that spring to get to the horses. Also, the king browns and goannas like the rocks near the water. They got easy access to the things they like to eat and if the country floods they got shelter.' Jack drew on his cigarette and butted it on the side of his boot. 'Both are a bloody nuisance around camps. The goannas smell the food and the browns get about at night. I've woke with one all coiled up beside me. Nothin cuddly about em.'

'It's a great spot, Jack,' I said. 'How'd you come to find it?'

'Looking for country. I got the maps and saw this was vacant land. If there were station possibilities I thought I might be able to apply for it, have the title changed and lease it. I swam the Charnley, too, for a look at Munja on the other side. Bob Dowling had it until 'sixty-eight, then abandoned it. When I contacted the Lands department they said the old feeding station area had been made a reserve, attached now to the Aboriginal reserve east of the Calder and north of the Charnley. Before the war Munja was run by the government as a sort of settling-down place for the tribes. They slaughtered a lot of cattle over there and when the government officer left in 'forty-six, the cattle went wild. These cattle I got here bred up from the old Munja stock.'

'This is no duffing job,' Jack went on for my benefit, perhaps worried about what I might pass onto Dad and Uncle Allan. 'The cattle have been abandoned, they're all cleanskins and with prices the way they are someone's goin to nab em. Might as well be me and Otto. Also there's a rumour in the industry the Yanks are going to enforce tuberculosis eradication. If we want to keep selling beef to the US we gotta clean up every herd in the country. The wild cattle they'll shoot. Could all start in four or five years.'

'You never goin to settle down in this place, Jack,' Otto said gravely, like a father to a son. Land title restrictions meant little to Otto. I'd almost forgotten he was there, except for the little red glow of his cigarette in the dark. We had all lit up.

'That right, ain't it,' he persisted. 'Bad place here. You buy the place you told me about.'

Jack got up to serve the meal and gave the boys a shake. 'Tomorrow, Otto, we're makin the first strike for that place. You grow old there too.'

'Me goin back to Beagle Bay and the women. No women out here in the ranges. They nearly all went barren at Munja. No kids, no soul. People just drifted away, got old and died. At Munja they blamed the water.' Otto shifted, sat up a little, as though he wanted to make a statement. 'There was nothing wrong with the water. It was the spirit people talkin to us.

We'd let the white man take our land and from there on it was all dead finish. But I'm not all dead finish. I get back with a woman and get more piccaninnies. I'm getting tired of ridin me arse off. No offence to you, Jack, but this last job. We get these cattle. I get my share and I got enough to go home.'

'Go and find her,' laughed Jack. 'No offence to me. I'm wearin out too. Need to pull this one off.'

FOUR

THE HESSIAN YARD CAMP

IT WAS CRACKING dawn when Jack stood over my swag. There was a good fire ablaze. Otto must have dragged in a log from beneath the rivergums. I could see the form of two saddled horses beyond the firelight and I heard Otto cough. He had a bad cough early. If you couldn't see where he was, you just waited for him to cough and spit. He was fetching the mules.

'We're goin back for the gear,' Jack said, in between puffs. His lacklustre tone said it all. Two more swims across that creepy river and eight hours on a salt plain so hot you could feel the moisture being sucked out of your skin. It would want to be a dream place Jack was aiming to buy.

'Be gone all day,' he added. He always addressed Peter too. In Jack's eyes, Peter was a man no different from Otto or me. Peter sat up but didn't say anything. 'Have a rest day. Make a damper and keep an eye on the horses. Just one job – saddles. Wash everything in the spring: saddlecloths and bridles – even yer boots. The salt water can bugger up the leather in a few days.'

He exhaled a thin column of tobacco smoke and drew deeply; you knew he had something serious to say when he did that. 'Don't go far from the camp. It's nesting time. I know they were pretty well shot out before the ban, but the hunters never bothered coming up into these creeks. They shot from boats. Any other way was too hard.'

The two men mounted up and left. It was a little sobering, watching them ride away in the gathering light. What if something happened and they didn't get back? It was just a brief shiver, nothing rational about it. All three of us were hungry and Jack had left the damper he made the evening before on some warm ash. With treacle and hot black tea we had a good breakfast. While Peter ate he often walked around, always on the lookout. Reared in the bush, he had developed an exceptional sense of hearing. He announced that he could hear a waterfall. It must be the swimming hole his dad had spoken of.

The excitement was too much; the saddles could wait. We wolfed down the last of the damper, pulled on our boots, grabbed our hats and left. It was easy walking across the flood-plain, following the cattle pads. Except for the mangroves on the salt creek, the timber was sparse and scattered. Big rivergums dominated, with bauhinia, quinine and the odd bloodwood. In a few minutes the sound of falling water guided us towards the spot. We crossed a salt creek. The tide was out and we estimated another two hours before it surged back.

None of us liked walking through the wet mangroves, but if we got nervous we laughed. This was an adventure, an exploration where the adults had no say. We hurried on amid the squawks of bower birds, a plain brown bird very vocal at our intrusion. We crossed the second tidal creek, slipping about in the mud. This second crossing put us onto higher, rockier ground, and we followed a low ridge to the main creek, which was flowing like a mountain stream after a storm. A wide rock slab came into view, then there before us was the waterfall. It fell about ten feet into an ugly tidal hole. The water spilling over the rock was pure and crystal clear, but in the hole it churned up black silt and was a dirty brown by the time it reached the channel through the mangroves, only forty yards from the waterfall.

The sandstone slab was like a natural spillway, holding back enough water to resemble a man-made dam. The water gushed over the lowest point and, standing on a hump of sandstone, we peered across an expanse of water fifty yards wide. There were little islands of pandanus and paperbarks, and here and there whirlpools and eddies. We ran to the edge of the water on the southern side where the water level neatly met the rock rim. It was only a few feet deep and you could see through the water as though the surface was glass and nothing lay between it and the sandstone floor. Two large fish glided past as we looked in. George couldn't contain his excitement. 'We can swim here,' he exclaimed. 'No salties come up here.'

We pulled off our clothes, boots and dived in. The temperature was perfect and the grimy sweat, sticky and stale around our groins and armpits, washed off the second we hit the water. A water monitor had been sunbaking on the far side and crept onto a raised strip of sandstone to see us better.

This was his territory and what were these pale-skinned mammals? He didn't watch for long, departing in a sudden splash and entering a gap between two stratums of sandstone.

Crossing to the other side looked hazardous. In the widest part the water looked tranquil enough, but towards the rock rim it suddenly surged as a torrent strong enough to pull an adult. We wanted to get over and climb up onto a high shelf of sandstone, high enough to see up into the next valley. I swam out towards the centre and immediately felt the pull in the water. That wasn't going to work, so we got dressed and walked up to an escarpment which promised to provide a similar view. The valley widened out in the form of a bowl encircled by the hard rock of the range. Away to the east was a gorge and to the north the range rose in a gentle slope, studded with a million boulders. On the bottom lay the blue grass flats and away from the noise of the water we could hear cows lowing from the timber, a contented call to their big calves, ever watchful of where they were, for this was dingo pack country.

By the time we got back to the camp it was stinking hot again. The humidity never eased off; even at daybreak your skin was moist and sticky, but when the heat rose with the sun you breathed as though at the door of a sauna room. We washed the gear, checked the horses, cooked another damper and headed for the waterfall again, only to be stopped by the tide. The creeks were full of seething, frothed up salt water. A croc could be crawling along in ankle deep water and you wouldn't see it. We returned to the camp, hot and slapping at mosquitoes. It would be three hours before we could cross the salt creeks and have another swim. It was too hot and uncomfortable to do nothing, so we collected firewood.

Jack and Otto rode in about an hour after sunset. It was about five days to full moon and the country was bathed in a partial light. Neither uttered a word. They dropped the load off the mules, unsaddled and poured themselves hot tea from the billy. George'd had the water simmering and when he heard the snort of one of the horses as they approached, he brought the billy to the boil. Peter sliced the warmed up damper and put it on a tin plate. The roll of corned beef lay in a cloth. They hadn't put the hobbles on, but I didn't like to say anything. A few minutes passed and Peter mentioned it.

'Hobble em in the morning,' Jack mumbled. 'They won't go anywhere tonight. We missed the worst of that mud yesterday – just by luck. This time we rode straight into it with the light goin. Bloody blue mud, sank to their bellies almost. Goin to have to watch it when we go out.'

He asked about our day and Peter told him we had found the swimming hole.

'No salty in it then,' he commented dryly.

'Didn't see one,' George said.

'You didn't see one.' Jack laughed. 'There's not one in there, that's for sure. Did you see many cattle?'

'Lots up in that valley; we could hear them.'

Next morning, no one stirred before dawn, not even Jack. Peter and George hobbled the two horses and I got the fire going. Jack was exhausted and lay full length on his swag.

Otto sat against the trunk of a bauhinia, smoking. He looked worried.

For breakfast we ate the last of the corned beef on warmed-up damper. I told Jack about all the fish we saw above the rock bar and asked if he had another line in his saddlebag.

'Ralph's got the only one I had. But we'll get a killer today. Boil the meat up in salt and that should do us. Last four or five days and hopefully we're out of here by then. Put the yard up tomorra and next day into em. Do it in three days.'

He tugged the tobacco roll out of his shirt pocket and began to roll the leaves. I took over a pannikin of tea, but I knew he wouldn't touch it before the first draw. Otto thanked me for his mug and I poured some out for the boys, too. It was planning time. I sensed we had reached that moment and I wanted to know. At Halls Creek we mustered to a yard, branded up, drafted out the fats – those ready for market – and drove them with us to the next herd and another yard. Then all the fats were taken to a holding paddock near the main trucking out yards.

'These cattle in here,' Jack began, 'will be in scattered mobs, dominated by a wild bull. There'll be some juvenile bulls too, but the big bloke chases them away when a cow's on heat. We'll gather a hundred or more each day and yard em. The big bulls we won't worry about. Once the pressure's on they'll break and we won't chase em. They're better gone. If we had a road and a bull catcher we'd throw and strap em, but in here, we don't want em. When we've branded up the calves and weaners we take em back to where we collected em.

That's their territory. The bulls will reclaim their cows. Then
the next day we go into other pockets and creeks and get out
another hundred or so. We may not get all the young cattle
done, but by branding I've made a claim on the herd. They're
my cattle and I can finish the job at the Hope Creek yards
before we box the lot. Hilton won't be happy, but we'll clean
up in one day inside the big timber yard.' He paused and
tasted his tea. 'More sugar please, one of you boys. I'm
knocked up. Never taken kindly to a long swim. Anyway, on
the fourth day we saddle in the dark and have em on the run
by dawn. Before heading for the river we load up the mules
with our gear and any tucker left. The yard we'll abandon.'

The boys and I washed the packsaddles and the two riding
saddles Jack and Otto used. That done, one of the boys
announced we were going to the waterfall and Jack and Otto
decided to come too. At the rock bar Jack told us to check for
drag marks before each swim. Looking down at the bare rock,
I wondered how you could ever detect any evidence of movement, but Otto ran his big hand over the surface and the
smoothing out of fine grit left a mark with the sun behind.

'Don't last long,' Otto said. 'Sun and a bit of breeze, all
gone. But them gators don't come up here anyway. Too bad
we don't have a line. Catchem barramundi here.'

Jack didn't respond. It would have been easier to catch a
big fish than chase a killer down. It was simply one of those
quirks of fate: he'd had a line and a jam jar half-full of hooks,
but gave it to Ralph, thinking we would never have time for
fishing.

There was no rest for Jack that day. After the visit to the

waterhole he saddled the spare horse, the light bay gelding, and rode towards the salt creek east of the camp. He said he wanted to ride around and see where the mobs were running. All up, there was only a couple of thousand acres of feed between the salt plains and the ranges. He intended to work out a mustering plan. The boys wanted to go with him despite the intense heat but Jack told them their mounts needed all the rest possible. Big Otto made himself a billy of tea and worked on the knives with an oil stone. The boys and I decided to go back to the waterfall. It would be better than sitting under the boab tree, feeling hot and bored. But the tide was back in. The tide ruled our lives.

I sat down and yarned with Otto awhile. The boys went off with a fire-scorched saucepan to gather some native gooseberries, a yellow berry with a citrus-like taste. The soft-stemmed bush was plentiful in damp, sandy soils. We had eaten a few the previous day.

Otto didn't like the mud he and Jack had encountered. He said it would be hard to steer a mob of 400 around it. They wouldn't go into it. Every beast, except maybe the young calves, would know about the blue mud, akin to quicksand. If they smelt it, there was no holding them.

'We gotta pray they follow the mules,' he said, somewhat despondently. I hadn't heard him say 'pray' before. Otto was probably mission-reared. 'Horses no good. Yer gotta kick em and spur em into mud. Them cattle see that and there's no foolin em.'

Otto's knives must have been razor sharp. He just kept working the stone, drawing on a cigarette and drinking black tea. We had to have constant fluid and water would have been better for us, but the tea had a taste and gave you something to do, apart from brushing off ants and swatting mosquitoes. I may have dozed off, or gone into the kind of heat-induce stupor when you lose all sense of time. Suddenly I was aware of cattle all around us. There must have been thirty of them, each one taking a distinct and individual interest in the camp. Some stretched their necks out and you could see their nostrils quiver, catching the camp scents. Others nosed the ground, their nostrils roving like an elephant trunk, testing the ground odours. They could smell the saddle grease. The boys and I had oiled the saddles on the ground and slung them into bauhinia trees on lateral branches. There were five or six bauhinias within thirty yards of the camp. Most of the cattle soon lost interest and began chewing their cud – a sign of contentment, that all was well.

'You wanta bring cattle up that seen no man before, or not seen one of us for a long time,' Otto said quietly. The cattle heard his voice and froze, eyes wide and watchful. 'You lie down on yer back and kick yer legs up in the air. They'll come right up and form a circle. Won't hurt yer. Just curious.' He smiled, 'you wanta try it?'

Just then we saw Jack. It must have been much later in the afternoon than I thought. The boys hadn't come back. They would have been swimming, taking the opportunity while the tide was out. Jack was skirting out around the mob and the cattle turned to face him. He had mustered them to the camp. For a few minutes Jack sat his horse, letting them get used to his presence. He had the revolver in his hand.

'Looks like it's skinning time,' Otto whispered. 'He'll ride in quiet and take one of them fat heifers.'

Jack came on very steadily. He could select one, gallop after it and drop it with a bullet behind the ear, but such a violent explosion of activity could upset the little mob for days and their fear and unease would be detected by any mobs they ran into. It was imperative he got close and dropped the targeted animal without fuss. And that's what happened. The shot was no more than a twig snapping, no echo in the high humidity and the heifer simply fell dead onto its belly then rolled over, the nerves quivering in her extended legs. The whole mob reacted to the revolver shot, spun a few yards one way or the other and stared at their fallen in utter astonishment. Otto was on his feet in an instant and jogged over to cut the heifer's throat. When he moved, the mob left at a gallop and went fifty yards before stopping and turning. Several fanned out, heads held high and though they shook their heads in warning, it was a bluff. With curled, sharp pointed horns, these were cattle living in a wild state. Safe and secure in numbers, they could drive off dingoes. One of their own was in trouble and the herd instinct had come to the fore, but it lasted only seconds. Nothing held their focus for long. The mob filtered away and only an aged cow hung back, occasionally mooing.

Otto quickly peeled the skin from the hindquarters to get the rump steak while Jack removed the delicacies. He took a tomahawk to the skull for the brains and sliced out the liver and sweetbreads. Everything went into an iron bucket, which had been carried in on the second load. Jack planned to boil the meat for an hour, take it out and rub salt into it, then boil again. The menu was liver for dinner and brains for breakfast. Both rich in vitamins, he said, and we needed a special treat for the job ahead. My idea of a treat was chocolate and strawberry ice cream.

With the butchering completed Otto took the bronco rope from his saddle and placed the loop around the bottom hind leg, then we all got hold of the rope and dragged the carcass for about fifty yards. Given the wind in the wrong place, that wasn't far enough, but it was heavy pulling in 100° Fahrenheit plus. Oh boy, I thought, my boots and hat for a fishing line!

Next day we built the yard. Jack selected a site between the camp and a small stony ridge on the edge of the inlet. It was about 400 yards from the camp, on an open plain. On either side it wasn't far to the marine salt plains. The open area was good for yarding; you don't want many trees in the way when working cattle into a yard they're not sure about. The problem was four anchorage points for the yard. There were two bauhinias we could use and two fan palms. Jack wasn't sure about the rooting of the fan palms. There's a lot of weight in hessian suspended along a wire. The palms had to be reinforced with stays. One end of the stay is placed in a small shallow hole, cut with a tomahawk, and the other fastened to the palm with wire. Jack and Otto went to cut the stays out of other bauhinias while the boys and I rolled out the hessian.

With stays twitched in tight and long wires in place, the laborious task of fastening the hessian commenced. We used string. If a beast panicked enough it might run straight into the hessian. The string would break, leaving the long wire intact. With me standing on the iron bucket, Otto and I did the top ties and the boys tied the hessian onto the ground wire. It took only a gentle breeze to lift hessian from the bottom if not tied, which spooked half-wild cattle more than anything.

It was a big yard, forty yards deep and thirty yards wide. Large enough for a bronco horse to work among a hundred head of cattle. The front of the yard, or the loading end, was left fully open. It was here the aluminium pickets came into play, a nightmare to pack and carry in. They were used to make a thirty-yard gate. After the cattle had been driven into the yard the loading side had to be quickly closed off. To make it was simple enough. Hessian was tied to one of the anchors, in this case a fan palm, and thirty yards rolled out. The pickets were tied onto the hessian about four feet apart, so that the hessian stood upright when rushed in to form the fourth side of the yard. While the cattle were being yarded it acted as a wing on one side, held up at the outer end by two forked poles. On the opposite side another wing was put up, using the five remaining pickets and two cut forks. The whole principle was ingenious for its simplicity.

The yard was up by midday and, the tide running towards low, the boys and I headed for the waterfall. The black tidal hole jolted us back to reality that day. Marks clearly showed that during the previous low tide a crocodile had waddled all the way to the foot of the rock bar and turned, following the rock into some mangroves. It would have been a steep clamber for him to make it up to the fresh water and it was most unlikely. But we were playing a form of Russian roulette and being young and daring we loved it. You never think you might die at sixteen – and at ten or eleven the thought doesn't even register. But it was not a crocodile that made us silent for a minute or two. Two big dogs stood on the highest rock perched at the top of the rock face on the other side. The centre flow of the stream was between us and them. They were dingoes; yellow, with pointed ears and a white tip on the tail. There was nothing threatening about their demeanour. Perhaps they had seen us on the first day and were curious. One faced us squarely, his eyes fixed in our direction and the tail swishing from side to side. The other, slightly smaller, had softer features. It was the mate of the bigger dog. She lowered her head over the lip of the fall – more a steep boulder scree than a cliff – and tried to gather more scent. They were bold, for dingoes. It occurred to me they felt safe because of the water. Then again, maybe that was wishful thinking. We went on swimming and diving and when I looked up again they were gone.

We forgot about the time and found the tide surging in when we arrived at the first crossing. There was no option but wade through as fast as possible. We were too hungry to sit around the waterfall for six hours.

Back at the camp something was wrong. Otto wore that troubled scowl I had come to know and Jack was squatted at the front legs of one of the horses. It was the spare horse, the light bay.

'There's a gator in that hole over there,' Otto said grimly. 'The spring hole. It's grabbed that horse. Not big enough to drag him down, but that leg, it bad. We down a horse. That horse gonna be no good.'

We went over to look. It was very distressing. The teeth of the crocodile had rasped into the flesh like a saw, flaying open the skin so that bone was visible and you could see the torn white sinew. Jack was bathing the leg with warm salt water. The horse was in pain, ears back and head down, his muzzle on Jack's shoulder. Jack was as white as a sheet. Not naming his horses might make you think that he was indifferent towards them. Nothing could be further from the truth.

'The bloody salty has come out of the water to get this fella. I heard a commotion last night. One horse squealed and the rest snorted. Meant to check at daylight and forgot.' Jack shook his head and stood up. 'Infection's the killer in this heat and humidity. No wonder no one ever stayed in this hell hole. We'll brand a hundred and go with em. We gotta at least do that many.'

That night the mosquitoes gave us no peace until Jack went out with his torch and collected some cow dung. He wouldn't let us use any more repellant; it had to be kept for an emergency, in case one of us got sick or injured. The smoke of the dung hovered over the camp, a sweet innocuous odour, not unpleasant to breathe. It drove off the mosquitoes and we slept until dawn. Normally the bad nights for mosquitoes were to do with the tides. Low tide at midnight left the mud in the mangroves exposed and on summer nights the mosquitoes swarmed in, but a rising tide carried a slight breeze, sometimes almost imperceptible but enough to disperse mosquito swarms. I made a comment about it while the billy boiled at dawn and Otto disagreed.

'It's building up,' he growled. 'It gone now, but back a few hours I seen lightning, way out on them islands. Out around Cockatoo and Karlan them storms be, that's why we got them mozzies bad. The rains are comin back.'

'Think yer right,' Jack said thoughtfully, lighting his second smoke since dawn and pouring a mug of tea. We were having baked fillet steak for breakfast. The ants had got into the brains, black mass of them. The fillet was meant to be for dinner. After the butchering Jack had washed the fillet, wrapped it in a calico bag and buried it a foot down, using the tomahawk to dig the hole. When he dug it up he washed it again, rubbed the whole piece with salt and popped it into the camp oven.

'We'll brand what we can today and tomorra,' he went on. 'On the third day we swim out. If we get some rough weather at Hope Creek it won't matter.'

We caught our horses and saddled up. The spare horse had a very swollen leg and could only hobble around. Jack said he would bathe the leg again when the day's work was over. He led the way back towards the Isdell. None of the tidal creeks made it as far as the range and we had an easy ride to the river. On the way back we rode into several small hollows, all walled in by the range. There were cattle in every one of them and by about 8.30 am we had 130 head walking straight towards the yard. We had them well covered, with Jack and Otto flanking a side each and the boys and me pushing the tail. Two bulls at different times emerged from the pack and broke for freedom, a red heifer sprinting alongside the second bull to leave. We didn't stand a chance to block that heifer and Jack raised his hand, holding his stockwhip at the ready. If we went after one heifer we would probably lose the lot. With one hundred yards to go, the mood of the herd changed. The leaders were eyeing off the hessian and sensed a trap. It was time to use the stockwhips.

'Righto, up em.'

Jack's order was just loud enough for us to hear. It's impossible to say why, but a human voice raised at the wrong moment can start a stampede among half-wild cattle. Whips, on the other hand, bully cattle into submission. They are frightened of whips and bolt away from the sharp cracks, so when the stockwhips were wielded this mob launched themselves straight into the hessian tunnel and the yard. Otto galloped to the end of the hessian wing with all the pickets, jumped from his horse and, with his weight leaning outwards, ran with the hessian gate to the opposite tree. It was a flimsy-looking yard with those cattle milling around in there. Like holding a possum in a paper bag. When we rode our horses away to the camp I wondered whether the yard would still be there when we got back. But there was no wind and when the hessian was motionless it must have looked as solid as a brick wall to the cattle.

At the camp we had a quick mug of tea and some cold damper while Jack and Otto loaded the branding gear into one of the packs. The bronco work was executed off Jacko and Paw Paw, in relay. They had the weight and strength to pull up weaners more than half the size of the cows. Otto did the bronco work and Jack the castrating, de-horning and branding.

It took nearly an hour to get ready. The boys and I had to gather small pieces of firewood and put it in a couple of the packs. They were too heavy to carry, which meant a pack-saddle had to go on Paw Paw. Otto saddled up Jacko for the first bronco shift. When we got to the yard the branding fire had to be lit inside, about halfway up one side. With the sun overhead the brand was red hot within minutes and Otto got to work. He was a master of the lasso, capable of a consistent bulls eye toss at five yards. To throw the loop any further could stir up the cattle. It was a skill of intense concentration. Once he'd selected his animal he worked it into position. If the animal was crowded into the mob, the loop didn't fall cleanly. Sometimes it took five minutes to get a clear, unimpeded toss. There was no cowboy action. A spin of the rope around his head might have plunged the mob through the hessian. It was a simple toss.

On contact the mule walked backwards, synchronising with the weaner's recoil towards the mob. With the mule anchoring back, the rope went taut almost instantly. At this point Peter and I worked as a team. We waited until the weaner was pulled up towards the little fire, then my job was to grab its tail and pull it over. The instant it hit the ground, Peter had to respond like a rugby halfback, seize the upper front leg and thrust it back towards the chest, with both his knees planted either side of the shoulder. Once the weaner was thrown and securely held, Otto slackened the pressure of the lasso, jumped off and ran in to help Peter. Jack did the castrating first if it was male, de-horned and placed the brand last. Little George's job was to pass the de-horners and the brand to his dad, plus stoking the fire.

In the air-locked yard the temperature lifted a degree

every few minutes. Trampled by the cattle, the thick cane grass in the yard the day before had vanished, replaced by fresh dung and urine. Buffalo flies buzzed in their millions and a pungent smell rose with the heat. Attracted by the malodorous yard, kites soon began to circle overhead. When Jack threw the first castrated testicle out towards the yard centre, it was only a few minutes before the first brown-feathered kite swooped. After several castrations it was like watching seagulls scramble for flakes of bread. They had no fear of us.

The throwing of the weaners took a toll. Most had been born in the spring and at six months of age weighed more than a heavy man. I managed to dodge most of the back-leg kicks, but when one connected it sent me reeling and I lost my grip on the tail. Almost worse than the pain was rushing in again, knowing the animal would be watching, waiting to let go again. Peter could count on several nasty kicks as well. When he dived onto the shoulder and locked the foreleg, I simultaneously seized the upper rear leg and pulled it straight, my bum on the ground and stretched out like a rower at the completion of a stroke. But some big weaners were just too strong. They thrashed and twisted and if the upper leg pulled out of my hands Peter took a whack anywhere from the chest up.

We drank copious amounts of water and worked on. I lost all track of time. Jack sent George back to the camp to make a damper and when he returned an hour and a half later we stopped for an hour. Peter and I lay flat on the ground, using our hats to cover our eyes from the sun. Otto and Jack were okay. Their job was a bit more satisfying than ours. The mules were changed every fifteen weaners. By four o'clock every young beast in the yard had a brand on it. Forty-five head, Jack said. He was delighted and said Peter and I had done a great job. I had so many bruises it was like listening to the praises of an AFL coach as the medic shuts the ambulance door. Worse still, the same game was on tomorrow.

Jack knew we were pretty well done in and let the three of us boys head for the waterfall, which was heaven after such a gruelling day. The tide was in and we waded hip-deep though the two salt creeks. We were too exhausted to care and knew the odds of a croc in the wrong place at the wrong time were exceedingly low.

Jack and Otto saddled their horses and drove the mob towards their territory haunts, between the camp and the Isdell. The mules were given a spell and when Jack returned he spent an hour bathing Salty's leg. The poor gelding at last had a name.

Next day we mustered from the other end, back towards the mouth of the Charnley River. It wasn't so straightforward. We had to cross salt creeks and, coming back with the cattle, had to wait for a tide drop before crossing. The smell of the yard created a strong deterrent for the mob not to go in and on the first occasion they broke. For the first time the heat was in our favour. They didn't go far and on the second attempt we got them. It was afternoon before Jack planted the first brand for the day. By then the whole western sky had darkened ominously. Thunder rumbled out towards Collier Bay and by late afternoon sheet lightning flashed on the horizon.

We branded forty-two and we all saddled up this time. Jack wanted to drive them towards the river, ready to collect at daylight in the morning. Cattle like to return to their own territory and there was a risk they might all go back overnight. But they were tired too and would probably lie up for one night, before working back.

The weather outlook gradually deteriorated. Otto said the slower it all came, the worse it would be. He was a Bardi man. If anyone should know it was him, but we were all too exhausted to be anxious. Not even the mosquitoes could keep any of us awake that night.

FIVE

THE SAVAGE TIDE

I WOKE FROM a dream so chilling I never forgot it. My mum and dad were on two mules, swimming the river. They hadn't dismounted to swim beside the animals and I was too far behind to see their faces when they looked back for me. I was swimming beside a pony I once rode around Derby and we were slipping further behind. None of us was making any progress and the first washed off a mule was my mother, but the mule kept swimming, high above the water like a small Arabian dhow, and when I lifted my hand again to shield the sun from my eyes the other mule had no one aboard.

The air felt sticky and very warm, as if it were the end of a blistering day, not an hour before dawn. I sat up, and for a while was mesmerised by the display of sheet lightning in the west. I wondered why the big storms seemed to stay put, gathering and gathering and not moving. I asked Jack, who was squatting by his little pre-dawn fire. All I could see was the tiny glow of his cigarette.

'Sheet lightning is usually a sign the wet's over,' he said.

'Bit like the build up in November, when it's all beginning. But this is the cyclone season, too, and a cyclone doesn't build overnight. They draw up into a core – it's called a vortex, someone once told me – and the circling winds gather speed. What do you reckon, Otto?'

'Them storms should have come over by now.' Otto sat in his favourite spot, his back to the boab tree, a few feet from the fire. The firelight caught the little tin mug which fitted into his saddle quartpot. Jack had already made tea. 'There's a big willy willy buildin. Boilin up in the ocean. Should head southeast, the old willy willy path. Might come straight at us too.'

The mosquitoes seemed quiet for the humidity and Jack said it was an hour off full tide, four o'clock. There was a breeze and when I stood I could feel it. It was more than a tidal breeze; whatever was brewing out beyond the islands was on the move.

'I've consulted my chart,' Jack said. 'We must be ready to cross at one pm. I want everything packed up by six o'clock. We'll put the packsaddles on the mules and hobble em out while we run the cattle out of that small valley up behind the waterfall. When we come back through here, we'll throw the packs on and drive everything ahead of us. Should have em all mustered and walking towards the crossing in less than six hours.'

Neither of the boys had stirred and Jack said he would only wake them with enough time to eat breakfast. He went on talking, while I groped around for my boots and lifted the billy off the ash to pour a mug of tea. It had been a full moon when I lay down on the swag the evening before. You could see the horses, the scattered trees and beyond rose the range, like a gaol wall. Now it was quite dark with not a hint of dawn. Jack said he was cooking a big stew of potatoes, onions and salted meat. The fresh damper we would take with us to eat after the cattle had swum the river. Then we would drive the cattle over the saltplains before thirst drove them half mad, through the freshwater wetland and on into the range. He didn't say when we would stop and sleep, only because he probably didn't know. Jack reckoned that by the time we got all the cattle in the river the tide would have turned. The horses and cattle could handle it and all of us, even Peter, would be okay but if George lost his grip the current might take him up river before anyone could go to his aid. The solution was a raft. He intended to wrap the four packs in the ten-by-ten tarpaulin, bind it with rope and put George on top. The rope left over would be the tow rope. Jack would take personal charge of it and tow the raft behind his horse, the rope wrapped around the saddlehorn.

'You don't reckon young George better hangin to his saddle?' Otto demurred. 'All them horses swim good. Him across in no time.'

'The worry is how long it's all goin to take,' Jack replied quietly. 'If we're slow and the tide becomes a savage rip, he might lose his grip. Take an Olympic swimmer to grab him and keep movin across.' He paused and looked at me. I could faintly see him near the fire. 'There's another reason why I want the packs off Jacko and Paw Paw. They don't mind the water. They're smart, knowin over the river is towards home and a spell. I want them to go into the river ahead of the cattle. If the lead walkers see em go in without a fuss, they'll follow. You got the job of leading them in, young Wann. Once they start to swim you let one go, but yer hold em in the water until the leaders have jumped into the river. Once a few start, they all follow. There's always a handful of lead cattle and they dictate what the mob will do.'

We sat in silence for a while, the light gathering quickly. Of all the uncertainties that lay before us, no one dare mentioned the darkest of them – the mud. It was unnatural for cattle to walk from firm earth into knee deep mud and beyond the mud was the dirty grey salt water, with the telltale froth of turbulence. Then there was the length of the swim. The opposite bank, right at the mouth of the river, had the look of an island about it. A swim to nowhere! Otto had told me that he and Jack had swum the mob over the Charnley River the previous wet season, but that swim was nothing compared to swimming cattle across the Isdell.

I had enough tobacco for two more smokes. We were heading home, so why not smoke one now, I thought. It soothed the nerves and today there was plenty to be nervous about. The dingoes on the heifer carcass bothered me too. The first rays of the sun had torched the range. The dingoes should have had their fill and been long gone by now, especially when we were camped only fifty yards away. Yet they were still growling and snarling over there when they should have been tucked in their lairs, bellies full.

As I listened, I got a long dry twig and lit my smoke from the ash. We all did that. Matches were too valuable to waste.

Standing near the fire I became aware of a delicious smell rising from the camp oven. It took my mind off the dingoes straight away.

'I'll wake the boys,' Jack said. 'She's about ready to serve.'

Peter was already awake and gave George a nudge. He asked his dad if there was time for an early swim. Their last swim at the waterhole.

'We gotta eat this and saddle up,' Jack said reluctantly. 'The time's goin to gallop this morning.'

'What's happening with Salty?' George asked, looking for his boots.

'He'll plod along behind us. I'll put a halter on him and when the last beast has the hit the water Otto can lead him in with the whip. Don't think he'll go on his own.'

Otto nodded. 'That'll be right, Jack. You watch out for young George.'

The packing didn't take long. I took the camp oven down to the spring and gave it a quick wash, mainly to get the heat out of the iron. Together with the steel bucket it had to go on top, with the big overall strap running between the handles and the steel. Both were too heavy and big to go in one of the packs. The problem was the heavy lid. At the last minute Jack found a spare rein to run through the finger grip and tie it on to the pack saddle. He said the packs didn't weigh much and decided to pack the mules before the valley muster and tie them to a tree. Fastening our swags to the back of the saddle was always a fiddly business. If they weren't perfectly balanced, the first canter would cause one side to drag and you had to dismount immediately. When

Peter and I had done ours we fastened George's swag. Even when he stood on his toes he couldn't reach the pommel of his saddle.

We were about to mount up when I saw Otto looking back towards the carcass. He was so much taller than all of us he had a much greater field of vision. Not satisfied with whatever he was staring at, he walked a few feet forward. Jack was making some adjustments on Paw Paw. I knew by the look on Otto's face he had seen something disturbing.

I couldn't contain myself. 'What's up?'

'I seen them dogs backin off something. Reckon all along them too cranky. Them dogs feed together. Not like them cats when the biggest takes all. They backin off from a big gator. Be the one that got our horse.'

Jack straightened and stepped back from the mule. 'Is he too big for a revolver shot?'

'I dunno.' Otto leaned against the trunk of a fan palm, as though his pulse raced from what he had seen. 'You sting him, he'll come at yer. On land they charge on their back legs, head six foot above the ground. It ain't a marvellous sight.'

'I'll use a tree for cover,' Jack said quietly. 'The trick is to freeze after the shot. Snakes need movement to detect the living. I think these bastards need movement too.' He walked to his mare to get the revolver from the saddlebag. 'I won't go close enough for a kill shot. I'll plug the bastard in the guts. After what he done to my horse I like to think he'll be a few days dyin.'

'He goin to be a very cranky gator,' Otto said anxiously.

Without another word Jack walked through the cane grass

towards the carcass. The sun was over the rim now and the light flooded the plain.

'Get on yer horses,' Otto growled. 'Get em up quick too. That fella gonna jump in the air and go faster than the fastest man in the Kimberley. If he don't see Jack he should go for his hole, but yer dunno what he might do with a slug in his gut.'

It was too exciting to hold back and not see it. As Jack was on foot and could do nothing if all hell broke loose, Otto felt partly responsible for our safety, but there was still a bit of boy left in him. We all wore that dare-devil grin as we rode forward just far enough to see over the grass. The horses sensed something was up. Maybe they could see the croc too, but I only saw it when the jaws went up and it swallowed something. It was probably feasting on the bloated intestines, good easy tucker for a croc.

Jack had reached a rivergum. The only rivergum for a hundred yards in that direction. He had used the trunk to stalk the reptile and with a light wind from the west there was enough rustle in the grass to cover the sound of his boots. The stink from the carcass ruled out any possibility of human scent reaching the croc. The dingoes saw him coming and slunk away, their tails tucked low. They trotted into the long grass and were out of sight, except when one stopped and I could see its ears cocked above the gently waving grass.

There was white in Otto's eyes when he whispered to us. 'Get hold of them pommels. He come this way we gonna be flyin and have no say where we stop.'

There were two quick shots. The horses stood, used to

whipcracks. The croc spun a full circle, looking for an adversary to savage. The sound it made when the slug hit was somewhere between the hiss of a wild cat and the sound of a calf when the branding iron hits. It made for its deep hole in the spring, just as Otto said, crashing into a fan palm. So crazed with shock and pain it wasn't seeing very well. The front of the reptile was raised high, the forelegs working so fast they were like propellers – you couldn't see them. If there was any creature on earth that could look like a torpedo a foot above ground, it was a crocodile. We heard a big splash and that was the end of it.

Jack returned triumphant. 'Been wantin to do that,' he said grimly. 'I loathe the bastards. They wait for the horses – and us. Spend enough time workin this sort of country it's only a matter of time.' He put the revolver back in his saddlebag and swung into his saddle. 'We can leave the mules tied up now. I didn't want to take em up into that top valley. Goin to be stony, I think.'

It was very stony. Most of the narrow valley floor was covered in ancient seabed rock. We walked the entire muster and let the stockwhips do the work. Luckily there was no other way out. We simply spread out at the top end, where the flats ran up against the boulder-strewn slopes, and drove the cattle ahead of us. The cattle on the eastern side of the creek had to be put over, but that was nothing. They had crossings in shallow water which they used every day. Near the waterfall there were several pads over the low escarpment onto the mangrove flats where our camp was.

The cattle bolted ahead of us and any estimate at numbers

was a wild guess. When I caught up with Jack he said more than a hundred. He was pleased, expecting to take out nearly 400 head altogether. If the prices at the meatworks held or only slipped marginally, it was enough to re-shape his life. Jack was in great spirits when he and Otto released the mules to follow on, and the cattle from the valley streamed out onto the salt plain.

Salty was very slow. In the bush, the horses and mules became an extension of your family. He was slowing us down and all of us felt anxious for him with the narrow window of time available. That he might be left behind was never an option, however. There was one salt arm which stretched from the inlet to within 500 yards of the rock. Once through that gap no impediment lay between the cattle and the river mouth. Jack left Peter and me to keep the tail moving. George's job was to stay with Salty and, if he stopped, to slide his whip through the halter and lead him. The leg was still very swollen, but Jack's constant bathing had saved Salty. He would recover.

Riding ahead, Jack and Otto aimed to clean out all the pockets and basins where most of the pre-handled cattle were holding out. I didn't have a watch. I guessed it was about three hours since the excitement with the crocodile, more than three hours up our sleeve when Jack and Otto disappeared from sight. Most of the cattle we had put through the yard were grazing on the young cane grass bordering the salt plain. The more edible blue grass had been chewed to the crown on some of the small creek flats. This was lucky. Had the cattle dispersed into the upper end of every little stream that striated the range it would have taken about four hours to clean them all out.

The size of the mob rapidly expanded and with it the mooing and calling of calves by cows already suspicious of our intentions. Jack and Otto had reappeared with the last they could find and immediately pointed the lead towards the river mouth. The wind had been gradually lifting all morning. It wouldn't blow your hat off, but it carried the smell of the sea and very soon Jack and Otto had to work either side of the lead to stop the bold walkers from swinging one way or the other. It wasn't as hot as the day we rode in. The western sky was neither a pitiless blue or darkened black from the cumulous of impending storms. It was a deep, charcoal grey, so thick that you knew when the sun arced over it, sometime after noon, there would be no sign of where it was and the mountains and the inlet would fade into an eerie twilight.

As we neared the river mouth, the mob became increasingly agitated. The wind was working against us. The tide was within an hour of dead low and you could smell the saline mud. The blue mud released a dead animal smell if you rode directly downwind of it. It was where stormwater ran off the salt plain and lay trapped in shallow lagoons. The sun warmed the water and the combination of tepid water and a salt-laden surface on top of organic silt produced a sun-bleached form of green algae. When the water evaporated altogether, a deadly blue crust covered all. It was bottomless mud, a death-trap to unwary animals.

The less time the cattle had to think about the crossing

the better. Cows have great memories. Swum across the Charnley a year or more before, they knew what was on. While Otto, the boys and I held them and tried to calm them, Jack made the raft for George. He folded the water-proof tarpaulin in half and lay the four packs in the centre, side by side. The four sides of the tarp were thrown over the packs, making a square bundle. To fasten it together Jack used his bronco rope, crisscrossing from a centre-line knot to tightly bind the loose flaps. The bottom side of the raft was smooth. It was wide enough to be stable, even if a few wave bumps moved up river while George was still aboard. The rope was perfect for him to grip.

Jack called to George, and the little bloke trotted over and dismounted. He half hitched the reins to the nearside stirrup leather. The horse stood for a moment, bewildered, then moved down the side of the mob to where Peter and I were holding the rear. A vociferous mooing filled the air and you had to shout to be heard. The big bulls had already broken away, long before we got anywhere near the river. Next would be the matriarchs. You could bluff them for a while, but once they decided enough was enough they were worse than the rogue bulls.

Together Jack and George carried the raft to the very point of the river mouth and a few yards to the inlet side. They disappeared from sight, then a few minutes later Jack came striding over the bank, untethered his mare from a mangrove and mounted. If it wasn't already dead low, it had to be only minutes away. Jack cantered around the mob and reined up beside me.

'Tie the reins to yer stirrup leather and grab the mules. It's time to go.'

Otto had taken hold of Jacko and I took the lead rope from him. The big mule led easily and Paw Paw followed. The mud was horrible. I was down to my ankles right from the edge and by the time I reached the water every stride was a mud-sucking drag from my shins down. I entered the river to my waist and waited. Jacko sniffed the water, blew into it disapprovingly and looked longingly at the opposite bank. I had to restrain him. The tide run had almost died. It was that eerie moment of tranquillity, when nothing moved. I scanned the placid surface for telltale bubbles, even though the croc men back in Derby always said that was a waste of time. A croc intent on seizing you is careful not to release air from his nostrils. I dismissed the thought and suddenly re-membered George. From here I should be able to see him. Preoccupied with the mud, I hadn't even glanced that way. He was sitting straight-legged on the raft and he gave me a wave. For a boy of ten, this was a great adventure. His faith in us all was implicit. I waved back and forced a grin. I thought he was a little close to the water, but with the bovine uproar just over the bank he would never hear me.

The whips began to crack and within seconds the lead was spilling over the bank. They reached the wet tidal mud and stopped as though there was a fence there. The lead seemed to be mainly young cows, juvenile bulls and heifers: the cunning old ones naturally at the rear. At Halls Creek I had learnt the good leaders were three and four year old bullocks. There wasn't a single bullock in this mob. No one had castrated and branded any beast in this herd for years.

Facing downhill into the river with whips pressing the

mob from behind, the leaders were soon forced into the mud and, venting their reluctance in a mounting crescendo, they sloshed down the slope towards me. It was looking good and I moved further out, the water up to my chest. When the first one jumped in, I intended to launch into the deep. Jacko would power me across nearly as fast as an outboard motor. I had never seen cattle swim. The Halls Creek country I was used to was semi-arid and rivers only ran after monsoon rain. Jack had told me they didn't just walk in and start swimming. In tidal rivers they sprang out of the mud, hit the water like a log up-ended and swam as fast as they could. They weren't stupid. They knew about crocodiles and had observed the tide surges when feed ran short and they ventured out onto the salt plains to forage on isolated high points of land.

Water to your waist is comfortable, but at chest level and holding a big restive mule on a squashy, shifting foot surface is just awful. Paw Paw, too, was fed-up and inclined to push Jacko forward. The leaders had reached the water but none wanted to take that first jump. Just when the whips were needed they had fallen silent. I glanced around Jacko's shoulder to see what was going on. They were working the whips like mad with no sound coming off the crackers. Suddenly I realised: the horsehair whip crackers were caked with wet mud. The three of them were yodelling and yelling their heads off. The seconds ticked by, and with the passing of each minute the possibility of a herd swim slipped away. They weren't turning back, but the pressure from the rear wasn't enough to force the leaders.

My situation had become intolerable when there was a

frantic yell. You could hear it over the noise of the cattle. It was George. At the same instant a wave swamped me and Jacko back-pedalled. He no longer wanted to swim. The tide had turned already. No sooner had I moved towards the cattle Jack screamed something inaudible, but from the pitch of his voice I knew something serious had happened. We weren't going to get the cattle across today so I jumped on Jacko and urged him back out of the water and up through the mud. It must have taken me twenty seconds to reach the bank on the point of the river mouth and from there I could see across the vast stretch of the inlet. George was on the raft, thirty yards from the shore and caught on a tidal inflow current. The raft was being carried along at a good eight knots and when Otto dived in, about twenty yards in front of the raft, I doubted he could possibly swim fast enough. His huge arms slicing through the water, he cut the gap to three yards and when he realised he couldn't bridge it he yelled to George for the rope, water filling his mouth and stifling the last word. George flung the little coil high, it unravelled and the end fell slowly – painfully slowly, as though it had a mind of its own. Otto had to leap for it, using one big palm to project his upper body out of the water. The rope end in his hand, he had the fight of his life to reach the shore, the raft pulling heavily against him. On all fours he struggled out of the water and up to his elbows in mud he made no effort to stand. Propelled by the current the raft spun to the side and George left it as though it were on fire. He wasn't risking another terrifying ride. The main channel was fast becoming a turbulent, seething flood of water. Covered in a grey, ominous froth, the whirlpools were already appearing. The water level jumps almost six feet an hour at Walcott Inlet.

The most pathetic sight was Jack. The mud was much deeper around the point on the Walcott side. He had tried to gallop his mare through it, hoping maybe he could get her to swim out. She must have floundered. I was too late onto the bank to see that. Now she was in mud up to her knees and just standing there, head down and sides heaving. Jack hadn't got much further. He had tried to run and had fallen into the slimy stuff, his hat lying upside down in front of him. He was looking wildly around, mouth open, trying to draw breath.

In the deep mud and stifling heat, time seemed to drag. No one could do anything in a hurry. Peter worked his way down the wet slope and took the rope from Otto, who was still winded. He tried to pull the raft from the rising water, but could gain no purchase with his feet. With a lot of urging I managed to get Jacko down to where Peter stood with the rope and he half hitched it to the nearside pack hook. Then I made Jacko climb up towards the bank. I wasn't sure he'd give his whole heart to it without me aboard. Whenever he stopped, Peter yelled at him and shook his whip. Together we got the packs to dry ground. By this time Otto and Jack had recovered and were forlornly dragging their legs through the mud, Jack leading his mare. George had gone to find his horse.

By the time we re-assembled with our horses, the cattle were halfway to the range. Most stayed with the herd but others, led by an aged cow, had peeled off and were walking as fast as they could swing their legs. If it were not for the heat, they would have been trotting.

There wasn't much to say. There was no hope now of the cattle crossing the Isdell. They knew they could beat us and it would take double or three times the number of mounted men to force a swim.

Only Peter asked George what happened. Why he didn't simply jump off the raft and hold it with the rope before it was swept out. George said he did, but the second wave after tide turn knocked him over and propelled the raft along with it. George said it dragged him and he knew that if he let go, everything in the packs would be lost. He pulled himself along the rope, reached the raft and climbed aboard. He didn't have time to dwell on the consequences of where he might be headed.

SIX

CYCLONE!

IT WAS A slow ride back to the camp. Salty was lamer than ever and we took turns to lead him. The cattle had made themselves scarce when they reached the range. Held by old bonds, the herd broke up into groups and headed for their various haunts. The wild bulls that broke away before the debacle were in a state of confusion at so many females and juvenile bulls heading in the same direction. They didn't want a fight, but they wanted their cows – and any bonus would be gratefully received. There was much bellowing and throwing up of dust. Had cows been cycling there would have been fights, but as we rode along, preoccupied with thoughts far from a bull's harem problems, it seemed to be a case of who could stir up the most dust from the unyielding crusted soil.

The wind dropped again by late afternoon. It was so humid it was like breathing steam. Something was going to break. The cloud had thickened and the ranges on both sides of the inlet lay under a grey blanket. The boys and I didn't wait for the billy to boil. We broke off a dry piece of damper from one of the packs, laced it with a bit of treacle and headed for the waterfall. The salt creeks were rising on the incoming tide. It had all become so familiar we didn't worry about the crocs any more. We never saw their tracks up the little salt creeks.

It was a very subdued campfire scene that evening. Jack hadn't uttered a word throughout the afternoon. He was thinking and while he weighed his options he bathed Salty's leg. It was his mental therapy. Otto slept. He was in his late forties and the rescue ordeal had flattened him.

We were all in our usual positions when Jack told us what he had decided. Otto with his back to the boab, the boys leaning back into the underfelt of their saddles, me on my side with one elbow on the saddle seat and Jack stretched full length, his head propped against the side of his saddle. Otto and Jack were smoking. I had enough tobacco left for one more and it was still damp.

'I think we've gotta give Hilton a go,' Jack began, addressing Otto. It was nearly dark and a stew simmered in the camp oven. The last of the meat had gone in. It was just as well or it would have grown its own legs and escaped.

'Down for the count here, hey,' Otto mumbled. A fighter for many years, Otto often used the expression. He was saying that Walcott was over, finished.

'We're not pullin out,' Jack corrected. 'We gotta start again. First on the agenda are Hilton's cattle. I want you to go to Hope Creek tomorrow, hold up there while this storm passes and then round up that mob and walk em to the King River. Once over the river, Hilton has gotta get his own mustering team together and take em onto the station. There's some good feed on the western side of the King.'

Otto's voice changed. 'Bring Ralph back with me, hey?' Then he frowned and added. 'If they went back to Oobagooma and see that willy willy brewin, they stay there.'

Jack was silent for a moment, uneasy. 'Too much at stake. Hilton wants those cattle. He must have some plans, because he wants the money. He won't have left the Hope Creek yards.'

The look on Otto's face said it all. He wasn't so sure. Hilton Walker wasn't a high risk taker and it was never easy for him to leave the homestead. Jack sensed the doubt and changed the subject.

'George,' he said, gently. 'You're goin out with Otto. You'll be an enormous help to him with the musterin and drovin. At the King you'll go back with Hilton to Oobagooma and he'll contact Mum. She'll arrange for someone to come out. You need to get back to school.'

'So does Peter,' George objected. He didn't want to be separated from Peter.

'I can't spare both of you. You're the youngest and that's the end of it.'

The boys knew not to take their father on and no more was said on the matter. Jack continued with his instructions to Otto. He was to load the two mules with supplies from the truck left at the King and he and Ralph were to get back here as quickly as possible. When they returned they would rest for a day, before mustering the cattle again and crossing the Charnley in the same spot the cattle were originally brought over. From there, Jack said, it was three days' droving to the northern point of the Edkins Range and a week or more to Mount Elizabeth. Then southwest along the old stock route to Derby, taking several weeks.

'It's a better plan,' Jack added. 'We don't have a mob split any more. That would have been a real bastard, separating them. Also this morning I noticed some very swollen scrotums but the big bull calves we marked will heal before the walk. And Salty might be okay to ride again in a few days.'

I didn't know the country we would ride over and had no idea of how far it was to Derby the long way. Otto said nothing. I'm sure he knew Jack Camp was a super-optimist and he must have liked working with a man who had such a positive outlook. They were great friends. When Jack finally turned to me and asked me how I felt about it all I didn't hesitate. I was learning more every day. I was seeing a lot of new country and more important than anything else, Jack treated me like an adult. At Halls Creek I was just the kid on the edge of everyone's boot.

It looked like Otto would be gone for at least ten days, given the storm – or rain depression or whatever it was on the way – would hold up mustering for at least three days. Jack kept reiterating that it was the end of the wet season and the heavy cloud build-up might amount to nothing. We would be kept busy while Otto was away, he said, bringing in small mobs to the yard and branding anything that had been missed. Jack was also handy with the lasso. I didn't relish the prospect of no Otto to help us hold the big ones down while Jack applied his marking tools. But in each little draft there wouldn't be more than four or five big ones and Jack said he was going to get Peter to do the ear marking and branding while he pinned down their heads. The ear marking was the worst: you could count on a fight every time. With the castrating, the bulls froze; they didn't kick much at all.

The next morning, the little group of Jack, Otto and George set off at about 10.30. The wind had got up again and overhead it was ominously dark. From one horizon to the other there was no difference any more. Before mounting, Jack gave Peter and me final instructions: Peter to bathe Salty's leg, me to wash the saddles and cloths – and both of us to erect the tarp to make a shelter and after that gather a big heap of firewood. He didn't tell us how to make the shelter, we were to work it out. When Peter asked how long he'd be gone, Jack said about six hours. He planned to tie the mare securely to a mangrove tree and swim across with George, both using George's horse to take them over. When George could touch bottom and was safe he would swim back to the mare on his own. The tide would have turned by then, he realised, but taking it steady with a bit of breaststroke, he didn't expect to be carried upstream more than a hundred yards before he touched bottom.

We held onto our horses while they rode away. Running together year after year, horses form strong bonds of attachment to one another. Salty pricked his ears and whinnied. He would have followed if he were not so lame. Jacko carried the only packsaddle going out and Paw Paw plodded behind with nothing but a halter. There was a spare packsaddle and packs in the truck for the return trek. Although Jack never said anything about it, there was always a risk something might happen and Otto not make it back. Without a packsaddle to carry our goods and no packs for storage, we could be left in a mess.

In a gale, a tarpaulin can gather as much power as a sail on a boat. The only thing that might work, we decided, was two heavy poles on the ground at either end and a raised centre ridgepole, one side faced into the wind.

We cut the poles with a tomahawk. On the steep slope running up to the bluff there was a jungle-clad gully, over the main salt creek. The only usable timber was juvenile river-gums, thin and straight. In the jungle, everything competed for light. We dropped two of them and a smaller one to be the ridgepole. It was heavy wood and we cut the sections down to ten feet, or the approximate width of the tarp.

The problem to solve now was what to use for tying the tarp to the ground poles. If the wind got up to sixty miles an hour, the light twine used on the hessian wouldn't hold. While we were cutting the poles I spotted a jungle vine. I sliced a section, put my boot on one end and tried to break it. No way, so we decided to strap down the tarp with jungle vine.

It was simple to erect. Using the vine, we attached the two heavy poles to the tarp, drove in two stakes either side of it, placed the ridgepole underneath in the centre and lifted it about three feet. The vine wouldn't bind tightly enough to hold the ridgepole in place, so we had to use double string to attach it to the stakes, after cutting a nick in them. Held

firmly by the ground poles, the tarp was taut and wind resist-
ant. The last thing we did was use the tomahawk to cut and
scrape a trench about ten inches wide on either side of the
tarp to stop the water running in from heavy rain. We ran
both trenches well below the shelter to make sure the water
got away. It was a bit of a cubby house – we had to crawl in
and out on all fours. But we were pleased with our effort and
felt we'd earned a couple of hours at the waterfall. It was there
that we noticed the cattle had retreated to the high ground.
Now that George was gone we had no compunction about
crossing the mid-stream current to the other side, where a
steep tangle of boulders rose more than sixty feet to form the
nose of a long escarpment. It was here that we'd seen the two
dingoes a few days before. We climbed to the same boulder
they had lingered on and peered across the blue grass valley.
There were no cattle anywhere to be seen. While we stood
there, buffeted by the wind, we heard the longwinded trum-
peting of bulls from accessible pockets in the range. Driven
by instinct, the cattle had already taken shelter.

Back at the camp Peter lit the fire and made a damper. He
knew Jack would be hungry when he got back – he had taken
no food with him. Kindled by the wind the flames chewed up
the wood fast and the smoke swept over the grass and into the
dark line of the mangroves. The salt creek was one hundred
yards away, but the flat spreading from the creek came
halfway to the camp and with it the mangrove trees. As the
hours passed, we both grew anxious. It got dark early and the
wind was so strong we were glad to be able to put our swags
under the tarp and take cover. What to do with the horses was

a dilemma. Salty wouldn't walk anywhere, but if we unhob-
bled Bluey and Peter's horse there was a good chance they
would take off, hoping to catch up with the others. We
decided to leave the hobbles on, confident the horses would
stay on the raised ground near the camp if the creeks on either
side of us came down after heavy rain.

Neither of us had a watch. I slept for maybe two hours and
when I woke I could hear the flames of the fire hissing in the
wind. Peter was crouched beside it and as I sat up he broke off
a piece of firewood with his boot. He was determined to keep
the fire alive, for fear Jack would not find the camp without it.

Something had happened. Jack should have been back two
hours before dark. I didn't like to say anything to Peter but
I had made up my mind he was drowned. Jack Camp was a
reliable man and worked to time. If he said he would do
something you could depend on it with your life. I noticed at
the waterfall he never actually swam. He washed himself, sat
on a submerged shelf for a few minutes and got out. He definitely could swim, but I doubted he was a strong swimmer.
After tide turn the water reclaimed the channel with a ven-
geance and I felt sure he had been swept away. Even if Otto
and George had seen it happen, they couldn't cross until the
next low tide after daylight.

It's moments like this you need something. Years later it
would be a stiff drink. Here in the little cubby house, so low
my head pushed against the tarp if I sat up, all I had was my
last cigarette. To be sure not to spill any leaves in the dark
I went outside and put my back to the wind in front of the
fire. I thrust the tip into the red coals for a light and inhaled

deeply. Peter sat on the ground with his legs drawn in and hat pulled down hard on his head. I couldn't see his face. After a while I went back to the swag and slept again, waking at dawn. Peter was in his swag, the blanket drawn up over his head. The wind tore through the trees and the cane grass looked as though a chain had been pulled over it. The heavy rain still hadn't arrived. I looked out at a gale-driven drizzle that cut visibility to fifty yards. I took my shirt off and pushed it under the swag to keep it dry.

Outside, it was an effort to stand against the wind. The fire was out and the horses stood nearby with their rumps to the gale, ears flat and heads down. They had been through it all before. In their view, you just stood and waited until it was over. I envied their resignation.

I carried the camp oven into the shelter and offered Peter some damper and treacle. Cold and dry, without hot tea to wash it down it was an effort to eat it – sort of stuck in the back of your throat. The one thing we didn't miss was the mosquitoes. I made a harmless joke about it, that the wind had done us a great favour and blown all the mosquitoes and buffalo flies to hell. Anything to break the silence. Peter hadn't uttered a word since I'd woken to see him huddled over the little fire and I was becoming worried about him. To my relief, when he came out from under his blanket he seemed in good spirits. He said Jack had told him the coming night would be the peak of the autumn king tides. Peter had concluded that the low tide turn might have a shorter dura-tion, perhaps only a minute – enough to force his father to abort the return swim. They would have camped on the other side, despite the terrible weather, he'd decided. Otto and George would have left at daylight for Hope Creek and his dad would wait for the next low tide at about 2 pm. It was a good theory, if indeed the tide did turn too quickly for Jack. He would have hated leaving his mare tied to a mangrove on the opposite side and they had no tarpaulin. Only one tarp came in with the packs. But that aside, I was grateful to Peter for his optimism. If we lost Jack we'd have to get ourselves back to Oobagooma and civilisation alone. There wasn't much flour left – we'd have to live on potatoes and onions. Luckily there was still plenty of tea and sugar and four boxes of matches.

But no cigarettes, nothing to read and no cards. Cards have always been the bushman's pastime in the outback. I'd never be caught without them again, but that didn't help the present. We lay under the tarp, listening to the wind gather ferocity and the rain rattling on our shelter. Soon it would be torrential and if Jack had indeed waited as Peter thought, I wondered about the salt plains. Basically the marine plains were a salt deposit laid down over thousands of years and I could picture them dissolving into a quagmire. If Peter proved to be correct, Jack had a more sinister problem to contend with. Low tide the day before had been one o'clock. Today it would be about 1.54 pm. I knew the daily tide adjustments from years of fishing. But it wasn't much help at the moment: a watch was another thing I had yet to own. We had both lost all sense of time and lay on our swags, staring at nothing and listening to the rain beat harder by the hour.

It was the horses that broke the good news. I had forgotten

about them since rising early and checking on them. The whinnies of all three rose above the noise of the gale. Jack's mare was calling them from far off, beyond our hearing. Presently we could hear her too, lively outbursts as though her survival depended not on humans, but the company of her own kind.

Peter jumped up and bumped his head on the ridgepole. His spontaneous reaction was to run out to his dad but then he clearly thought better of it. You didn't express emotion in the world of Jack Camp. Peter dropped back onto his swag, clasped his knees tightly and waited. When Jack appeared, I thought to myself that I'd never seen anyone look so wet, even his hat hung like a rag on his head. As always, it was business first and chatter later.

'Them horses hobbled?' he asked, his voice a bit croaky from exposure.

Peter began to explain he didn't know whether to hobble or not. Without a word Jack left, returning a few minutes later.

'I've taken em off. That bloody freshwater creek's already belly-high. They won't go from here.'

He got under the tarp and, pulling off his wet things, dried himself with a towel from the clothes pack, then started to put on some dry clothes. I wondered if any of us were going to stay dry for long. The rain was so heavy a fine mist was drifting under the tarp and water from the ground was starting to seep through our swags. If not for the little trenches we'd dug, our swags would have been in the water already.

'You boys did a good job with this,' Jack said, dressing quickly. He was cold. After extreme heat you can get hypothermia in the tropics if you're exposed to heavy rain for too long. 'We'll get a bit damp, but the main thing is to be out of the rain.'

Jack was also starving. He said he hadn't eaten anything since daybreak the day before and it was now late afternoon. He had to raise his voice. We were in the grip of a cyclone, he told us, and the gale would get much worse. He was very impressed with us for thinking of the jungle vine, saying it wouldn't break unless the cyclone increased to a category three. He estimated the wind to be at about sixty miles an hour, which he said was a category one. The worry was the king tide due at 8 pm. Under torrential rain, the range would be awash with water and the tide could hold it back.

He told us what had taken him so long. They had reached the crossing point about half an hour before dead low and were just making final gear adjustments when Otto spotted a salty on the other side. It was in the water and very difficult to see. He said he should have realised the smell of the cattle would have attracted the crocodile. The odour from droppings could drift for up to two miles. Just why the salty was on the other side was a mystery. Could be ambush tactics: Jack said crocs had an extraordinary brain when it came to stalking prey.

With the low cloud and heavy rain, it had become quite dark and Jack asked Peter for the torch. He shone it onto his right hand and we were shocked at the wound there. The webbing was ripped open an inch and the gash gaped nearly all the way to his wrist. In town it would have been a rush to hospital and ten stitches.

'Don't know what got me,' he sighed. 'I kept the smokes dry. Get yer to roll me one, Pete. The matches are wet. Some more in the pack.'

Peter rolled his dad a cigarette and lit it for him. We waited to hear the story, but all we got was the smoke of his cigarette. It had a nice Log Cabin smell. I think the cigarette fell out of his mouth before he'd finished. He began to snore. We had no handkerchiefs to dress the wound with – no one carried such things. We only had dirty rags and it wasn't worth the risk of infection.

It was pitch dark before I dozed off. When I woke, I knew I hadn't slept for long; maybe three hours. There was a faint light. It was a relief to be able to look out and see the dark shape of the boab trunk and the wide spread of its foliage. The wind had been roaring through the boab leaves when I fell asleep. Now the tree was silent. We were in the eye of the cyclone. I recalled Dad talking about the cyclone's eye: the eerie silence, waiting for the gale to return from the opposite direction. The rain had ceased too. I lay for a while, hoping to go back to sleep, but the silence bothered me. Water off the range would have flooded the creeks on both sides of our camp and I should have been able to hear a rumbling sound as thousands of gallons spewed into the inlet. But what I did hear chilled me. I didn't want to admit it; I wanted to pretend I was mistaken, but the lapping of water is a distinct sound and everyone has heard it one time or another. It was coming from very close by, then as I sat up the water was suddenly across my lap. It came that fast. Jack and Peter came off their swags spluttering and confused.

'Bloody hell!' Jack yelled. 'We're underwater. The king tide's held the flood! I've heard about this, but shit –'

Peter exclaimed he couldn't find his boots. We had a panic rush. We had to find everything before it floated away. In a flurry of hands we salvaged the boots before they floated away.

Jack was aghast. 'The bloody pack with the food! Can't see it.' He threw the gear pack at me. 'Hang onto that! We gotta bolt for the ridge. If the water rises any more we'll have to swim most of the way.'

Jack had great presence of mind in a crisis. The torch was where he had left it under his swag and it still worked. The food pack was nowhere to be seen. There was a current. Not strong, but enough to carry a floating object quickly away. Our swags were now afloat too. Jack didn't waste any time – probably thought we were too short, anyway. Grabbing the swags, he ran through the water and jammed them high into a fork in the bauhinia tree. Then he whipped the long blade from his belt sheath and slashed the tarp free from the anchor logs.

'We gotta have this tarp!' There was a desperate edge to his voice.

Peter helped him stretch it out and they folded it over. Spread out, the tarp floated and Jack was able to quickly roll it. Once rolled, however, it was inclined to sink so Peter held onto it while Jack rummaged through the pack I was holding for the rope.

The water had risen to our knees – in Peter's case, to his thighs. Working quickly, Jack took the rope underwater and wrapped it twice around the tarp bundle. He half-hitched it and had enough rope left to pull the sluggish bundle through the water, and we set off. For most of the way we were knee deep but gradually the level rose as we approached the fresh-water creek and spring.

'We'll have to swim!' Jack gasped. 'When the tide starts running an elephant wouldn't stand against it. I hope the horses got out.'

I was sure they had. If they had instincts anything like cattle they would have waded out a couple of hours ago. But I must admit that, as the water rose to my chest and I had to dog paddle with one free hand, I didn't give them much thought. The gear pack had a little buoyancy, but the cook-ware had weight.

The water was cool, most unlike the tepid sea water. If we had to be in it for any length of time hypothermia would grip all three of us. We reached the edge without further mishap and lay for a while on the wet ground, all heaving for breath, unable to speak. When we sat up and looked back towards the old camp, all we saw was water in the faint cloud-smothered moon-light and no sound save the gentle slap of tide-stirred ripples.

I don't know how Jack managed to both tow the tarp and swim. It didn't float. When he heaved on the rope it rose to the surface, only to slowly sink again.

'There's a spot up here,' Jack said, when he'd caught his breath. 'I camped on it a year ago. It's marked with a boab too. Come on, we'll see if we can find it.'

The ridge itself had become the bank for the massive flood. We left the water's edge and climbed onto steep ground, boulders all around us. The ridge was wooded, too, and it was very dark under the trees. We could barely see and stumbled and slipped on every second step. Jack said the water level would only be three or four yards below his ridge camp and by keeping close to the water he would find it. After several bruises and many curses, Jack reached a small piece of level ground. An area about the size of a small room had been cleared of rocks. It was a bleak outlook. You didn't have to think about it very much to realise this little patch of bare dirt among the boulders was going to be home for some days, no matter what happened from here on. Possibly with nothing to eat.

Jack unrolled the tarp and spread it out in the darkness. The torch had slipped out of his badly cut hand back at the camp. I wondered what he was doing for a few minutes then realised he was feeling around for rocks to hold one end down. When he'd found enough of them he told us to get under the tarp and take off our wet clothes. All three of us were shivering and I think it was as much to do with our desperate situation as the cool floodwaters.

The ground was saturated and quite cold on bare skin, but after a while the air under the tarp, which covered us like a blanket, warmed and became tolerable. We used our wet clothes for a pillow. It wasn't long before the gale and heavy rain returned. The ground must have had a slight tilt or the water would have poured in where we lay. Jack had correctly anticipated the direction of the wind and the rocks held the tarp. We lay there for hours. This time none of us slept. The gale lost its velocity sometime next morning, but the torrential rain on the tarp above our faces made me think of the end of the world. A world of water and no dry places. When the tide ran we heard it, a frightening sound like several rail locomotives departing all at once. I often peered out when the tide was running and the whole narrow valley, from our ridge to the bluff where Peter and I had chopped the rails to size, was a mud-stained river of choppy waves, surging currents and whirlpools. We could say good-bye to the food pack. Thank God Jack'd had the presence of mind to jam our swags high into the bauhinia tree which had shaded our old camp in the afternoon.

SEVEN

THE WAITING

THE DAY FOLLOWING the cyclone was as depressing as any I can ever remember. All three of us knew what it was like to feel hungry: a muster that went too long or a slow trip on the rough Kimberley roads, but you knew there was always a meal over the next horizon. This time there was not only nothing to eat but no immediate prospect of anything to eat. Add to this sopping wet nakedness and you come up with utter despair.

It rained in torrents all day and the combination of King Leopold run-off and high tide pushed the flood level within three feet of our new camp. From the beginning, Jack looked beat. I don't think he had slept the night he was away and he'd only had three hours in the night just gone. The reality of our situation had sunk in. To make matters worse, he had tobacco but no matches. The box Peter used to light Jack's cigarette the evening before had gone into the food pack. The contents in both packs were the only things dry before the flood. The food pack was lost and the gear pack soaked. Jack searched it for matches, wishing in vain one of us had put a box in there.

It would have been soaked anyway. At least we still had our hats, although they were sodden and crushed. Jack had sometimes lectured us about the consequences of losing our hats (sunstroke being a major concern) and we always slept with them beside our heads, otherwise we would surely have lost them in the flood.

The initial hunger crisis dissipated after a few hours. The hunger went in cycles, our bodies driven by instinct when we would normally eat. It would become an insane craving then diminish. I grew listless and lost all track of time. We hated being under the tarp and to urinate came as an enormous relief. An excuse to step out into the driving rain, and kid ourselves we could put up with it. The water cascaded off our bodies. It wasn't cold, but we were cold and dispirited, and each time forced back to our dark and drenched refuge.

The rain eased to showers the next day. We pulled on our wet clothes, careful to shake out desperate occupiers. Rain you couldn't see through had flushed out every living creature, and spiders, centipedes and scorpions were very happy to crawl under the wet clothes and get warm. The moment the heavy rain ceased, mosquitoes bombarded us and this time there was no escape. We put our hats on rocks to dry out.

It defied logic how quickly the water got away. The out flow of the tide took it all. Our old camp was in the centre of a large island. The hessian cattle yard had gone, not a trace of it could be seen.

'The gooseberries are goin to give us the trots,' Jack mumbled as we stepped over boulders and rocks looking for the horses. 'But they'll keep us alive until we can get a killer.'

The berries were in scattered clumps along the bottom of the ridge. Many bushes were still in the water. Peter and I plucked the little yellow fruit and wolfed them down, regardless of the consequences. Jack was more careful. He knew what to expect.

We seemed to fill up quickly with the berries, as though the gasses were at work. The hunger settled for the moment, we continued to search for the horses.

Jack looked as white as a ghost and his eyes were all sunk in hollow sockets. It frightened me to look at him. Surely no man could look like that and last long. To cover his injured hand, he had cut a strip from the tail of his shirt.

'The horses will be out here on the point,' he said, leading the way and stumbling a lot. I was lightheaded too; a strange sensation, as though separated from your body. 'Bit of ground there free of rocks, but high enough to miss the water.'

They were there, about 200 yards from our new camp. Heads down and just standing, not eating. They looked miserable. Mosquitoes covered Salty's wound like a black scab. In swift, angry rubs from his nose he could dislodge them for a second, a little cloud rising from his leg, only to settle back.

'When sun comes out it'll be the flies,' Jack murmured in despair. 'There'll be millions.'

Each of us went to our particular friend and gave a rub behind the ears. They loved that. I spotted Jack scanning the immediate area and then he walked to the edge of the water and examined a grey-blue bush. It looked as if the horses had half-eaten it.

'Walkabout bush,' he said in disgust. 'The rain's buggered the bit of grass up here. They're goin to keep eating this stuff and there's nothing we can do to stop em. It'll kill em.'

It was a chilling thought. The horses were the key to our rescue. When the Isdell dropped back into its banks we could swim over it and ride home. I felt sick, though it wasn't just dread. My stomach was churning oddly.

'Why don't we try and find our saddles and just leave,' I said. It was the first time I had ever put a proposition to Jack.

'Don't take any store from the fast drop in the water here,' he said patiently, appreciating my feeling of desperation. 'Massive water coming off a range is gone in a few hours. But the rivers . . .' He shook his head. He almost looked undressed without his hat. 'The Isdell will have a big run for weeks. None of these horses will make it now they've eaten that bloody walkabout. The Humbert will be as wide as the Congo. Otto and George couldn't have got out, the cyclone came a few hours too soon. I told Otto to get to Hope Creek. If Walker left I reckoned on him leavin food behind. I dunno for sure – just goin on what I would have done. But they wouldn't have got there. That steep gutter we rode up from Hope Creek would have been a ragin torrent before they got there. I reckon Otto's tryin to get back here. I gotta saddle up and ride over. Wait for em. Gotta get George back safe.'

'They got any food in the packs?' I asked.

'I gave em nearly half – I had this bad feelin. I had this feeling that Walker and Ralph had gone, taking all the tucker with them, thinking they'd be back.' He slapped his wet shirt pocket where the tobacco was. 'I gave Otto a packet of matches too.'

I wanted to ask Jack how he thought we might get out. In the coming days the river was going to be too big for the horses, then when it dropped they would be too sick. The range was too rough for us to walk out. Jack must have sensed my reticence, that I didn't want to corner him with a question he couldn't answer.

'We're not entombed here. Otto will be back. We'll eat what food's left and go out with the mules. They either don't eat walkabout or it don't affect em. Not sure which, but they'll stay strong. George can sit on top and the rest of us can get a tow over the rivers. We'll get home.'

The fate of the horses was sealed. Looking at them, you couldn't help feeling very sad about it. No one was to blame. Out here, we were all very small and helpless. I didn't have time to dwell on it. The diarrhoea from the berries struck and I bolted for the nearest boulder that offered some privacy. Minutes later Peter was heading up the slope too. Jack hadn't eaten so many and seemed okay.

'You gotta eat a few at a time,' he said.

The complaint persisted for hours and we refrained from eating any more of the berries that day.

After another wretched night, the creek between the ridge and the old camp had drained away enough for us to wade over and see what we could salvage.

The ground was surprisingly firm. It was as though the weight of the water had packed it down. There were fresh-water billabongs everywhere, water flowing in at the top end and out on the lower inlet side. With the low cloud retaining sound you could hear the waterfalls up in the mountains. The whole area seemed to be rumbling under the discharge of water.

At the old camp the saddles hadn't moved. We were lucky the strong currents were confined to the creeks. Even the saddle cloths had only been dragged a few yards. We found the food pack about thirty yards away in a clump of debris washed up against two bauhinias. The straps had been left undone. It was one of those oversights that normally wouldn't have mattered. Inside there was just one item, the Sunshine milk tin containing the cooking fat. We searched the debris for anything else that might have got caught, but the silt washed up on the sticks and fallen branches was more than a foot deep where the two trees formed a barrier.

The swags were still in the tree. Jack had worried that the constant deluge of rain might have dislodged them. He pulled them out of the tree fork and tossed them into a pile with the empty food pack. Then he opened his saddlebag and removed his revolver and the ammunition.

'The firin caps will be wet,' he muttered. 'Could take a few days in the sun. We'll have to get a killer with the rope.'

'Eat the meat raw,' I said, nearly gagging at the thought.

Jack looked at me as though I was a kid released from his mother for the first time.

'You eat the liver while it's warm. The brains too. It digests okay. I'll cut off some steak, wash it in salt water and hang it in a tree to tenderise it a bit. Take a day to go rotten.' He looked grimly around. There were no cattle anywhere to be seen. 'A killer every second day and we stay alive until Otto gets back.' Then he chuckled, more to himself – the irony of our situation not lost on him. 'Expensive tucker. Hundred times dearer than any posh restaurant.'

We had to make two trips back and forth through waist-deep water. First we carried our soggy swags to the new camp, then the saddles, bridles and cloths. The bridles were never a worry – we'd always kept them on a special hook in the bauhinia tree near the camp.

There was no sign of any crocs. Jack said he didn't know what they did when floods hit, but assumed they swam up into the backwaters. There was nothing we could do about it. Everything in the wild had been displaced. The snakes seemed more confused than anything else. You could see them rippling through the water, little heads up like mini-ature periscopes.

'The bastards love an easy ride,' Jack laughed when one swam towards us. 'Splash the water. Let em know yer not a floating log.'

The water monitors were everywhere – starving I think. The edible insects had vanished and the small rodents were scarce. They have a tremendous sense of smell and one was halfway into the food pack when we got back with the saddles, lamenting the lack of provender as much as we did. We didn't know where the dingoes were, but after the first killer was taken we expected to have eager rivals for the spoils.

The new camp had a bit more character about it. Three or four yards up the slope, an oblong shaped boulder straddled two larger boulders, forming an arch just wide enough for three to squeeze in and sit down. Perfect protection from an electrical storm. On the southern side of the little stone-free patch we had another boab – a baby compared to the giant at the old camp. A definite plus was a good seat each, which the flat top boulders provided in abundance. We had our own toilet spots, too, and to clean ourselves we used nice round sticks broken from the stunted trees. If our tummies didn't get used to the berries I could visualise us stripping the whole ridge of its vegetation.

We needed meat urgently. For the moment, irrespective of the consequences we had to keep eating berries to get some energy but once we had meat we could shy off them. Before we saddled up to go after the killer Peter and I picked half a billy full.

In the meantime Jack got his rope from the gear pack and made a lasso. His hand was useless. He made the knot with one hand and his boot. With reins in one hand and the lasso in the other it looked an impossible task.

'Like me to drop the rope over one?' My saddle had no roping horn. I would have to jump off and half-hitch one end around the butt of a tree.

'Gonna drop the loop from a bauhinia. We get a few together, get em walkin along a pad and I'll canter ahead and get ready. Won't be easy and it might take some time.'

I was relieved. The ground was wet and I knew it took considerable practice to rope a beast from horseback. Nothing more was said and we struggled over the boulders with our saddles. The horses hadn't moved. We saddled up, urged them through the belly-deep creek and rode up past the old camp towards the waterfall. The salt creek was a banker from high tide and water off the range. The horses hated going into it, thinking they might have to swim at some point. Full tide was better than half in or half out, because there was no flow. But it was deep and discoloured; a croc's dream and the horses knew it. They ploughed through, water to the saddle for a couple of yards.

We continued through shallows towards a roar of water ahead. Our swimming hole was now a giant whirlpool, the water spinning against the top of the rock bar before it surged over into the saltwater hole. The stream was only a few yards wide, but at least three feet deep. Most of the higher shelf was underwater. Where the fresh struck the salt it created a stationary wave. To avoid the whole treacherous scene Jack spurred his mare up a steep slope and we rode right around the side of the swollen creek.

Up on the flats we found the cattle. The butts of the blue grass were bursting with new growth. If it were not for the cattle, Jack said, the fresh stems would push up two to three inches each day. The problem was the ground. It was boggy where the soil was heavier and deep cattle tracks crisscrossed in all directions. Stony, too. Jack changed course.

'We'll head over to the foot of the range,' he said, the rope and reins in his good hand. The bad hand hung in his lap. He said nothing about it and didn't like personal questions.

It wasn't far. When we got to the boulders and rocks, a small group of cattle were in the shade of some salmon gums. Some stood, others lay on their stomachs, alert and watching us. A pad had been hoof worn through the rocks from the wide creek flat. Jack reined in. Peter rode behind him and I followed.

'There's a bloodwood coverin the pad,' Jack exclaimed in a whisper. 'Bloody perfect. Look at the leaves on it and that big overhangin branch. If I was a leopard I'd have me serviette on.' He turned the mare round to face Peter and me. 'They'll only want to come this way, on the pad. You boys skirt right out, three hundred yards away before yer work in behind em. Lead the horses if it's very rough, but don't tie em up. While the cattle see horses they'll be okay, stay where they are. See you two on yer own and they'll bolt down. I need em to walk down, single file. I'll tie the mare here on the flat and while they're watchin you two I'll sneak up the bloodwood. When you get behind em, advance slowly.'

'You going to tie the other end to a branch?' I asked, knowing he couldn't possibly hold the animal.

'Yep. Among the three of us we'll toss it somehow.'

Peter and I skirted out. There were enough trees to give us cover and there was more loose stone than boulders. The horses picked over it and up behind the cattle we mounted. We couldn't see Jack in the tree. He was beautifully camouflaged. The cattle reacted to plan. Those lying down stood when we approached and some of them had that wild eye look about them. I thought they would take off down the slope.

Peter had developed great instinct with cattle. He raised his hand and reined in. All of them turned to face us. It was an exercise in patience. Any moment, one would become unsettled and head down the pad. It was a juvenile bull, black and tan and cruel horns. Worth a lot of money in Madrid, but not even the cost of a slug out here. It was good he led first. Jack wouldn't want him and the first to go might be the most watchful. With all mammals it's very much follow the leader and hope for the best. Next to start down was a heifer, a fat one weighing a third of ton. What a waste, but we had to eat. The rest were cows and small weaners. It would have been hard to drop the lasso over the head of a small weaner and pull it tight before it jumped out of the loop. Jack dropped the eye neatly over her head and she jumped forward, causing the lasso to lock instantly. She reared over, got up and charged uphill towards the stunned cows behind and when they fled down-hill she tried to follow, the noose throwing her once again.

Jack had half fallen out of the tree and was waging a futile battle before we could dismount and run to join the fray. I got hold of its tail and Jack grabbed it as well in his left hand. The heifer lashed out and we took a hoof each. We wrenched hard in anger and still she wouldn't fall. She was too big. In a bronco yard a mule would be backing up, applying the tension. Here there was no such constraint. It ran in every direction and carted us along like mongrel dogs. Somehow Jack held the knife in his crook hand and threw it handle first at Peter, who had been waiting for the heifer to fall before sizing up where he could be most effective.

'The throat!' Jack gasped. The hoof he collected had winded him.

Peter had no hope while the heifer charged from one side of the tree to the other with Jack and me going for the ride. When she leaned back, tongue lolling and choking for air, he got his chance. If she jumped forward she'd rake him and spill his insides on the rocks. They weren't long horns which pierced and flung, they were the more dreaded devil's rake: go in one side and when the crazed beast jerks its head to the opposite side the other horn penetrates. The action can disembowel a dog in two hard thrusts.

Peter drove the knife in deep and instantaneously Jack darted forward, grabbed one horn and seized the knife handle with his crook hand. He yelled out in pain as he thrust downwards, opening the heifer's throat. It was over quickly then. Blood spurted all over us and the poor thing staggered to its knees, fell over and died.

Doubled up, Jack stumbled away, his face contorted. The rag had come off his hand, which was red and swollen. All three of us sat on the ground, gasped for air and tried to wave off the fly swarms. The cattle dung had brought the flies in their millions and they wasted no time. The head and throat of the heifer was already black with them. It looked an ugly mess with the flies all over the blood on the ground.

'We can't do this again,' Jack gasped, slapping away both flies and mosquitoes. 'It's not worth the struggle. She's nearly kicked my guts out.'

I nodded. I hated the whole spectacle. When you can butcher properly it has a civilised feel about it. What we'd just done was savagery and in a little over an hour this heifer would be a bloated, rapidly rotting carcass.

Jack rose painfully, holding his stomach with his good hand. 'That was great work, Pete,' he said to his son. 'We were getting nowhere. The bitch had us just about beat.'

Jack never gave the boys credit for anything and Peter

smiled. It was rare for him to smile. I don't think he and George ever had a childhood. They worked from the day they were strong enough to carry a bucket.

The flies rose in a cloud as Jack opened the stomach and drove the knife under the ribs. The first titbit out was the liver. He let it slide down the blade to the hilt and carried it over to the nearest flat bottom boulder. There, he sliced it into strips and invited us to start. With blood running down the side of the rock it looked revolting, but we were starving and bit off chunks of it.

'Hey! Slowly,' Jack warned, but too late. My stomach repelled it within seconds.

'I'll slice up some sweetbread,' Jack spluttered. He was struggling himself, holding his stomach. 'It's not nausea, just sudden pain.'

The neck sweetbread, or thymus, is a pale pink piece of fatty meat which sits either side of the windpipe, near the lungs. It's far more appetising to eat raw than the liver.

'Give that a go,' Jack said, after he had sliced it up. 'Gotta get some of this down before it turns rotten.'

After that first vomiting spasm I was okay. We chewed on the sweetbread and the liver for about an hour. Following Jack's instructions Peter cut off several pounds of rump steak before we left the carcass to the flies and went to find the scattered horses.

Much of the next two weeks is a blur in my memory. It's not just that it's so long ago now. A medical fact provides the explanation for my inability to recall the fine detail of that time: we were starving and rapidly developing beri-beri, a tropical disease caused by an acute deficiency of thiamine, which manifests itself in gross swelling – called wet beri-beri. In addition, the constant fight with insects, infected bites and merciless humidity and heat resulted in listlessness. It all served to destroy our sense of time and contributed to memory loss.

We didn't get much out of the rump steak Peter carried back. Being the taller – though not by much – I cut a spike in a quinine tree at the camp and skewered the meat. Taking it in little pieces, we got a stomach full out of it next morning – before a sea eagle swooped and took the rest. It was already flyblown. A couple of days later we tried to get another killer with the revolver. The firing caps had dried out. The problem was Jack's physical condition: he couldn't hold the gun steady, and missed. The horses, too, were deteriorating and Peter and I couldn't keep running mobs up to the ambush tree on horse-back. After two attempts, Jack abandoned it for good.

Until he became too weak, Jack rode to the Isdell nearly every day. There was a bend at the foot of the range, he said. He'd made up his mind that Otto would arrive there and wait for him to appear before attempting the dangerous swim with George. I think it was a way of dealing with his remorse and grief. Remorse, that he didn't keep George at the camp; that he should have sent Otto out alone. And grief. I believe that deep in his heart he thought George and Otto had perished. He suffered in silence, his good hand shielding his eyes for hours at a time.

To protect his badly gashed right hand Jack cut a long

strip of cloth out of a spare pair of trousers. It must have throbbed for days. From a small branch he shaped a forked stick to rest his wrist in, his whole arm raised higher than his head. It relieved the pressure on the wound, which constantly wept. Each day Peter got a billy of salt water from the tidal creek for Jack to bathe his hand. But for Jack, not being able to smoke his tobacco might have been the greater torment. He kept it in a buttoned shirt pocket and sometimes I'd catch him smelling the tobacco in his good palm.

My clothes became a serious problem. They were old to begin with, and after being wet for days, not to mention the high humidity, the shirt and trousers I'd been wearing simply fell apart. Jack couldn't even make a temporary bandage from them. By the second week I was wearing my spares. The stitching had rotted in both boots and when the soles flapped I cut them off. Wherever possible I walked barefooted.

After the two abortive attempts to shoot a killer, Jack didn't have many bullets left. About twenty, he said. They had to be saved for an emergency, which I realised was the horses. The first to be put down was Salty. Not as mobile as the others, he'd probably eaten more of the walkabout. It poisons their livers and the walking in circles that gives the plant its name is the horse's pathetic attempt to try to escape the symptoms. Horses with chronic colic lie down, roll and grunt with agony. Walkabout poisoning is not as sudden but there's no cure, and it's thought the poison eventually affects the brain and eyesight.

Peter was our champion for picking the gooseberries. We soon cleaned out the camp area and by the middle of the second week Peter was walking halfway to the Isdell to find them. The little acidic berries were all we had. They must have been bad for us. The excretion was almost white, but it was a stark choice between certain starvation and a chance to survive.

Each day Jack made us go up to the waterfall and wash. Before the cyclone we loved going there. Now we had little energy. Jack used to wash in a billabong nearby. He wouldn't let Peter or me wash there, laughing that he was too tough and lean to interest a salty.

The weather didn't let up. Some of the worst thunderstorms were at night, with lightning raking the ranges in a myriad of deadly strikes. Jack said it was as bad as being in a bunker under fire. But it was a good sign, he added, ever the optimist. While the lightning spat fury all around us we could take comfort that the wet season was coming to a close.

By the end of the second week Jack had shrunk to a skeleton and Peter and I were expanding with beri-beri. Peter's stomach was so distended you could have sworn he had a four-gallon drum inside. I had hives and the march flies were constantly buzzing and biting. Another new parasite on the scene was the shellback tick. Add mosquitoes and flies and there were times when it was tempting to raid Jack's saddlebag and blow out your brains. But there were far more sinister maladies than skin irritations and beri-beri. Peter and I had very raw throats and even the gooseberries were becoming difficult to swallow. With Jack it was his eyes. His sight had faded only a little, but it was a disturbing symptom of advanced malnutrition. This was when he had to abandon his

Isdell River vigil. On his last ride to the river Peter and I had to help him mount and when he rode away he was drooping in the saddle. It reminded me of those scenes in the Hollywood westerns when the cowboy took an arrow in the stomach and sagged forward gripping the pommel, knowing that if he fell off he would be scalped.

Then one morning he woke us at daylight and instructed us to catch our horses. We were leaving. Otto couldn't have made it, he said. They were both dead. We had to ride over the range and head for Mount Hart Station.

I wondered whether he was delirious. He had been talking in his sleep and eating next to nothing. The plan had no logic. Even if there was a way over the range, the horses were too far gone. Peter's gelding in particular was very sick.

'Don't you think, Jack,' I posed, tentatively, 'that we should stay put? It's two weeks now. Hilton will know something's wrong and organise a search plane.'

'I don't think he could have got out either,' he said hoarsely. 'I've been in the north all my life and never seen such a deluge. The Humbert would have flooded from one range to the other. The King the same. No one in Derby knows where we are.' He was silent for a while and I noticed that his sunken cheeks were a bloodless white. 'We're on our own, and if we stay here we'll slowly starve on the bloody berries.'

We didn't take much. Peter and I rolled up the tarp as tightly as possible and fastened it to the back of my saddle. Two swags were tied onto Peter's saddle and the other we put behind Jack's saddle. It was a case of trying to distribute the weight equally among the horses. The thin blankets in the swags were coming apart, but at night they were the only defence against the marauding mosquitoes. Everything else we left.

'It's the last place on earth I want to go.' Jack mumbled as he walked towards his mare to mount. We went with him to help. 'Last time I saw him I jabbed the point of that gun into the side of his neck.'

I didn't know who he was talking about. Mount Hart had always seemed to be a taboo subject for Jack. Sometime in the past couple of years there had been a fierce stand-off about cattle ownership. Bizarrely, the thought of actually arriving at Mount Hart seemed to trouble Jack more than our hopeless prospects of getting there.

We rode up past the waterfall and followed the creek for an hour until we came to a gorge. The horses were listless and, although we hated to do it, had to be spurred along the whole way. Stops were frequent. The diarrhoea was constant. In the gorge, we passed through jungle half trampled by the cattle. The creek here was like a narrow river, deep and continuous. There were more fish than I can ever recall seeing before or since. We just sat on our horses and stared at them, twenty pound barramundi catching the light as they fleetingly broke the surface. Otto would have been able to make a spear.

We rode on, the gorge narrowing. Ahead, the sun caught steep bluffs of red rock. It was a dead end, but before we arrived at the first heap of boulders Jack suddenly reined in and pointed. 'Watermelons!' he exclaimed.

I followed the line of his arm and sure enough there on the

opposite bank was a watermelon vine, about twenty-five yards from where we sat the horses. Peter and I slid off and went to the edge. We intended to swim in our clothes. The mosquitoes were terrible in that gorge.

'Wait,' Jack croaked. 'I'll ride along a bit upstream.'

We were impatient and already had our boots off. Peter had gone one further and unsaddled to get the cloth. He was going to bring some melons back for Jack. The exciting prospect of something decent to eat blinded us to the croc threat. We didn't have much faith in Jack's eyesight, either.

Jack rode up for about forty yards and stopped for a long while. Whether he was in pain or watching I couldn't tell. Then he came back, head down so that you looked straight into the crown of his hat.

'Very big croc,' he said quietly, disgusted with our luck. 'Big enough to take a bullock.'

'Throw the saddle on again, Pete. We'll ride downstream a hundred yards or more.'

The trick was not to take long. Bull crocs claim territory over long sections in a river. They can smell a mammal through the water 200 yards away.

Jack dropped off his mare and took the .38 from his saddlebag. He walked to the edge and looked carefully over the water.

'Pick em quick and swim straight back,' he said anxiously.

With a saddlecloth each, Peter and I swam over together. We went as quietly as possible using breaststroke, hands and feet under water. There were five melons. The swim back was the mouth-drying one. To hold the melons, we were forced to swim on our backs with one hand free and propel ourselves with our feet which made a few splashes. Hunger drove us to do it. If that croc had followed the horses down, one of us was dead meat. Jack may have got an opportunity to shoot but the odds were stacked against it.

When we got out of the water, Jack wasn't there. He was sitting on the ground leaning against a rivergum, bandaged hand over his chest. Peter asked him if he was all right and he nodded, but it wasn't convincing. He handed Peter his long blade and within seconds we were eating the melons. The sappy pink fruit seemed the best thing we'd ever eaten.

'Seeds from old Munja,' Jack remarked. 'Carried by birds. Be little watermelon patches scattered across the range.'

We ate all but the rinds. When Jack rose he doubled up in pain. Before he said anything I knew we were going no further. Peter and I had to help him mount and we rode back to the campsite. Jack's condition had distracted me – I'd intended to put the melon rinds in Jack's saddlebag to eat later. We dismounted and unpacked with a pervading sense of hopelessness. By now it was midday, hot and the mosquitoes bad. I fell asleep with my hat over my face. It seemed hours later when I woke. Jack was propped up against his usual boulder. His couch, he called it. He moved his head a little when I sat up. Peter was gone, out on the gooseberry run.

'I'd better get a few too,' I said rising and scratching myself. The hives made me scratch all the time. Sometimes they bled and flies homed in.

'Leave it,' he murmured. Fully awake now, I looked at him. He was lying in the sun. The insects didn't bother him.

Tough-skinned, he didn't seem to sweat much. He was tough right through.

'Yer boots have had it,' he went on. 'They're gonna fall right off yer feet any time.' He got up and moved to the shade. I think he must have been in a heavy sleep too. 'It's Peter's way of copin. While he's picking the berries, we're safe. At his age there's no thinking through it. Just one day at a time. He's lucky I suppose. You and I know the devils are diggin.'

He must have seen the look of horror on my face. I hadn't thought it would get to this either.

'Teenage bodies are very resilient,' he added quickly, as though he had drifted away and suddenly realised what he'd said. 'Someone will find you before it's too late.'

Peter returned before sundown. He had a billy-full of the berries. No one ate any. You ate a handful and went running. Only when the hunger hit hard did we give in and eat them.

We seemed to be sleeping far too much. In one way it was relief: those hours asleep passed the time and waking hours were full of torment. When I awoke again it must have been two or three hours before dawn. Jack was delirious again. He mumbled about George and Betty, his wife. I lay still, disturbed and fearful. Peter was asleep. Apart from the beri-beri he was in much better shape than Jack or I.

Jack went silent for awhile before groaning loudly and I could hear the rasp of his breathing. I asked him what was wrong and he said chest pains.

'I think I'm goin to peg it.' He could barely speak. Between breaths he issued some chilling instructions.

'Don't try to bury me. Just go, on foot. Mount Hart's about

thirty mile away. You'll be rescued there – decent people and a good airstrip. But it's all cliffs and gorges for the first twenty miles. Bad as it can get. You gotta look out for a mountain higher than all the hills for miles around, then cross the Isdell and head southwest.'

I didn't say anything. We would never find Mount Hart even if we could walk that far.

Jack fell silent after a while and, despite everything, I drifted off again. At daylight I threw off the blanket and with dread looked over at Jack. He wasn't there. I called out and he answered from the billabong below. Unbelievably, he was having a wash and yelled out for me to wake Peter and both go up to the waterfall for a swim. Jack had become obsessive about personal hygiene.

The sudden change in Jack was hard to take in. He'd definitely had a bad turn of some sort, perhaps a panic attack. But whatever it was, he now seemed none the worse. In the end we all headed up to the waterfall.

After the swim and a few berries, Peter announced he was going to ride back and get the melon rinds. Jack was all for it. He said we could make them palatable by dipping them into the jar of fat. In the meantime he was going to ride to the Isdell again. I thought he'd lost it properly then. If Otto had made it back he would have swum the river and come to find us.

Jack mounted without help. It was staggering what a little food could do, even watery melons. I had to tie Bluey as the others rode away in opposite directions – the grey didn't like being left on his own. We didn't hobble any more. Jack said they wouldn't go anywhere and, with the walkabout poison spreading through their organs, the hobble straps would have been another source of misery. The cane grass was now a foot high and quite succulent, but it was too late for the horses.

EIGHT

THE MAGIC OF FIRE

OUR ONLY CHANCE of rescue now was from a smoke signal. Sooner or later there would be a search plane. You don't just disappear from the face of the earth and no one raises the alarm. The problem for the authorities would be where to search. Those who knew just a little, such as my dad and uncle, would have said somewhere on the top end of Oobagooma. Hopefully, one flight would make it over the range to Walcott Inlet. The build up to the cyclone was slow and Walker would have wanted to be by his young wife's side when it struck. But if he'd got out, why hadn't he raised the alarm already? There should have been a plane days ago.

There had been at least three boxes of matches in the food pack. There was a remote possibility one of them had got snagged in a flood debris heap, down from the old camp. When we searched after the flood the debris heaps were like mounds of mud; now they were dry. The mud crumbled easily and I was able to pull the heaps apart. I got a tingle of excitement when I found the remains of a Billy Tea packet. It was coated in silt and, walking past, no one could have seen it. I shook it for tea leaves then threw it away. I pulled more debris apart. The silt fell apart in my fingers like an old bird's nest. I worked in the hot sun for more than two hours before I saw something that set my hands trembling. It was tiny and square shaped. I scraped the silt off with a fingernail and saw the familiar red top. The box was as flat as a postage stamp and there wasn't any carbon left on it. I used my knife to gently prise it open to see if any matches remained. The box ends had disintegrated and most of the matches had floated away. But there were three left and they were okay.

While I was down on the flat, Jack had returned. I knew he couldn't have reached the Isdell in such a short time. He had unsaddled the mare by the billabong and left the saddle on the ground. The mare didn't appear to have moved. She stood there listless, head down a little and ears back. Bluey wasn't far away in the shade of a bauhinia. I went up to the camp and found Jack half lying, half sitting in his usual position. When he saw me it took him a while to focus.

'Matches,' I croaked, trying to catch my breath. There was a flutter in Jack's eyelids, as though he was trying to break out of a dream. I looked around for Peter. He wasn't back.

Suddenly awake, Jack echoed me with disbelief: 'Matches?'

'In the debris. Three left and I think they're okay.'

Jack staggered to his feet and I gave him the little crushed box.

'That big dead tree just along a bit,' he said breathlessly. 'It might burn for two or three days. Put up a bit of smoke.'

The tree was a big rivergum near the foot of the ridge, thirty yards from the camp and opposite the lagoon. We got busy heaping sticks and dried leaves against the dead trunk. We had a bit of a pile stacked up when Peter returned. His horse was nearly beat too. He unsaddled and left the saddle where it lay. He had the melon rinds in a billy. Coming towards us he wondered what the hell we were doing and was most excited when we told him. He dropped the billy and helped us. When there was a pile of sticks and small logs big enough to light the trunk, Jack dropped to one knee and drew the first match. He had a nice little bundle of leaves to take the flame.

The first one wouldn't strike. It wasn't the match; it was the lack of carbon on the box. On the third attempt the match snapped. Jack cursed. He drew the second match and, holding it in his bandaged hand, he angled the matchbox carbon to the sun. It was an hour before the sun peaked over-head and getting hotter by the minute. Satisfied the box was warm, he tested the second match. It flared and going very slowly, so as not to catch an extinguishing draught, Jack lowered the burning match into the leaves. The flame had reached his fingertips by the time he got to the leaves.

The leaves burst into flame and Jack stood back. He had a big smile on his face and it must have been the first since we crossed the Isdell nearly a month ago. It was short-lived though. In the heat the leaves burnt as though doused with diesel, too quick for the sticks to catch. The morning dew dampened everything. The leaves on the ground dried like paper in the hot sun, but the sticks held the dampness until noon. In the end it was the sordid, homemade bandage from Jack's hand that caught the dying flame. He ripped it from his hand and got it onto that last gasp of flame. The rag burnt slowly, long enough for the sticks to catch. In five minutes there was a roaring fire.

Having a fire was like a shot of adrenalin. All three of us suddenly felt alive again.

Jack unbuttoned his shirt pocket and snatched out the Log Cabin packet. It was soiled and on the point of disintegration. With trembling fingers he shook enough leaves for a cigarette out into the palm of his swollen hand. A black crust closed the wound, the flies around it so persistent that several got into the tobacco. Then he retrieved the papers from the same pocket. He pulled a paper with his teeth, laid it flat in his good hand and placed the tobacco, a couple of flies not escaping. He lit the cigarette and passed it to me.

'You first. You found the matches.'

I took it and drew in sharply. The sense of levitation was almost immediate and the addiction cemented forever. Reluctantly yet gratefully, I passed back the drooping, fragile cigarette. Peter had gone back down the slope to retrieve the billy with the melon rinds.

'Come on,' Jack said. 'We'll eat these rinds to get some energy and go after a killer. I saw a few cattle this morning not far away.'

Jack opened the old Sunshine tin of fat, which was soft and runny from the heat. He dipped a strip of rind and passed it to Peter. He took a mouthful, tried to chew it and spat it out. His throat was too sore to swallow anything like melon rind. I was the same. Our throats were getting worse each day. Perhaps it was another symptom of beri-beri.

'If we don't get a killer we'll soak em,' Jack said. 'We won't waste time now. In the heat of the day they'll be camped. Might get a close up shot. Our horses are too gone for any chasin.'

For a fit horse it was only an hour's ride to the gorge where we found the melons. I was so excited about the matches it didn't occur to me Peter had been away nearly five hours. When we walked down to get our horses the chestnut was walking in a tight circle, sweating profusely. As we watched, he walked into a tree. The horse's muscles were twitching in spasms.

Grim-faced, Jack looked at me. 'Take Pete back to the fire for a moment.'

Peter knew, of course. He'd seen it all before. Hard choices are part of life in the outback.

The tree was ablaze when we got there. At some stage the top trunk and branches would fall in a shower of sparks. It distracted us for a moment, until we heard the shot.

Riding close to the ranges, Jack and I rode in the direction of the Isdell, where Jack had seen cattle earlier in the day. We had to leave Peter behind. He was a brave kid, but Jack didn't know how to handle it, so nothing was said about his horse. Jack just told Peter to keep away from the tree until the top of it fell in.

It wasn't long before we put a mob up. They were lying down in a clump of bauhinias. With low spreading branches, the bauhinias were the last shade trees before the rocky escarpment. We reined in to discuss a plan.

'They're on their feet already,' Jack muttered. 'Didn't think they'd be that touchy. They're gonna run too. You swing right out and ride to the edge of the salt pans. They'll watch you and stay. I'm goin to go back a bit, ride to the edge of the range and backtrack to those bloodwoods over there, then wait. There's a cattle pad through the trees, saw it this morning. Give me about twenty minutes.'

The bloodwoods at the foot of the range were about 600 yards away and about 300 yards from the mob. When I pushed them out of the shade there was no certainty the mob would run that way. But it was a good bet and on horses that we had to treat gently, there were no options.

'It'll be a shoulder shot,' Jack added before I rode out towards the salt plains. 'If it don't fall, don't chase it. The grey – Bluey as you call him – is the only healthy horse we got. We'll follow the blood.'

Half-wild cattle never respond to please you. When I thought the time was right, I rode slowly towards the bauhinia clump. Jack was right, they were touchy. Predictably they trotted towards the bloodwoods. It was their pad in among those trees and all looked to be going perfectly to plan. I couldn't see Jack mounted on his mare, which was better still. But the lead beast must have seen him or smelt the horse. The smell of horse sweat is exceptionally strong and although I couldn't feel a breeze, it doesn't take much to carry scent to a wild animal.

From 200 yards I couldn't tell whether the lead beast was a

cow or one of the juvenile bulls. It baulked and ducked away to the right, cantering with its head turned towards the bloodwoods. Another drew alongside it and the mob broke into a gallop, tails in the air. There were about twenty of them. With Jack's instructions in mind I had no intention of doing anything until I noticed a fat cow lame in the hip. She was tailing from the start and each second left her further behind. When I took off I had no plan. It was pure predator instinct. If I could reach her before the narrow valley up ahead, where rocks and trees would frustrate any pursuit, I might be able to do something. Block her until Jack arrived – even throw her.

Bluey collared her in a single burst, legs stretched like a racehorse. He wouldn't have felt like it, but gave everything. Beaten, the roan cow swung around with extraordinary speed and charged. The grey was a seasoned camp drafter and spun easily away. It unbalanced the cow and she fell onto her hip. She bellowed with rage and was a little too slow to regain her back feet. With the image of a sizzling streak to spur me on I jumped from Bluey onto her hip, pulling her tail up between her rear legs as I did so. She thrashed the air with her legs and bellowed in fury. The thought of her tossing me off and raking me with her evil horns was a helpful incentive to fight her and hang on. I knew Jack would be coming as fast as he could and he didn't let me down. In fact, I never even saw him, but heard the shot as though it were at the base of my skull. The cow's legs suddenly flexed before the whole body broke into a spasm. Jack cut her throat and we shook hands.

The cow had nearly made it to the rough country. The rocks and boulders would have taxed her too, but pursuit on Bluey would have been impossible. Dropped to one knee, Jack spat on the nearest stone and rotated his long blade through the saliva. There was just the sound of steel on stone and the massing of flies. Satisfied he had a good enough edge, he made a neat cut around the ankle on the foreleg and began to skin from the shoulder down. Perplexed, I asked him what he was doing.

'Gonna peel the leg and pull it off like they skin rabbits. Makes a good carry bag and keeps the flies out.'

He went on skinning, me feeling useless. Jack was a natural skinner. He loved it. There's something therapeutic about skinning, but I hate to think what psychologists might have to say about that.

'It's tight on the leg,' I said. 'You'll have to skin all the way. What if I take out the rump?' I was itching to have a go.

Jack kept skinning. 'The horses, they need a drink bad. Hop on your bloke and lead the mare to a spring. Up in that pocket valley you'll find water.'

In my excitement I had forgotten about them. Bluey was in a lather of sweat, still breathing heavily. He stood a few yards away, head lower than his wither and half the reins looped on the ground. The mare, too, hadn't moved. I didn't like the way she was standing, slightly splay-legged. She nickered pathetically as I picked up the reins. The sense of victory and elation evaporated. We would ride them until they dropped dead.

I found water and let them have a long drink. By the time

I got back, Jack had removed the pelt from both front legs. The wet skin bags were ideal for carrying the meat. Cut around the cow's ankle, the hole at the base of each bag was quite small. To prevent the chunk of steak and the liver slipping out, Jack slipped the narrow end of a shank down into each, effectively plugging the hole.

'Goin to boil up the shanks,' he said. 'Make some broth for you and Peter. It will settle yer throats down.'

We were ready to leave. I suggested that Jack ride Bluey and we tie the two pelt bags onto the mare and I lead her. I'd had a long drink and a dip at the spring and felt better than I had for days.

We were about two miles from the camp. Halfway back, slogging through the fresh cane grass, the mare began to stumble, falling onto her knees and staggering pitifully. Doggedly she tried to follow me, but by that stage even a helicopter lift with a vet aboard could not have saved her. She was finished. I untied the pelt bags and put them on the ground. Jack dismounted.

'We'll put the bags on Bluey. Lead him away a bit and wait.' His voice was hoarse, I thought choked.

The shot echoed up through the valley where I had taken her for a drink. There were ten bullets left. Since Jack last counted them my brain automatically registered a count after each shell used. I looked at my grey's big floppy ears and for some moments fought back the tears. Bullet number nine might be his. The first of us to die would be Jack. Would he choose to die in the heat, with the flies crawling in and out of his nose, or would he use bullet number eight? I felt cold standing in the hot sun, holding the reins and Bluey nudging me with his nose. He knew.

A minute passed and I made myself look to see where Jack was. The cane grass had swallowed the mare. Jack was coming towards me, floating in the heat haze. A small, fragile figure under a hat doubled in size by the heat distortion. Rain and humidity takes its toll on a hat. I used to see him re-working its shape. It's said some men are obsessed about dying with their boots on. If there's any truth in it, Jack would pass on in his hat.

'You leaving the saddle?' I enquired gently when he stopped by Bluey and gave him a rub behind the ears. He wouldn't look at me. His hands were shaking but his voice was measured and slow.

'I thought we'd get back to Pete as soon as possible, have a big feed and then I thought maybe you could ride this fella bareback for the saddle and the bridle.'

I nodded and we walked slowly back to camp, leading Bluey. Peter had set a small cooking fire at the camp while Jack and I were away.

'Not half an optimist,' Jack said to him, forcing a grin. But Peter was looking behind us.

'She didn't make it,' Jack said harshly. He was determined to maintain a tough front.

Peter sat down on his boulder, his private chair, and stared into the fire.

'I see the tree's gone,' Jack added, trying to get him talking. Peter nodded. His hat was much too big for his face.

With fresh meat to fry in the pan we should have been set

for a feast. The problem was that Peter and I were struggling to drink water let alone eat solid food. Jack chopped one of the shanks in half and boiled it up in the camp oven. We had lost the steel bucket in the flood. While he waited for the water to turn to broth he talked about our next attempt at escape. I had no faith in any plan, but it was better to go somewhere than languish in the heat, tormented by mosquitoes and flies.

'Why don't you have some steak?' I said. I was ravenous and I knew he was just as hungry.

'After what we all been through I can't eat alone.' He smiled ruefully. 'It's not the meat tormenting me right now. It's the tobacco. I've got an urge to smoke them all one after the other, but I've got to stagger them. There's only five left.'

He told us we must take full advantage of the energy we would get from the meat. In the morning we would put the packsaddle on Bluey, load the meat and shanks, our bit of gear, hang the other saddles in a tree and head towards the ruins of old Munja. He had lost track of the tides and his watch had stopped. A couple of miles below where the Charnley flowed into the inlet there was a rock shelf crossing. At the first low tide we would swim across, taking our fire and meat with us. The destination was Panter Downs, about three days' walk. There would be no one there. During the wet months the station was abandoned. But all stations had a storeroom and tinned food might be left behind. Jack said he thought we could rely on it with our lives.

'Who owns Panter Downs?' I asked, simply curious, not expecting complications.

'Same bloke who's got Mount Hart. There's a couple of others in with him.'

'We'll be trespassing in a big way,' I said, trying to make a joke of it.

Jack nodded grimly. 'You can say that again. It's one thing to wander into Mount Hart and say we're lost, quite another to make ourselves at home at Panter without askin.'

'But he won't know.'

'Oh yes he will. That's where we're goin to get rescued. There'll be a two-way there, unless they took it out with em.'

'What's it matter? We just tryin to get somewhere to get help.'

'It couldn't matter more. Rumours will spread I went to Panter to lift cattle and got caught in the cyclone. I'm a contract musterer. A rumour like that could finish me up here in the Kimberley.'

The water bubbled and the steam rose. It must have taken an hour for the meat on the bone to dissolve into a beefy soup. Jack poured it into our pannikins. He wouldn't let Peter or me touch the camp oven when it was hot. One careless fumble was a third degree burn, he said.

'Let it cool,' he warned of the broth. 'It'll soothe your throats and then eat a fill of steak.'

He fried the steak in the pan. We had nothing to barbeque it on and green sticks made into long forks burst into flame too quickly. To make sure an eagle or goanna didn't make off with our meat, Jack tied some rope around the wide end of both pelt bags and, by managing to toss the other end of the rope over the lowest branch on the boab, he hauled both bags into the tree. The small hole at the bottom of the pelt bag let air in, keeping the meat fresh for a few more hours.

After a painful but very satisfying feast, I rode Bluey back to the mare for the saddle. Perhaps it didn't matter, I don't know, but I didn't want Bluey to see her. I tied him to a tree and walked the last hundred yards.

Back at the camp the effect of getting some solid protein into our bodies made for a much happier camp. With a bit of daylight left Peter and I took off for the waterfall. It would be the last swim there and I think we both knew it. One horse left, cartridges nearly spent: no matter what was in store we had to leave.

Jack was cooking again when we got back. More broth and more steak. We were hungry again, too. There was a spark in Jack's eye and, although he was almost a skeleton, that fire in his eye gave me great confidence. He was talkative too.

'We'll cross where the army did in 'forty-two,' he said. 'When the Japs were thought to have landed out on Doubtful Bay. Almost straight across the inlet from here and over a low range.'

'They dropped plenty of bombs,' I said. 'Never heard of a landing.'

'Well I dunno either. I was reared in north Queensland. The old people from Mount House told me the story so I guess it's true.'*

* For the full story, see Appendix II

NINE

THE TRACK TO PANTER DOWNS

IT TOOK EIGHT hours to reach the narrow section of Walcott Inlet, about one and a half miles below the Munja ruins. Jack dictated the pace. Before we left he lit a cigarette, saying he had enough tobacco for four more. Wordlessly he passed it to me for the first couple of puffs.

Trudging along, stopping for a minute or two every three or four hundred yards, we must have looked a pathetic sight. Our clothes were torn and my boots were not going to see it out. If a farmer wanted a scarecrow Jack would do if he simply stood still. Peter and I, on the other hand, looked grotesquely bloated. Little wonder a pair of wedgetails circled as we walked.

Jack and I took turns carrying the firestick. He'd found a dead branch off a bauhinia and placed one end into the flame. Bauhinias are a hardwood variety and a thick rounded stick will only burn quickly when totally consumed by flame. To get enough charcoal at one end Jack had to leave the stick in the flame for about twenty minutes. It was difficult to juggle. The trick was to maintain a tiny flame. If the flame grew too big we had to stop and hold it up until it tapered off, and if the charcoal looked to be cooling we pointed the stick to the ground to catch the gentle updraught from ground level. The worst part was its weight. We were nearly too weak to walk, let alone carry a heavy firestick.

Peter Camp was the pathfinder. He led Bluey, who was clearly in low spirits. All Bluey's friends, bonded for life, had vanished, and he was still sick from eating the poisonous walkabout plant. When he stopped and wanted to walk no further I clicked him on from behind. Jack was listless and struggling, breaking his silence only to direct Peter. Sometimes he slapped his shirt pocket, the button long gone. He was checking the tobacco, as though it were all he had left in the world. I knew this morning he was suffering what I called in my mind 'the George remorse'. At the camp I'd catch him staring at the point of the ridge where it ran down to the salt plain, grappling with an anguish known only to bereaved mums and dads, and made all the more terrible by not knowing what happened.

The worst of the trek was the salt creeks. There were eight in total. The mud filled our boots and several times I stopped mid-stream, scraping the bottom for a boot that had come off. The last creek was more like a river. Jack called it a tidal estuary, another perfect backwater for a bull croc to claim for himself. All three of us scanned the surface. It was about forty yards wide and the tide was in. Jack simply lifted his right hand. A scab covered the wound now and the flies were less interested. It must have been still very painful, for he never once held the firestick in his right hand.

We had turned to walk towards the range when Jack pointed to a fin out in the centre of the stream. It wasn't a big shark, but it didn't have to be.

'Keep goin, Pete,' Jack mumbled. He didn't want us to stay and dwell on it.

The range tumbled to the plain as though some quake had shot it to pieces in past millenniums. To get clear of the tidal waters we had to find a track through the boulders at the base of the range and urge a reluctant Bluey through the narrow gaps.

Once on the salt plain again we plodded on, directly towards what Jack called the Walcott ankle, before the inlet widened again like a giant heel and tapered off to the very toe of the inlet at the confluence of the Calder and Charnley rivers. The range curled right into the ankle of Walcott. In fact the crossing, if anyone could call such a stretch of water a crossing, was an extension of the sandstone to the very heart of the main channel.

Exhausted from another struggle through the boulders – more than a mile – we arrived at the crossing about mid-afternoon. Jack still had his watch pouch fitted neatly to his belt and sometimes he'd take the watch out and look at it, forgetting the salt water had got into it, or maybe hoping it would just start ticking again. We didn't know the exact time – or what day it was.

The tide had been flowing out for a while and Jack's guess was two hours to dead low.

'Be near sunset,' he muttered gloomily. 'My sight's shot when the sun dips.' He sighed, exhausted. 'We gotta go through. If Bluey don't get a drink he'll drop dead on us.

When they got that poison in em they gotta have a lot of water.'

The tough eight-hour trek had taken its toll on Jack. His problem was cramps. He sat on the silt plastered sandstone, leaning against the packs, and shared two cigarettes with me. The fine grey silt and the rock reflected the heat back into our faces like a radiator.

It was a broad sweep of flat rock where we waited. At the height of the tide it all went under. Two hours after tide drop the sun burned the wet silt to a thin dry crust. None of us could stand the thought of the water left in the billy and we shared it, consoling ourselves the heat would dissipate with the lowering of the sun and on the other side there was a spring, somewhere. Jack said it was near the Munja ruins. Could we find it in the dark, I wondered? Well, we had to. We never seemed to have options. Suddenly Jack shot a leg out and rubbed his cramping thigh. 'I need salt bad,' he gasped. 'You boys need it too.'

'You haven't got an old dog's chance of swimming, Jack.'

'I know.'

He was looking out across the inlet while he rolled another smoke. I think it was his second last, having smoked two with me.

'I'll have this smoke and get to work,' Jack said. 'The raft will be difficult to shape with only two packs to work on. I'm aimin to sit square in the middle. The thirty-eight in one hand and the firestick in the other.'

A small flame kept reducing the length of the firestick. About five feet long when Jack first lit it, it had shrunk to about twenty inches. Jack said it was an ideal length on the raft, when he would have to hold the wood aloft from the water. When we got across he intended to light a fire, then find another piece of suitable wood in the morning.

It took a lot of skill and patience to make the raft. Jack had made tarp rafts many times, but always with four packs, not two. He didn't want any help from us; it was a one-man job. When he'd finished, it looked stable enough. The swag blankets had become little more than torn rags, which filled the two packs along with the canvas covers. When the tarp was neatly folded with the intent to float, the big bundle was about five feet long and three feet wide. The first wave after tide turn would throw Jack. He knew it and we knew it. We had to reach shallow water before tide turn.

Daylight to dark is swift in the tropics. When our own shadows were long Jack said it was time, dead low or not. I dragged the raft to the water's edge and Peter led Bluey. Jack followed with the firestick in his crook hand and the .38 in the other. With only two packs to facilitate buoyancy, dead-weight items such as the frying pan and the tomahawk had to be left behind. The camp oven couldn't be left and Jack had managed to fasten it to the packsaddle on Bluey by running a strap over the handle and the little hand grip on the lid.

With two or three minutes' start we had about fifteen minutes to get across. First in was Bluey. He didn't want to go in all alone and we had to wave, shout and slap his rump. It left a nasty taste in my already bone dry mouth. Once in, he trudged into the deeper water and began to swim. Right behind and as quickly as possible, the three of us launched the

raft and it was a tense moment as Jack awkwardly straddled
the floating tarp. If it didn't sink a little into the water under
Jack's weight, it would roll. But it did, and with a leg either
side Jack said it felt quite stable.

We pushed off into thigh-deep water. Me in front and
Peter behind. It was easy to begin with, wading and towing
the raft by pulling on the centre rope. Jack looked comfortable. Smoke rose from the firestick, conjuring up images of a
prehistoric scene – man carrying his fire over water – but
there was no time to dwell on such reflections. Suddenly we
were in the main channel and swimming. The raft buoyed
Peter and me to some extent, but the only instrument of
forward propulsion was our free hands. We had to work hard
to gain any movement, me pulling and Peter pushing. Jack sat
as still as possible, watching out for a dreaded fin or a creepy
reptilian snout.

With only our heads out of the water, Peter and I had
no sense of distance from one side to the other and a minute
felt like half an hour. My heart sank when Jack muttered
'Halfway'. The tide rush had to come long before our feet
touched the mud on the other side. Midstream was the
danger point too. If anything was about, we could expect a
visit while in the deep water. I'm sure Jack was more
concerned than he ever dared convey to us, because whenever
I glanced up at him he was electric, his eyes everywhere, the
.38 raised. And it was just as well. I didn't see him take aim,
but the report whacked my eardrum and the echo rolled away
across the water. My heart leapt; something must have been
bearing down on us. There was a great splash, as though a

forty-four gallon drum had been pushed off a boat. I glanced up – 'What the hell?'

'Shark!' Jack yelled, and added gleefully: 'Plugged the bastard too, base of the fin. Seen a couple of crocs. Small though, weighin us up.'

Then he straightened his arm and fired again, the report echoing away. 'Another shark. Think I got him. Paddle boys! Paddle all yer got. How yer goin, Pete? I don't dare look behind for fear of upsettin the balance.'

'How am I goin!' Peter spluttered, and he started to laugh, stopped suddenly by a mouthful of water. He was a fearless young boy.

We kept on. The shark terror had pumped some adrenalin into my veins and for a couple of minutes I felt no fatigue. Just a desperate urge to get across.

'Bluey's out,' Jack announced. 'He's shakin himself. Thirty yards and you'll feel the bottom.'

My legs seemed to be working through the water much better than at the beginning. Then I realised: my boots were gone. On the previous swim, across the Isdell, the elastic was strong. Now it was rotten and my boots had come off after Jack shot the sharks, when I swam and pulled with everything I could throw into it.

When the tide hovers at the point of balance, in those few minutes when there's no pull either way, Walcott Inlet is as tranquil as a lake. But we had enjoyed the lull for what seemed too long. You could hear it, a frightening, rumbling sound as the tide rush gathered momentum. The first wave seemed certain to topple Jack. It was three feet high and racing towards us. When it struck, his skill as a horseman came into play. He raised the arm with the .38 to hold balance, like a bronco rider, and with his crook hand he clutched the firestick.

Peter and I went under as the wave passed. I could hear Peter spluttering and coughing. There was another wave nearly on us. It was going to be a disaster if we didn't soon touch bottom. The second one hit us and Jack rose as though high in the saddle. A moment later I felt the mud.

'Bottom!' I yelled.

Jack jumped off. Submerged to the chest, it was a super-human effort for him to hold both the .38 and the firestick above the water – and the third wave was hissing towards us. It was an eerie sound. On a beach a wave is almost silent until it gathers and breaks, but the tide change waves at Walcott have a sinister, intimidating energy all their own.

Jack had to make a choice. He couldn't stand against the third wave and hold both the firestick and the .38 above the water. The capacity to be able to cook was critical, so he jammed the .38 into his belt, below the water, and clutched the raft with his free hand. It saved him from being swept off his feet and in the next instant he was standing on the under-water bank of the channel, where the water was only knee-deep. Peter and I kept towing the raft, slipping and slid-ing in the mud, knowing the shallows would be transformed within minutes by a tide-driven torrent. We stopped for a few moments, bent over and trying to get our breath.

'Come on,' Jack growled. 'I know how buggered you both are, but right here will be several foot under in no time. We gotta slog it for a long way yet. Drag the tarp and I'll carry the firestick.'

We were covered in mud. It was smeared over our faces and in our hair. We pulled on the ropes, still trying to catch our breath, and we couldn't budge the raft. I looked for Bluey and saw him struggling through the mud, still a hundred yards from the mangroves and solid ground. He was probably about beat anyway.

'We'll let the tide lift her,' I gasped to Peter. 'Use the tide all the way over. You go on. I can do it on me own.'

Peter wouldn't leave, so we did it together. Jack struggled to beat the tide with only the firestick to carry. A couple of times he stopped and turned around to look at us. Without the meat and our few possessions we couldn't survive.

It was a terrifying struggle towards the finish. A wave would elevate the raft, sweep us off our feet and in a swirl of grey water we were jetted upstream. Then we'd regain our purchase and pull like mad until the next wave struck. Still fifty yards from the mangroves, Jack appeared to be half a city block to the west of us. He looked to be in knee-deep water, the tide almost coming too quick because he wasted time watching us. It must have been a photo finish who reached the shore first.

We pulled the raft into the mangroves and flopped. Nothing could have rallied us this time. I was aware of a dreadful thirst and a pounding heart. The light was fading and it was merciful, I thought. The fight to live could be stalled until sun up.

I woke from a shake, a hand gripping my shoulder. It was Jack. I think he was on one knee, his back to a pale strip of light I knew at once to be dawn breaking over the Edkins Range. I must have slept with my mouth open for when I went to swallow I couldn't. My mouth felt as though someone was aiming an oxy-torch into it.

'We gotta get going,' Jack croaked. 'Gotta find this spring. Bluey's nearly cast it. We gonna be close behind if we don't find water and get away from this plague of mozzies.'

I went to speak and couldn't. I wanted to tell Jack my mouth felt like it was full of razorblades. Up on my feet I looked for Bluey in a tangle of thick growth. Some of the mangroves grew above the normal high tide level, their lower trunks submerged in salt water when the much higher full moon tides swept the Kimberley coast. He lay flat on his side, half hidden among juvenile mangroves. Then I smelt the smoke. Jack had cleared a patch on the dry silt and made a fire with the debris. The little pile of ash smouldered, wisps of smoke drifting up into the mangroves. I half tripped in the undergrowth rushing to get my face into the smoke and hopefully some relief from the mosquitoes.

'I found some driftwood, quite a bit on this side,' Jack went on. 'You two boys were dead to the world so I let you be. Too dark to look for the water anyway.' He paused, staring across the dark mud flats. The tide had rushed in and rushed out again since Peter and I slumped onto the bank. 'About an hour to the fresh water, I reckon. Then boil up another couple of bones for you and Pete. Ease yer throats.' He walked over to where Peter lay. The boy was asleep over a pile of flood debris, covered in mosquitoes. Healthy and strong you could have lain on it for a week and not got five minutes of sleep.

Jack had to get his stockwhip out of the gear pack to get Bluey on his feet. Whatever happened, I was sure we couldn't save him. If we were not in such peril ourselves we would have left him to die in peace. The band of shoreline mangroves were only twenty yards deep. The poor horse stumbled and staggered as he tried to step over the curly mangrove roots. Somehow Jack had got the packs off the night before and carried them to the edge of the salt plain. The packs on, our wet swags still stuffed in them, we set off for old Munja. We went as before, Peter leading Bluey, Jack and me following, taking it in turns to carry the firestick. Jack had cut another stick into shape and lit one end.

At the Munja ruins all that was left was heat-twisted roofing iron, brown and rust-eaten, lying around a cast iron stove, set in homemade cement slabs. A memorial plaque had been screwed onto the old stove – for Harry Eastman, Jack said. We didn't pause to read it. He was the first white settler at Munja, later taken by a crocodile. It was a forlorn, desolate place and we didn't stop until we reached the lagoon. This was the lagoon, Jack told us, used by the government manager Harold Reid to irrigate vegetables and fruits for the Munja settlement in the 1930s and '40s.

Our tongues were swollen. It was nearly fifteen hours since we'd shared the billy of water before crossing. Just 200 yards from the salt water, the lagoon was a perfect habitat for crocodiles, but we threw caution to the wind for that drink. The bird life was very disturbed at our presence. Flocks of ducks, magpie-geese and brolgas circled overhead while we drank and washed the salt from our bodies. The brolgas in particular trumpeted their displeasure at our arrival, not that we took much notice of them or anything else. Famished as we were, it hurt to drink and it took quite a few minutes to consume any quantity. After our fill we lay among the waterlilies. I closed my eyes and tried to tell myself I was in a swimming pool; that I could get out and dry myself with a soft towel and cross the street to a store and buy an ice-cream. The fantasies of the moment saved my sanity I believe.

Bluey slurped up the water too, standing in it belly-deep. When he staggered out it looked like someone had opened him up, rolled in a forty-four gallon drum and stitched him together again. Already weak, the weight of all the water he'd drunk was too much. Jack yelled at him from the water, but Bluey was on his knees and with a grunt, dropped to his stomach with the packs still on. We all got out then and managed to get the packs off. Bluey wasn't going to get up for a while. His bottom lip almost touched the ground, a sad, resigned acceptance of his fate. I felt sad too.

The stomach cramps were inevitable after fifteen hours without water and then a sudden gutful. I lay on my back and drew my knees in; it helped a little. Jack doubled over and clenched his teeth, suffering in silence. Peter held onto a paperbark, his head bowed. I think it lasted about ten minutes. The mosquitoes were all over us and swarmed onto my hive sores. So far my feet were okay, but I didn't dare dwell on the next forty miles.

Jack undid the straps on one of the packs and took out the

meat. Submerged in warm salt water the steak had turned a shade of green, despite pre-cooking in the pan before we left. The risk of food poisoning was too high, Jack said, and I told him I couldn't swallow meat anyway.

Using the firestick Jack lit another fire, half-filled the camp oven with water and placed it on the flame. We didn't have the tomahawk any more to chop the bones, so Jack removed one of the stirrups and struck the bones until they broke in half, some going into the oven to make broth. The rest he rolled up in wet canvas for next time. The meat and the bones had a sour, stale smell.

While we waited for the broth to form Jack produced his tiny roll of tobacco, bound tightly with a spare stockwhip fall. He did a great job keeping the tobacco and the papers dry in his shirt pocket. Careful not to waste a single leaf, he took his time.

'You carried the firestick on the raft for the last cigarette, didn't you,' I teased. I felt we had become close enough for a bit of ribbing.

'Now listen here smart arse,' he replied quietly, 'you won't get a puff.' He looked gaunt. In fact he looked terrible, but the glint in his eye would remain until his last breath. 'Mind you, every man needs a bit of incentive and we're not going to find gold at Panter Downs.' Then he stopped smiling and studied my feet. 'Cut a bit of meat off and rub the grease into yer soles.' He lit the cigarette, took a long draw and passed it to me.

It took ages for the broth to form and about five minutes to smoke the cigarette. We just sat there in the rapidly increasing heat, listening to the water bubble and pop in the oven. If we thought we should be counting our blessings to make it across the inlet it was nothing compared to our dip among the lilies. The ever watchful eye of Jack saved one of us for certain. The crocodile was half out of the water, several yards away. He looked to be poised to rush one of us and by instinct we knew not to run, which would trigger the charge. Jack had been sitting on the ground, leaning against one of the packs. It was the pack with his saddlebag in it. Slowing moving his right hand, he worked it into the pack, felt for the leather bag and ever so slowly withdrew it from the pack.

'Don't move,' he muttered.

The straps were fastened on the bag and it took him another few seconds to undo them and extract the .38. His hand neatly clasped over the weapon he took careful aim and pulled the trigger. To be threatened by one of the earth's most dangerous predators and hear an innocuous pop as the cartridge misfires, isn't a pleasant situation.

'Bloody water got into em,' he muttered fiercely. 'The lead's in the barrel.'

He dropped the gun and slowly reached into the same pack for one of the stockwhips. He risked another glance at Peter and me. We were sitting on the ground, close together.

'Stay rock still!' he whispered savagely.

Using his crook right hand he let the whip stream out, spinning over the top of Peter and me, and with a hard thrust from his wrist the lash travelled faster than sight and cracked sharply about six feet from the croc. In the swing now and stepping boldly forward, the second crack was right over the croc's snout. It didn't wheel and crash back into the water, rather, it back-paddled, mouth open; the exposed teeth looking like an old-time crosscut saw. It had no intention of going far.

The whip cracking stirred Bluey onto his feet. Peter led him away about thirty yards to the shade of a rivergum, and I followed with the packs. Then we both went back and got the billy and the oven. Everything moved, Jack coiled up his whip and joined us.

'He's smelt the bones and thought that's how we would taste'. Jack shook his head and grinned. 'A special treat for his larder. I tell you what, they'll rue the day they stopped shooting these bastards.'

It took half an hour for the broth to cool. For our raw throats, the liquid had to be lukewarm. It had a pungent flavour, which must have been the marrow in the bones. It soothed our throats but did little for the hunger. Between three of us, a tea billy wasn't enough. The last drop drained from our pannikins, we tossed the packs up onto Bluey.

It was going to be very slow. Bluey was weaker and I was barefoot. It had been okay from the inlet to the billabong, as I walked mainly on dry silt from the flood. Carrying the fire-stick made my bare feet thump into the ground. One of my heels was already bruised and I knew that once we lifted out of the low floodplain we'd be back in the stone country. Jack relieved me as much as he could, but he'd deteriorated since leaving the main camp. To begin with, Peter had to walk in front and Jack flicked the whip at Bluey. He said he didn't think there was any walkabout weed at Panter and if Bluey could struggle along he might just recover there. The horse was listless and not eating, but he didn't have the chronic symptoms the others had. It was a morale booster for Peter and me. If Bluey could make it, we could.

The first day from the Munja billabong passed without incident. Angling back towards the Calder River, Jack found signs of the old vehicle track to Mount Elizabeth. The spear grass was head high and haying off. The sharp barbs penetrated between my toes, forcing me to frequently call for a stop. At least fresh water was no problem: a few miles above Munja we left the upper limits of the tide behind and Peter often pushed his way through the thick grass to fill the billy from the river. He led Bluey and carried the billy.

It was apparent from about noon that Jack couldn't walk all the way. He seemed to almost welcome my call for a stop, when I handed him the firestick and dropped onto my backside to withdraw several barbed seeds from my feet. Sometimes it was so difficult to keep the lighted end out of the grass, I suggested we put it out and push on with nothing to eat.

'Just won't make it to Panter on an empty stomach,' Jack argued.

We stopped at sunset and Peter led Bluey down to the river for a drink. The horse was going okay, but it was Jack who wasn't. He lit another fire, lay down and fell asleep almost immediately. Peter carried a fresh billy from the river and dropped a couple of bones into the oven. The waiting was the worst. You have to boil bones for an hour or more to make wholesome broth. When it was ready we woke Jack, concerned it took a lot of shaking to get a response.

They howled close by at dawn, a whole pack of them. Struggling to wake and face the day, at first I took no notice. It was only when we got going I grew nervous. The dingoes trotted along behind, thirty yards or more back. They were hungry. After the big flood, game was scarce and the evening before they must have picked up the scent of the broth a long way off. The boiled-up bones that we'd tossed to the side of the camp had been snatched while we slept. Looking back, I saw the lead dog several times; a long-legged creature with a yellow pelt, hard to see in spear grass the colour of wheaten hay.

'They're scavengers,' Jack mumbled when I drew his attention to them. 'They know we're weak and the diarrhoea you two got is like a blood trail to a feast.'

We travelled light now. The fire had gone out. None of us woke to stoke it and I was having too much difficulty with my feet to carry another firestick.

Jack's energy was slipping away. We had only covered about a mile when he fell to the ground in a seizure of leg cramps. He was in agony and it took several minutes for them to subside. There was nothing for it but to dump the swags to compensate for Jack's weight on Bluey. Mortified, poor Jack knew it had to be. Peter and I legged him up and he rode on the packsaddle with his legs astride the two packs.

Late in the morning we arrived at the junction of Red Bull Creek. Jack said we had to part with the river and head due north, following the creek. In the distance we could see the unbroken cliff rim of the Harding Range. From the low flood-plain we couldn't see the gap, but Jack assured me it was there. And once over the gap it was only about nine miles to Panter Downs. There was a safe swimming hole near the junction and we bathed in it for half an hour before starting north.

The sun arced across the sky and at dusk we fell to the ground, exhausted. Jack had broken into delirium again and Peter had to shake him out of it to get directions. The soles of my feet were worn to the flesh and bleeding. They felt hot and numb and I had given up on the barbed seeds unless one sank deep between my toes. Bluey, too, was not going well, stumbling badly at times and Jack only staying aloft by his hard grip on the packsaddle frame. Thankfully, water was no longer an effort to collect. Along the Calder, Peter had to slide down a steep bank and tackle heavy undergrowth to fetch our water – and he had to get water for Bluey as well. Red Bull creek had a constant flow with easy access.

At dawn next morning the dingoes were back. If I held my breath I could hear the grass rustle where the pack waited. Then one howled so close I thought his mouth was by my ear. He could smell my bleeding feet. This was our end, I decided, more sad than scared. Totally drained, I realised you could die devoid of emotion. The lead dog, the one just yards away in the grass, would heel me and draw more blood. Then the rest would home in.

While I was peering through the thick grass, trying to see the rest of the dogs, Jack struggled to his feet and with one hand leaned against a tree. Grimly, he looked at me.

Peter was still asleep.

'We'll give them the horse when he drops.'

'No – please!' I gasped. 'Not my Bluey!'

'Better than being eatin alive.'

I looked at Bluey standing motionless, his head down, and at Peter peacefully asleep.

'We'll be okay,' Jack said tiredly. 'Just go slow and steady and dream about something. Think of a pretty girl, warm and cuddly.'

'It don't help Bluey.'

'Think I'm not sorry too? He's my horse.'

Bluey walked for two hours before he dropped onto his knees and slowly collapsed onto his side. Jack had ample time to step off. I undid the girths and Peter and I pulled off the packsaddle and the two packs. Then I removed the bridle. Bluey took several laborious breaths and as I watched, his eyes glazed over. Poor old Bluey. Never had an animal given so much for nothing in return. There was just one blessing. He died without the help of the .38.

Jack still carried the long blade on his belt. He flicked open the sheath strap, drew the knife and pinched up the loose skin on Bluey's brisket. In one stroke he slashed a huge gaping wound. I had to turn away.

Driven by the smell of blood the pack split and sidled out on both sides, still partly camouflaged in the spear grass. Ten or twelve of them, they wanted to feast on the dead horse and if any one of us got in the way we could expect to be an entrée. The dog I had seen always in the lead, carried his head high and white-tipped tail curled upwards, level with his backline. He bared his teeth; no sound, no growl. It was their way – a deathly silence. Totally focused on them, we walked away from Bluey and got about twenty yards before I remembered the .38.

'The gun!'

Jack spat, bile that had welled into his throat. 'Leave it,' he growled hoarsely. 'They're onto yer blood. Your feet are bleeding and to them yer mortally wounded. They got no fear of humans any more. The tribes are long gone and we whites pass by just once a year.' He stared ruefully back at the wild dog pack, some already tearing at Bluey's open brisket. 'They're crossbreeds, genes goin back to the cattle dogs at the old Munja feedin station. Believe me, dangerous as hyenas once they've tasted the blood. Anyway, I'm too weak to carry the gun.'

We rested often. Towards noon, the cliffs above petered out away to our left and we headed for the gap. On higher ground we could see a prominent bluff. Jack said it was called Lushington Bluff, after an explorer. It was a positive marker, he told us, and he thought we only had about eight miles to go.

The last threads holding my shirt together let go and I threw it away. The cotton fabric was so rotten from sweat I couldn't even use it as a temporary bandage on my feet. Flies clustered onto my sores. Jack took off his shirt and made me put it on. He said flies would turn the hives septic.

When darkness closed around us, we dropped and slept. I woke with the sun in my eyes and my tongue swollen. Red

Bull Creek was behind us now and the next water might be the Sale River – Jack couldn't remember. He was propped up against a boulder and delirious again, mumbling something about the station they took off him. I shook him out of it and tried to speak. I wanted to say if we didn't get there soon, we'd die.

It took him a while to focus and then he asked me about my feet. Could I use his boots? I shook my head. We had already tried sharing boots; he'd forgotten. Jack's boots fell off my smaller feet on the first step and Peter's were the other way – tiny. When my feet warmed up I could tolerate the pain. It was the setting off again; cold, that was agony. This time I couldn't stand the weight of my body. Jack saw me grimace.

'Better take the shirt off,' he sighed. 'I'll cut it into strips and wrap it around your feet. It might last two or three mile. Reckon it's only four mile now.'

It took ages for Jack to cut the bandages. He was determined to get me to Panter Downs and didn't think I could walk any further on raw soles.

We woke Peter and pushed on. We stumbled onto a creek and drank until it made us nearly sick. After a drink I could speak again, but my throat was on fire. There was so much hurting I couldn't define what was worst sometimes. All three of us were in a bad way as the beri-beri worsened and Peter was wilting noticeably for the first time.

When Jack drifted off into delirium yet again I took hold of his belt and tugged him along. Each of us fell over at different times, knocking off skin – to the delight of the swarming flies. Night fell again before we reached the Sale River. We weren't even making a half-mile to the hour and we knew that if we stopped it was all over. The rags wrapped around my feet fell off.

It was the horse paddock fence that let us know the trek was over. Peter, leading at the time, walked straight into it with no harm. The fence was on the southern side of the Sale River. It was a plain old wire fence and minutes later we found ourselves stumbling down the riverbank. The Sale was flanked by a tangle of scrub and cane grass, snaky as it gets. We waded into water waist deep before scrambling up the opposite bank. The grass had overtaken all the open ground and we nearly walked into the wall of a shed. The homestead was nearby. Despite the bouts of delirium, Jack had still managed to read the shapes of the hills and distant mountain ranges correctly. He was truly a super-bushman.

TEN

DELIRIUM AND FEAR

THE FLIES WOKE us early. They were in millions. They crawled into our noses, eyes, ears – and when you opened your mouth enough of them to fill a dessertspoon fell in. Why they were so much worse at Panter than at Walcott or Munja flabbergasted even Jack. If we didn't find food we had trekked to our graves, but it didn't take Jack long. He found a five-gallon drum with a few pounds of tapioca, which I'd always known as frogs eyes. The hard white grains are made from the tuber of a tropical plant called cassava. Mixed with water and cooked it becomes a soft, slippery substance and is mostly used to make a pudding. Jack warned Peter and me to take a little at a time, but he needn't have said anything. Unsweetened, it was unpalatable stuff.

The only other food Jack found was a chunk of corned beef in the meathouse, black and rock hard. He found matches somewhere in the house and boiled it for hours in a big pot, until it disintegrated into a broth. He nearly went demented searching for tobacco, without success. Our sole luxury was tea.

For three days we lay about on the verandah, tormented by the flies in daylight and mosquitoes at night. There was no gauzed-off area in the old slab home. Jack was very irritable. It was more than physical weakness and the dwindling supply of tapioca that bothered him. He'd been to the radio room and predictably the batteries were flat, but he said he hoped to work something out when he felt stronger.

Jack could barely walk, those first three days at Panter Downs. He sent Peter and me to the river for water twice a day – we carried a tub between us. My feet were crusted underneath with scabs and I resented the ordeal, but deep down knew Jack was trying to help me. The protein in the tapioca instantly aggravated the scores of hives over my stomach and groin. Add a plaster of flies on the weeping sores and I was on track for septicaemia. Jack boiled the water, let it cool and tipped it into a larger tub mixed with salt. Taking it in turns in the tub, he made Peter and me bathe twice a day. Peter had also developed sores. We must have looked a pitiful sight in that tub with our grossly distended stomachs. Jack said our immune systems were rock bottom.

On the third night I discovered what was worrying Jack more than anything else. With food he had become more lucid and his bouts of delirium were shorter and less frequent. He complained his sight was still poor, with objects at a distance difficult to define.

'They'll arrive any day now,' he said to me grimly, leaning against the slab wall, his legs stretched straight. 'On horseback and packhorses. No one will put a vehicle to the washed out tracks in the coming dry. They'll ride in, muster and walk the cattle out through Beverley Springs. When they find me here, unarmed –' He hesitated, his eyes squinted against the flies. 'The riders will be sent ahead and the bloke with the contract.' He brushed away the flies and stared at me, hard. 'You got to get the thirty-eight for me.'

'I think that's a bit extreme Jack,' I said, desperately wanting to convince myself. But I knew the stakes were high and this was Australia's last pocket on the edge of law enforcement. There were white men out here with blood on their hands and no fear of ever having to confess or face a jury.

Jack didn't answer. His eyes narrowed back to slits and he seemed to be far away. It was a long while before he spoke again. We both just sat on the floor leaning against the wall and constantly brushing the flies. Peter lay on his back, asleep.

'There are some old horses hanging around,' Jack began again. 'You boys must have seen them down by the river. They'll be the ones Frank Lacy used a few years back. He was Bob Dowling's manager. No split in them days. He was here before the equal wages came in, when most of the black ringers were turfed off the stations. They worked the Kimberley, the lifeblood of every station. It all went arse up after equal pay. It's how split mustering came about.'

'They might send Frank out to look for us?' I posed. Frank Lacy's father, also called Frank, owned nearby Mount Elizabeth Station and was regarded as a Kimberley pioneer legend.

'Be good, wouldn't it. Good man in the bush, but he won't come out here again. He broke his leg not long before he left. Anyway, thanks to him there are some quiet horses around here. I want you and Pete to catch a couple at daylight and ride back for the thirty-eight. Get everything we left. The dingoes won't be around after the sun gets up a bit. Full of meat, they'll lie up in their lairs, high up in the range.'

It was a long ride and unnecessary, I thought. We weren't going to be shot down like dogs. Still, it was strange no one had come looking for us. The cyclone was about four weeks gone and not a single plane had been heard. To me, the conclusions were inescapable: either Walker had met a similar fate, or he was pretending ignorance of our location. And Otto and George hadn't made it. It was always on Jack's mind, for when he succumbed to bouts of delirium George's name was uttered every time.

I looked across at Peter lying asleep on the floor boards. He wasn't a good colour and sores were starting to blotch his thighs and stomach.

'Think he should ride that far?'

Jack grinned. 'Try and go without him. He's turned the corner. Might be shit food, but it saved him. The beri-beri was nearly on top of him.'

There were a dozen or so horses running together as a mob. They seemed to like being around the sheds and the cattle yards, probably because of supplementary feeding when the mustering team arrived. The problem was to catch a couple. They didn't know us and there was no grain in the tack room. The saddles had been taken, but we managed to find a couple of old bridles and, with a bit of patience and slow talking, we coaxed two into accepting us. Both aged geldings – shading about twenty, I thought – and not the most attractive equine specimens. The bloke I caught for myself had a big lump on the side of his head. It looked like a growth, but it didn't affect him. They both walked along well – and just as well: riding bareback and still very weak, we were at their mercy. Horses not ridden for many months and in prime condition usually try the rider out on the first day. I think the angels caught these two for us.

Walking and a bit of slow cantering, it took three hours to cover what had taken us two days on foot. Lushington Bluff was our principal marker. When Bluey collapsed, the red cliffs of the bluff stood about due west. All we had to do was pick up the game pad, which Jack thought was the old bridle track between Panter Downs and Munja.

There wasn't much of Bluey left: bare skeleton, shrivelled up hide. His tongue had been chewed out and crows had pecked out his eyes. A bitch with pups was snarling at two big wedge-tailed eagles when we burst through the grass. On horseback our mere appearance was enough. The eagles took a funny little run and, with the sound of sheets flapping on a clothesline when the wind is up, they rose in slow motion. The dingo bitch bolted, tail between legs and pups scurrying behind.

It was a grim scene and we wasted no time. I checked the gun was in one of the packs and as Peter was on the fitter horse, we clinched the packsaddle to his mount and fastened the packs. We expected to be back at Panter about mid-afternoon.

Riding bareback is very tiring and I think that's why we got lost. The game pad petered out in places and we somehow rode northwest instead of north. We should have kept Mount Kitchener to our left, instead of riding over its western flank. We weren't off course much, but enough to put us into the Berckelman River valley and not the Sale where the homestead was.

When night fell we decided to tether the horses and wait until morning. At first light we mounted again and retraced our tracks, me struggling to choke down a feeling of panic. We hadn't been riding long when my horse began to reef, pulling hard to the left. Peter noticed it too and we agreed to let him have his head. He strode along confidently, his mate keeping pace, ears pricked. They knew all right. Within an hour Jack's smoke signal could be seen, rising like a dark pencil line out of the Sale valley. It was ink black from old truck tyres. Poor Jack, we realised with considerable apprehension, must be nearly off his head.

Jack was in a pitiful state when we got back. He roared at us, and then broke down. To see a hardened bushman weep is an unsettling experience. The only human habitation within ninety miles was Mount Elizabeth and he knew we didn't have a clue where that was. He knew, too, that we didn't know one river from another. In our vulnerable physical condition he thought the worst: he had lost George, now Peter, and he didn't even have the gun to end the horror of it all.

While Peter and I were away and before Jack realised we were probably lost, he got to work on a little motor which was used for charging the radio batteries. By draining the dregs of all the petrol drums he could find, he managed to salvage a pint, which he kept in a jar with a lid to prevent evaporation.

There was plenty of kerosene and he filled the fuel tank with it. But the petrol motor wouldn't start on kero, so he had to wait until I got back – starting the motor was a two-person job.

I'm sure this added to his torment: he'd sent us off on an unnecessary mission that might have been fatal – and he couldn't start the battery charger on his own.

I pulled the starter rope while Jack tipped a few ounces of petrol directly into the carburetor. It fired and after a few splutters ran quite well on the kero. There were about eight gallons of kero, more than enough to charge the batteries several times over, but they were bone dry and dead flat. The best we could hope for was a tiny bit of accumulative charge in the batteries. Jack opted to run the motor on and off for three days before trying the radio. He said no one would expect us to be at Panter Downs and he had to be able to send a clear message.

The radio room and office was a separate building. The radio was a two-way provided by the Flying Doctor Service. It was connected to the batteries outside by wiring through the wall. The batteries and charge motor were connected by leads, alligator clips at each end. At the end of the first day with the charge motor running, Jack said he could hear some chatter when he put the earphones on. It all depended on the batteries. He had carefully checked out several discarded batteries and put water in the cells of the two he selected.

The next day there was a little more sound. He thought he recognised the voice of Dr Lawson Holman, the flying doctor who operated from Derby who until recently had owned Oobagooma. I could barely contain myself. I wanted Jack to have a go, put his voice to the air. But I knew how difficult it was for him. Once the word was out, that he was at Panter Downs, the gossip mongers would be set alight. Jack had gone there to cut out a draft, got buried by the cyclone and was calling for a rescue by air. For Jack it was one thing to get the radio working, quite another to use it.

The tapioca would last two more days and Peter's beri-beri condition couldn't go on indefinitely. If the radio failed, I would have to start shooting the horses for meat. Jack couldn't see well enough, I had never used a revolver and there were just six bullets left. And worst of all, the concept of shooting the horses for food was sickening. Our lives depended on rescue via the radio.

The open air time was called the 'scit', when anyone on a remote west Kimberley station could consult with the Derby-based doctor. If the line was quiet and not many people required medical advice, the Flying Doctor Service permitted some neighbourly chat. Air time was from 10 am to noon.

On the third day Jack decided to try and tap into the frequency. Together we started the motor and he fitted the earphones. It was uncanny what happened next: Hilton Walker's voice came through the radio. He seemed to be talking to someone on another station. Fearful Walker might suddenly go off the air, Jack interrupted: 'Hilton, it's Jack. We're at Panter Downs. We need help, mate – over.'

There was no response. Jack again said, 'Over to you, Hilton.' He repeated it several times. You would hear the frequency fading while Jack waited for Hilton to come in. Stunned, he wrenched off the earphones and looked at me, ashen. I leant forward and switched off the radio to save the little battery energy left.

'Perhaps he didn't hear,' I suggested.

'No, he heard,' Jack rasped, disgusted. 'He heard because he stopped talking.'

As bad as things were, I had never seen Jack look so crushed. I was almost speechless myself.

'He got out, the bastard,' Jack went on, 'and he knows I couldn't possibly know the fate of George.'

'He's watchin his back, Jack. Most of the stations hook up for the scit show and he's scared yer gonna ask him if he had a crack at taking out the Humbert Creek mob. You said yourself they probably belong to Mount Hart and he shouldn't be touchin them, cleanskins or not.'

Weak and shaken, Jack raised his hand. 'No, I wouldn't have stumbled that bad and he knows it. Why wouldn't he come in? Just to tell me if George is okay?'

I saw the tears in his eyes and looked away. Peter had walked outside, totally bewildered, poor kid. There was a slight naivety about Jack for all his toughness. Years later I came to realise that some people from the outback don't comprehend the dark side of the human spirit. But even at sixteen I knew how ugly some outback men could be.

Suddenly Jack buried his face in his hands and silently shook. 'George's dead,' he sobbed. 'That's why Hilton didn't answer.'

I walked outside and wept myself.

Jack ran the charger motor all day and at 10 am the following day he had another go. On the first attempt he reached the Derby base operator. With only seconds' worth of sufficient energy to carry his voice, Jack simply gave his name, location and said that two people required urgent medical attention. I couldn't help smiling, because I don't think Jack ever thought he was sick, yet of the three of us he would have been the first to go.

Jack waited for a reply, but all he heard was distant chatter. He switched off the radio and looked at me blankly.

'We just got to hope. I think it went through okay.'

'How's the runway?' I asked. 'We should have checked it.' The station had its own landing strip behind the buildings.

'It'll be good. The owner flies everywhere and the station itself is on all maps. This country doesn't wash either unless it's a gully or a downhill track.'

For the rest of the day we went on with the routine. It was better to be doing something than just lying about, waiting. The days were mild and that helped enormously. Peter and I carried the water up from the river, Jack bathed our sores and kept a small fire going to heat up the tapioca, warm the tub water and make tea. There was plenty of tea and salt.

Very few words passed between us. Jack was grieving. I never heard him say anything to Peter, and when he said to me that George was dead Peter had been outside. He wouldn't have heard his father over the charger motor. I didn't agree with him about George. Walker was a big loser over the cattle.

It was about nine o'clock the next morning when we heard the chopper. Peter and I had just finished a small helping of the tapioca. Our throats were much improved from the broth Jack made, but the swelling in our stomachs was no better. We raced out into the sunlight and stared into the sky, up river. The trees blocked our view and the sound was a long way off. I climbed onto a tank stand, hopped up onto the tank and from there onto the roof of the house. I watched it disappear, a mere speck in the blue void.

'It's gone!' I yelled.

'It's not the Flying Doctor mob. Be a mining company, chartered a flight somewhere.'

But it hadn't gone. I was about to step back onto the tank when I heard it again, far to the north.

'It's still out there!'

'By golly it might be for us.' Jack started to run up onto the verandah but fell over.

'Pete!' he gasped. 'In the bathroom there's a small mirror leaning against the wall on the timber, near the basin. Get it!'

Blood dripping from his knee, Jack was slow to rise. 'I wonder who it is,' he groaned. 'If they've come for us they don't know the country. Anyone west of Gibb River would know Panter's on the Sale.'

Peter ran out with the mirror and tried to get onto the stand but his stomach was too distended. I stepped down onto the tank and took it.

'Flash it in the sun,' Jack said, his voice hoarse from strain. 'Don't matter if you can't see the bloody chopper. The pilot will see a flash ten miles away.'

I heard the chopper again for a few minutes and then nothing.

'If he was going somewhere up north you wouldn't have heard it again,' Jack said. 'He might have put down to get a map fix.'

'What about a fire?' I suggested. The frustration was worse than twenty hives all itching at once. 'Those tyres you burnt sent up a great spiral of smoke.'

'I burnt the lot,' Jack lamented on his haunches, head down. The felt top of his hat was about to fall away.

We heard the chopper again, out to the northeast. Then I saw it. It had to be within six miles or I couldn't have spotted it. It was heading south. Three minutes at eighty miles an hour and it was gone. All I could do was hold the sun in the mirror. If the chopper hadn't been out to the east the mirror would have been useless.

I didn't see the chopper turn. It slipped from sight and with a sinking feeling in my stomach I sat down on the ridge pole of the roof. But the sound left nothing in doubt. Helicopters are noisy machines and suddenly the three of us were standing straight, arms raised. I can't express the excitement of those last minutes as the helicopter raced towards us.

There was a wide space between the homestead and the outbuildings. The pilot cruised in a bit like a fixed wing plane and left the engine running, the big blades idling. His head ducked, he walked quickly towards us. I was already off the roof.

The pilot, a middle-aged man with sandy hair, had a wide, relieved sort of grin.

'I'd just tipped in the last of the fuel,' he shouted, 'and was heading back when I saw the mirror flash.'

'Is George alive?' Jack yelled.

The pilot nodded. 'He's in Derby.'

Jack seemed to lose his balance and the pilot grabbed his shoulder. 'It's okay, fella,' he said, his reassuring tones almost drowned by the noise of the machine.

There was a brief spell while the pilot looked at us, one at a time, as if taking in the enormity of the rescue.

'No room for any gear and we're low on fuel. It's all aboard, right now.'

'We've got nothing.' Pitifully, Jack tried to laugh it off.

Jack did have something though, his saddle bag with the .38 inside. The .38 was the only item to survive the whole ordeal. He clutched the little leather bag to his ribs like a mother might hold an infant.

Crouched low, Peter and I hurried over and took our seats. I began to think about all the things I'd missed for so long – ice-creams, steaks, my mates and the girls. I hung around with several girls, but at sixteen I didn't have a steady one. I was still at the age where girls were perceived to be fun, but often got in the way.

Seated in the chopper I expected to see Jack scrambling into the front seat, beside the pilot. But he hung back. When the pilot saw he hadn't moved he went back, running this time. There was an altercation about something. Jack wanted to get something sorted out before we went anywhere.

A couple of days later Jack told me, my dad and Uncle Allan, what he had to sort out with the pilot. He knew the destination would be Derby and told the pilot to put us down at Oobagooma instead. Yelling over the noise, the pilot tried to explain he was under instructions to return to Derby with all three of us. That since George and Otto had been found we were listed as missing with the police. But Jack refused to board until he agreed. With no time to argue – every quart of fuel is precious, even when the machine's idling – the pilot reluctantly consented. There was an aviation fuel dump at Oobagooma and he would tell the authorities he had to divert there for fuel and his passengers were too ill to travel onto Derby. All the more plausible when Hilton Walker's wife was a trained nurse.

When we landed at Oobagooma I did think it was to take on fuel. The pilot put down beside the forty-fours and shut down the engine. Despite the excitement and an adrenalin charge from being rescued, all three of us were sick and to me it was inconceivable we would be dropped anywhere but Derby. But Jack motioned us both to get out and that was it. I was stunned. I thought Jack would have wanted to see his family as soon as possible. I certainly wanted to see mine. Then when I saw Jack walk unsteadily towards the homestead, the saddlebag in the left hand with its straps undone and his right hand free, I knew.

'You all right, Jack?' the pilot called out.

He stopped and slowly turned around. So preoccupied was Jack he'd forgotten to thank the pilot. He raised his free hand, fingers limp and emaciated.

'You saved our lives.' Slowly he turned again and staggered on. I expected to see someone emerge from the house any moment. Peter shook hands with the pilot and followed his dad.

'You still going to Derby?' I asked. It looked like every man for himself now.

The pilot looked uncomfortable. He wasn't at all happy about Jack's stand.

'No, I've got a job at Fitzroy. I was supposed to go there this morning.' He paused and looked over at the homestead. Walker's wife had come out to meet Jack and she had his elbow. He seemed to be swaying.

'She's a trained nurse I believe. You'll be all right here.'

'Tell Mum and Dad I'm okay.' I fought to hold back the tears. I didn't deserve this. I wanted to see my mum and dad and friends.

I could see the pilot was really torn. I began to wonder whether he was really going to Fitzroy. If he arrived with only me, he was left with nothing plausible to say to the authorities.

He put his arm over my shoulders. 'Yes of course I'll tell them,' he said at last.

'Jack's got a score to settle here. I'd prefer not to be around. Take me with you to Fitzroy.'

'I can't. I've got two sick people to collect.'

'Is Jack in trouble?' He could settle with Hilton any time. Derby was where we should have been going.

'With cattle at boom prices, cattle rustling is rife across the Kimberley. The police want to know why he was at Panter Downs.'

'We walked there from Walcott, to look for food and rescue. We were desperate.'

The pilot shrugged. 'Well that's all he had to say. Five-minute interview, that's all it would have been.' He bent down, up-ended a drum and fitted a spanner to the bung.

'It's just a simple matter of pride. He doesn't want people to see him the way he is. Not his wife, his kids and all his friends. When you're my age, you'll understand.'

The pilot fuelled up and left. I went inside expecting to hear Jack and Hilton having it out. But Hilton was nowhere to be seen. His wife was running water into the bathtub for Peter and directed me to undress as well. She said she had taken Jack to the spare bedroom. He had almost collapsed.

I spent two days at Oobagooma. With an expansive medical kit at her disposal, Hilton's wife provided care equal to any country hospital. She got through to the police station on the radio and they contacted Dad. He and Uncle Allan drove out next day. It was the same morning Walker showed up. He had a mustering team working somewhere on the station and came in for supplies. Jack was sitting on the front verandah, smoking. Every station pantry carried salt first and tobacco second. When Hilton's vehicle drew up Jack ordered Peter and me to make ourselves scarce. I was glad he didn't have the saddlebag with him. Jack was his rational old self again.

I regret to this day I never heard the row between Jack and Walker that morning. Some swear words drifted over to the yards and if it were not for a raucous barrage of squawking from the corellas in the rivergums I might have heard the whole heated exchange. It lasted about ten minutes, then Walker went inside. Luckily, Dad and Uncle Allan arrived soon afterwards. They were shocked at how we looked.

'You should have seen us three days ago,' Jack said dryly, shaking hands with them both. 'We got clean clothes on.' Then Jack added: 'Thanks for coming out. We won't hang around here if it's okay with you blokes.'

My dad and uncle were placid men by nature, not ones to press questions. It went without saying everything had gone as bad as it could go. George had been taken into Derby by Walker. He had at least done the right thing with him. No one knew where Otto was. He hadn't been sighted in Derby.

About five hours after leaving Oobagooma we arrived in Derby and Dad took me straight up to the hospital to see Dr Holman who didn't mince words. I had dysentery and beri-beri. I should have been dead, but as I wasn't I would recover quickly with high doses of vitamin B_1 and I didn't need to be admitted to hospital. Dad dropped me off at Mum's place, there was a tearful reunion and more than ever before I felt saddened by their separation. It was the fishing that took my mind off it. The breeze was up, the tide rolling in for a peak about an hour before dark – perfect for hooking mangrove-jacks. That was my dream, anyway – in reality it was bed and rest for some days.

ELEVEN

THE MOWANJUM MEN SADDLE UP

Mike takes up the story again

THE INTRIGUE WHICH motivated me to write this story began with Otto Dibley. Having nearly perished himself in the aftermath of the flood, he knew his good mate Jack Camp and the two boys had to be in some degree of trouble, yet he failed either to make it back to Walcott Inlet with supplies or send help. All I could discover more than thirty years later was the rumours circulating in the Mowanjum community that someone threatened to kill him if he tried to return.

Bardi man and Elder Roy Wiggan knew Otto quite well. He said Otto had got involved with a shady group of *kartiyas* (white men), tracking mobs of cattle for them and guiding them through the various mountain passes. The *kartiyas* took cleanskins from Gibb River, Mount House and Mount Hart. In hidden, makeshift corrals they slammed on their own brands, then walked the cattle to the nearest legitimate stock route and onto the Derby meatworks. The owners of the pastoral leases knew they were losing cattle and as cattle prices rose, so did the level of frustration at not being able to catch them.

Once the cleanskins were branded there was no possibility of a counterclaim, and to cover the use of a brand the *kartiyas* were always careful that one among them owned a block of land or had a lease.

Roy knew the names of all the *kartiyas* who rode the ranges at the time and Jack Camp was not among them. He believes it would have been Otto who took Jack to the Munja reserve. Otto knew the *kartiyas* had never been able to get the Munja cattle out and if anybody could do it Jack Camp was the man. Otto didn't ride for wages. It was always a share of the spoils – 'the split'.

These days it might seem incredible that Otto didn't at least raise the alarm in Derby about Jack Camp's predicament. After all, Otto and Jack were not only business partners but great friends. But in 1971 the psychological dominance of white over black seems to have still existed in the Kimberley. It wasn't until the 1980s that Aboriginal people gradually began to reclaim their identity and self-respect.

There is a wall of silence surrounding what happened to Otto. At least a couple of locals do know what happened but they will not talk about it. The only telling comment made to me on the subject was: 'Otto packed the mules and left. Didn't get far before some white fella pulled a gun on him.' That certainly confirmed what the old man from Beagle Bay told me. But it would be wrong to draw a conclusion from this about who threatened Otto: after all, he had a reputation and plenty of local pastoralists wanted him to leave.

Otto took a job at a backyard abattoir near Derby for a year or so, then went back to the peninsula for good, living in Beagle Bay until he died. He and Jack Camp were never known to ride together again.

During his few years in the Derby district Jack Camp had demonstrated an extraordinary capacity to work and survive under difficult conditions and that was Betty Camp's reason for not going to the authorities. Jack hated any fuss relating to himself. He was totally self-reliant and always left instructions that the authorities were not to be contacted if he was overdue on any of his mustering forays. It was only when Otto and George turned up nearly dead at Oobagooma that family and friends realised Jack must be in trouble. Betty chartered a Cessna fixed wing plane and invited Hilton Walker to fly with her and guide the pilot. But it seems Walker carefully guided the pilot everywhere but where Jack and the boys were camped.

Sadly, Jack Camp was never able to materialise his dream of owning a Kimberley cattle station. After Walcott it appears his life was a struggle until the end, in 2000. His oldest son, Peter, went on to manage Carlton Hill Station, one of the world's largest, and later acquired two Kimberley stations of his own. George Camp lives in Wyndham.

Peter Wann recovered quickly from beri-beri. Two months after his return to Derby he rode in the annual rodeo, reaching the final in the bull ride tournament. The rodeo was run in conjuunction with the Derby Cup race meeting and festivities continued for some days. It was towards the end of the carnival that fate delivered Peter another harsh blow. While attending an out-of-town party he was hit by a car and this time Dr Holman did have to admit him to hospital. The vereran flying doctor was forced to undertake two operations to set Peter's leg, who remained in the Derby hospital for some months.

In the following years Peter tried his hand at cray fishing near Dongara, worked at the Mount Newman mine for five years and then in 1983 signed on with Rio Tinto Ltd. He has been a heavy machinery and transport operator ever since and lives in Karratha, Western Australia, with New Zealand-born Ngaire and their two daughters, Jenna and Kayla.

When the story came out, Jack Camp's cattle mustering expedition to Walcott Inlet aroused a lot of interest in the Derby community. With the cattle market soaring to record prices, the herd at Walcott Inlet sparked an urgency akin to gold fever. The first on the trail were the tough Mowanjum stockmen.

In 1956, a mission encompassing 200 square miles had been established eight miles from Derby, It was named Mowanjum, which means 'settled at last'. A most appropriate name, as the Ungarrangu and Umiida people had been constantly disolocated since the impact of white settlement. The first mission was Port George in 1910, followed by Kunmunya in 1915. Plagued with water supply shortages, the northern mission was closed and a government ration station was opened at Munja in 1927, decades later to be closed in favour of Mowanjum in 1956.

Fifteen years after the final move to Mowanjum, the

station carried a commercial herd of more the 500 cattle, and as a result of the flood rains in March 1971, there was grass available for a lot more.

The Mowanjum Elders made a claim on all the cattle at the Munja reserve – which was supported by the Department of Aboriginal Affairs. In 1927 the reserve had been gazetted by the government for the purpose of 'Use and Benefits of Aborigines'. The local tribes looked upon Munja as a meeting place for the clans, where they traded a whole variety of goods and performed ceremonies. It appears leprosy was not widespread at that time, but by 1935 the disease had filtered into every pocket of the region. It struck fear among the tribes and the government system of finding and incarcerating diseased victims shattered inter-clan contact and age old social disciplines. By the 1950s only a handful of old nomads remained in the Munja area. No single clan lived on the reserve and it became a free for all. Between the time of the closing of the Munja ration station in 1946 to the TB eradication program in the late 1970s, so many cattle had bred up on the rich river plains of the reserve that crocodile hunters (black market operators) used to simply shoot a beast from their boat for meat.

The Mowanjum Elders formed a joint business venture with an American known as Bud Crockett. Bud owned a cattle barge with a capacity for fifty head. In the winter of 1971, a few weeks after Jack Camp and the boys had been rescued, boss Mowanjam stockman Watti Nardoo, together with a band of experienced horsemen, left Derby with Bud Crockett to secure the first load. A handful of saddle horses were loaded to round up the cattle.

Anecdotal evidence suggests the cattle Jack Camp handled were never tracked. There were so many cattle on the Munja reserve the Mowanjum men had more than enough without going further. On horseback they cut out fifty head and drove them across the Calder River above the tidal limit. Once on the old Munja side the cattle were walked to the lagoon for a drink before taken to a holding yard. The yard was built on the inlet shore with a chute to the high water mark. The cattle barge only needed three feet of water and at high tide could be piloted to the chute entrance. The yard was about two and a half miles south of the Munja landing strip, which was in disrepair at the time. Derby Elder Sam Lovell knew the spot and said it was close to where Jack and the boys swam the narrow ankle of the inlet.

The procedure was simple enough. The barge was piloted to the yard chute and when the tide dropped it settled into the mud. A drawbridge mounted on hinges was lifted by a cog-chain and lowered onto the bank. The rails of the chute closed off either side. The cattle were loaded in a few minutes. To avoid stress and unnecessary standing in crowded conditions on the barge, the loading was not carried out until the first sign of the incoming tide.

The most testing part of the whole exercise was at Yule Entrance, where Walcott Inlet converges into a narrow strait about three and a half miles long and one and a half miles wide. The barge captain had some delicate navigation once committed to this narrow, twisting passage. At the yards the barge lifted off at high tide and, taking advantage of the strong tide run, the captain opened the throttle and powered down the wide section of the inlet at fifteen knots an hour. Upon entering the strait all life depended on the skill of the barge captain. As the tide dropped, the giant whirlpools gathered and as the minutes passed the ferocity of these massive eddies intensified. Large vessels were known to have got caught in them, spinning in ever widening circles until either its weight enabled the vessel to break free or the skipper deliberately broadsided the vessel, applied maximum throttle and powered across the perimeter of the swirling water. With stationary cargo the whirlpools were manageable enough, but having cattle on board, made a capsize more likely.

Upon reaching Collier Bay and the open sea, the barge captain still had no cause to call for a noggin of rum and relax. Ahead lay the tricky Buccaneer Archipelago of more than a thousand islands and reefs. It took another ten hours to zigzag through this little known paradise of tropical islands and coral reefs before swinging into King Sound and heading direct to Derby.

At Derby the Mowanjan stockmen constructed an unloading platform at the high water mark. If the tide was rising they could wait, but if they arrived on a dropping tide the cattle couldn't be contained any longer without water. The cattle were jumped off and the horses with saddles on them went too. The men braved the crocodiles and swam. When the horses found ground and left the water, the Mowanjum men swung aboard and went after the cattle, all bewildered by being in a town for the first time. On one occasion it was quite a melee, with confused cattle heading back out into King Sound. But only one was ever lost. The difference between white and black can be strikingly apparent on these occasions. The Mowanjum men loved it. One man was known to swim 200 yards out to turn back a frantic beast, much to the delight of a cheering crowd.

Gathered up from the streets and in hand once again, the cattle were walked to the nearest watering point and onto Mowanjum. By winter, the grasslands in the vicinity of Derby have lost most of their nutrition and the cattle were never held long before going to the local meatworks.

In total about 300 head were barged out from Walcott Inlet. Most of the barge trips took place in 1972. In 1974 the cattle market crashed and the operation ceased. About three years later the TB eradication program began in earnest, right across the continent. Cattle prices dropped to such low levels most of the Kimberley leases were unviable for some years. Thousands of cattle were shot from the air and among them the remaining herds at Walcott Inlet.

EPILOGUE

By July 2005 I had written the first draft of Peter Wann's experiences at Walcott Inlet, only to realise that to be able to best relay his tale of adventure I had to go to Walcott Inlet, set up camp in the same locality and experience the hostile environment for myself.

The helicopter reconnaissance with Peter Wann had taken place in February. It was the monsoon season with volatile weather that changed daily. It would not have been wise to undertake anything more than a one-day excursion by air. On the whole it was a successful trip. Specifically I had wanted to find the two campsites used by Jack Camp. Peter spotted the first from the air, marked by one of the largest boab trees he and I had ever seen. For convenience we named it 'hessian yard camp'. We landed and searched for the second camp, which we referred to as the 'refuge camp', without success. We landed at Panter Downs (now Pantijan), saddened to discover that all the old historic buildings had been lost to bushfire. We saw the huge spread of a full moon high tide at Walcott Inlet, flew over a flock of magpie geese taking off from a wetland, watched as a slow-flying jabiru drew close to the chopper for a stickybeak, saw crocodiles charge into the water off the banks of the Isdell River and, after taking off from the Hessian Yard Camp, we flew low over the tiny waterfall and string of fresh-water waterholes where Peter spent so much time. The Kimberley has hot dry spells in the wet and the rivulet flowing over the rock bar was a mere trickle compared to March–April 1971, Peter told me, as we flew over – my intrepid wife Sal leaning out of the chopper taking photographs. Minutes later we were in the forbidding Isdell Gorge, sometimes weaving from cliff to cliff in the expert hands of pilot Grant Wellington. Only Sal had the stomach to keep working a camera. By 2 o'clock that afternoon we were reliving our experience in the Derby King Sound Hotel, relishing a steak hamburger and cold beer. It was a different story six months later.

'Okay mate,' Morgan the pilot said. 'I'll shoot through now. See you blokes next week.'

The chopper blades cut the air, Morgan opened the throttle and Pat, Nelson and I watched the little machine rise to tree top level before it sped away and out of sight. The gloom of the mangroves settled around us and the heat was like an invisible weight. It was only 19 August, still winter on the Australian calendar, but here on the sixteenth parallel the sun had already retracted enough from the northern hemisphere to turn the range-locked Walcott Inlet into a natural baking bowl.

It was Pat Lowe who broke the spell we all seemed to have fallen under. She picked up her rucksack, single blanket, camera and water bottle and turned to trudge upstream through the deep shade of the mangroves. Luckily the tide was out or Pat would have thought it too dangerous to wade through knee-deep water in crocodile territory.

Sharing a wilderness with just one or two companions was nothing to Pat. With artist Jimmy Pike she had lived on the edge of the Great Sandy Desert for some years. She was a passionate environmentalist, an author and clever at identifying most species of flora and fauna. With a mutual love of the Kimberley, Pat and I had become good friends, and her mission on this mini expedition was to collect dung scats to identify the mammals in the area. I don't use the term 'expedition' lightly. This was no pleasure trip. We didn't expect to be comfortable – or entirely safe. I could only afford the smallest of people-carrying helicopters, flying at $715 an hour. With safety utmost in his mind, Morgan permitted us just a few kilograms per person, all stored in a little cavity under the seat. We had a blanket or sleeping bag each, a medical kit, spare change of clothes and a few packets of freeze-dried meals. Gourmet – I am a great believer in good tucker in the bush. Nothing erodes morale faster than boring or badly cooked food.

Close behind Pat was Nelson Berunga, an Elder from the Mowanjum community near Derby. Nelson was a Worrorra man. His tribal lands were a little to the north of where we now were, and encompased the Glenelg and Prince Regent watersheds, but Walcott Inlet was so close he looked upon the whole region as home. He had come to see his country again for what might be the last time. With only one lung, any physical exertion was an effort for Nelson.

I followed next, lumping what remained. We had selected our campsite from the air. It wasn't a difficult decision: it was the only fresh water for many kilometres. In some deep, almost permanently shaded gorges, we did observe a trickle of fresh water. But these narrow defiles were little more than fissures eroded in the hard red rock, and all that we saw were inaccessible. Jack Camp's precious little waterfall was the only refuge in the entire area.

It was only about 500 metres to the shelf, or rock bar, and the waterholes beyond but the thick damp reeds, the sticky saline mud and the heat quickly took a toll. For Nelson it was a real battle – he coughed and wheezed as he crept along. Pat remained with him and I went ahead to look for a likely spot.

The rock bar was about two metres high, forming a barrier between the tidal salt water and the pristine fresh water. The big water hole below the rock bar was ugly and had a sense of danger about it right from the start. The tide was about halfway out and during the low tide cycle the previous night a large crocodile had crawled up to the rock bar, turned and retreated. So deep was the drag marks and the claw imprints, the high tide just gone hadn't washed the tracks away. More sobering still was the damp high tide mark on the rock bar: it was almost level with the sandstone shelf. With a spring tide due in two days' time the salt water might inundate much of the wide shelf, suggesting a crocodile could easily swim to the edge and clamber onto the shelf. No matter where we camped, there was nothing to stop it from becoming an unwelcome guest. In 1971, crocodiles were considered endangered. Quite the opposite applied in 2005, with demands from tourist operators to impose a cull after a spate of fatal attacks in the Northern Territory.

The rock bar was about ten metres wide. On the southern side it dropped a metre onto an expanse of flat sandstone. On the western side the rock bar disappeared into a low sandstone escarpment covered in boulders and spinifex. It was just as easy to walk around the side and avoid the big jump. I startled a water monitor and running on his hind legs, head a metre above the ground, he looked quite comical. Ahead was a deep depression in the sandstone, full of water. A perfect swimming hole roughly twenty metres square, provided of course it hadn't been claimed by a crocodile. I walked to the edge and saw that it was only a metre deep and transparent. It was an enormous relief, with the late morning heat already reaching 40° Celsius. By mid-afternoon it would be impossible to look at that lovely cool water and not take a dip.

Beyond that pool, a mere five metres of flat rock in between, was a much bigger waterhole with pandanus palms on either side. It was deep and shaded, a perfect hole for a lone bull croc. To the right was a wide strip of sandstone. If we could be safe there it was the ideal spot for our camp. I didn't know the tick situation then, but in northern Australia wherever there are wallabies and kangaroos, there are ticks. The way to avoid them and still sleep under the stars is to camp on bare rock.

I dropped the few things I was carrying to check out the hole immediately. We couldn't come here if there was a croc living in that hole. It was a big responsibility. If I got it wrong one of us could end up croc tucker. I have had some close encounters with crocodiles and don't mind admitting I loathe them.

It was a difficult job. If there was a croc in there he would already be watching me through his waterproof eyelids. They are territorial and don't tolerate any intruder. I had to keep well away from the water and rely on tracking skills acquired over fifty years. Even with the thumbs up we wouldn't be swimming in this hole.

It was creepy in the pandanus and the jungle vines. The north side was clear and I stepped through a shallow swamp to the south side. Here, the blue grass grew as high as my shoulder. I moved forward, the broad sweep of rock I wanted to camp on only forty metres away. There was no telltale sign of a saltwater crocodile. They always come out of the water for a brief period. Whether it's a territorial thing or to sunbake, I have no idea. I was no croc expert. But if a croc had claimed a hole with vegetation around it, a tracker should be able to find the clues.

With twenty metres to go and already feeling the tension draining away, excited that we had these dual waterholes to ourselves, the wall of grass in front of me exploded as something very large burst out. I don't think my heart's ever leapt like it did that moment. I had visions of a four-metre croc tearing the grass down, jaws open. Phew! All in the mind. The animal in the grass was an antilopine or Kimberley wallaroo. The reddish tan males are usually solitary and it is rare to see more than three or four together. Sadly, due to incessant Kimberley fires, the species is now listed as endangered. The buck which hopped away from me through the long grass had a large head and a square jaw. He seemed more robust than the eastern wallaroo bucks, but when an animal moves quickly and it has given you a scare to begin with, appearances can be exaggerated.

We planned to stay five days. If one of us got sick or was bitten by something, Pat had a satellite phone to call the helicopter company. In such a beautiful setting, however, it was hard to envisage trouble of any kind. I caught three black bream out of the pandanus waterhole for dinner and when we lay down to sleep it was under a full moon. The barking owls were the first to rent the languid evening air. Loud as they were, the answering calls were rhythmical and I was almost asleep when two curlews began to pierce the night with their scream-like whistles and jerked me into wakefulness. Soon after, there was a strange sound from the blue grass at the edge of our camp.

Nelson was awake, also listening to the night sounds. 'That one the female king brown,' he said in a tone bordering on a whisper. 'It's the mating season.'

It's an easy sound to describe: think of the hiss of gas escaping. Listening to this snake hiss intermittently was as though someone was quickly turning the gas on and off. It's not a sound you want in your ear. I dozed off and when I woke I did indeed have the sound right in my ear. The snake was so long I thought for a moment it must be a python. Slowly, I lifted my head off the rolled up coat I was using as a pillow and stared at the snake's head, about 30 centimetres from my face. It was the distinct head of a king brown and she was very persistent with that rather creepy sound. The moon was so bright I could even see the little forked tongue, busily slipping in an out of her mouth. I didn't feel very comfortable. Survival instincts kicked in and I lay still, hoping she would soon tire of my lack of response. She did eventually, but it took at least five minutes. Then I wasn't very keen to go to sleep, thinking she might come back and coil herself beside or even on top of me. Later a wildlife expert told me no one in Western Australia had died from a king brown bite in recent years. They are a non-aggressive and much vilified snake – but I didn't know that at the time. We decided to call the king brown Gina and the water monitor we'd seen on arrival, Wally. Wally cleaned up all the fish scraps.

Finally I fell asleep and at dawn was awakened by the howling of a solitary dingo. Nelson was already up and I lifted my head to see the flames of his little fire casting shadows on the water-smoothed sandstone.

I had wanted to confirm how critically hemmed in Jack and the boys were once all the rivers were in flood. Neither Peter Wann nor Peter Camp were sure where Jack had crossed the Isdell with Otto and George, except that it wasn't at the river mouth. However an Elder in Derby who knows the whole area better than anyone else alive claims that Jack had a secret passage over the range close to where the Isdell cuts through, but it was very rough. So our mission on the first day was to try and determine whether it might be possible to ride horses through the range country on the eastern side of the Isdell River, immediately south of Walcott Inlet. From the diaries of explorer Alexander Forrest I knew the deep rock fissures which streaked the tableland rock surface to the west of the river were impenetrable on horseback. Forrest lost a quarter of the expedition's horses trying to cross the King Leopolds near Walcott Inlet. Peter Wann and I had carefully examined the rocky surface for a possible horse passage from the air the previous February, without success.

Pat and I set off about 7 am. Both bushwalkers, we were looking forward to an invigorating walk along the range. The temperature had dropped to about 16° Celsius at dawn and it was still pleasantly cool. We were going to take our time, Pat collecting her scats. The long thin ones interested her most. I was more interested in the big round ones – bigger than any marsupial droppings I had ever observed. Along the way I photographed all the different trees for later reference. What we hadn't bargained on was the broken nature of the terrain. From a distance the quartz-capped rock appeared to offer easy walking and I kept saying to Pat: 'It will get better as we get higher'. But it got worse. The whole surface was a myriad of deep gutters full of prickly spinifex. A long step, a hop, a jump and either a climb up or down. It soon wore us out plus the heat was building rapidly. From a high point we noted that the range never altered in character. No horses or cattle ever crossed these ranges. Using packhorses, I took tourists into the Warrumbungles in the 1970s and thought one of my trails was bordering on being irresponsible, yet the country was a pensioner's backyard compared to this. After four hours we gave it away and headed for a large waterhole on the upper stretch of the creek we had camped on. Once off the range and onto the narrow floodplain, we encountered the blue grass. It's called the 'big blue grass', growing head high. It was vital to step carefully. The snakes I saw were small, but fast moving. In Australia, venomous snakes tend to be the fast-moving ones.

At the waterhole a flock of whistling ducks heralded our arrival, along with loud splashes as the freshwater crocodiles launched off their favourite sunbaking perches. It seemed mean to be disturbing everything. I didn't think the hole was big enough for the freshies and the salties to mingle together and felt quite safe on the water's edge. Suddenly Pat exclaimed that she had ticks on her. I opened my shirt and discovered the same. The blue grass was loaded. It was too hot to climb back up the range and clamber out the way we came. There was nothing for it but to slog through the long grass and jungle-like pandanus, sidestepping snakes and being almost showered with ticks. The image of our tropical paradise was completely blown.

Our little camp near the pandanus palms and paperbarks was like being near a furnace with the coking door open. There was no adequate shade anywhere, except on the very edge of the larger of the two pools, where the banks were shaded with mixture of river gums, pandanus and, underneath, blue grass. I sat in the relief of the shade for a few minutes, only to discover ticks crawling over my clothes, searching for my skin. Pat had found a single paperbark casting some shade over the rock and appeared safe from the ticks for the moment. I looked around for Nelson. A cough soon gave his position away. He frequently broke into spasms of coughing. He was under a rock ledge, sharing Wally's home.

Wally probably didn't care much, as it was his sleeping time as well. I couldn't find any other rock crevices, and settled for sitting in the sandstone rock pool, submerged to the neck, shirt and hat on.

By four o'clock we were bored witless. The heat had dropped a little and Nelson had left his shelter to boil up the quart pot for tea. The entrance to Wally's home, where Nelson had been sleeping, was only about ten metres from the tidal saltwater hole. While Pat and I had been away he had walked over to the hole at low tide. The crocodile had been back, he said, no doubt alerted to our presence by the odour of the fish cooking on the coals the night before. Nelson confirmed what I'd feared: that the high spring tide due the night after next would ebb up onto the rock shelf, giving the crocodile access to our camp. There's no set rule about how far crocodiles will travel on land for prey. Malcolm Douglas, who owns Broome Crocodile Park, says strong odours will entice the reptiles to leave the water for a snoop around, but they rarely seek prey on dry land. However, in the crocodile park he has a croc called Bluey, captured in the Victoria River in the east Kimberley. Bluey left the water one night and crawled to a set of yards to seize a quarter horse weanling, belonging to a young boy. It was a horse yard of a very basic type where the lowest rail can be up to forty centimetres above the ground – enough room for a croc to drag a small horse through. The croc dragged the horse for at least one hundred metres back to the river, which suggests easy prey is sometimes too tempting. One of my most frightening experiences ever was on the bank of a Queensland Gulf river. It was a perfect campsite and I thought my tent twenty metres back from the water's edge was ample space. It was the smell that woke me. Not a horrible smell; simply unmistakable. I knew if I didn't move I was okay. If I did, I think that bull croc might have grabbed the tent and shot into the water. He was known, this reptile, and said to be four metres, the same size as Bluey in the Broome crocodile park. The terror was listening to the dragging sound, a mere 30 centimetres away on my side of the tent and my young son beside me asleep. If the smell woke Tom he'd stir and possibly sit up. That's all a monster-sized croc would need. It was a nasty half-hour. I think the tent saved us. It was heavy canvas, originally French Army stock. I don't think the little light plastic tents in use these days would bluff a crocodile.

We decided to accept the danger and just watch out for ourselves. With the tide on the run again I suggested to Pat we search for the location of the refuge camp while we could duck through the mangroves without wading through salt water. She got her scat bag and we set off.

The mangroves and adjacent floodplains were an entirely different ecosystem. Pheasant coucals darted from one copse of mangroves to another. They are nearly as large as the eastern lyrebird, but lack the colour. Everywhere, bowerbirds squawked at us and on the higher levels of the floodplain, scrub wallabies bolted for cover. I headed for the same high ridge Peter and I had spent a few minutes on back in February. We were not over keen at the time. Our pilot said it was the crocodile nesting season and the high patches of ground between tidal creeks were the perfect location for nests. The females ferociously protect their nests and the immediate area.

With time on our side, it wasn't hard to find Jack's refuge camp. On the entire eastern side of the ridge there was only one place where a swag could be rolled out on bare ground. It was exactly as Peter Wann described: a small area about four metres above the floodplain. Rocks had been thrown to one side to clear a space of about ten square metres. There was a balancing boulder nearby, which Peter had also mentioned. In the wet season it would have been the best spot available, with a freshwater spring flowing along the base of the ridge. It was a bit puzzling Jack Camp didn't choose this site from the beginning. Either he thought is was too far from the hessian yard or thought the greater danger of a crocodile attack was an unnecessary risk. Dry now and full of cane grass, there was a waterhole near the ridge when Peter and I inspected the area. We had to walk through shallow water to reach the ridge as well.

Night comes suddenly in the tropics and Pat and I headed back before the long shadows sucked in the darkness and increased our exposure to crocodiles. I had to catch fish for dinner too. As they had never been targeted before, it took little skill to catch a half-kilogram bream. A tiny piece of dried apricot on the hook and a single hand cast. The slowest part of the job was the gutting and scaling.

On the way back from the mangroves I cut a bundle of dry reeds for our beds. With just a thin mat each, the rock was too hard. The reeds made all the difference and we were able to lie listening to the night chorus in reasonable comfort. Gina slithered around the camp for much of the night and Wally gathered up the scraps.

Next morning Pat and I set off again, but much more subdued this time. Pat had taken on board about fifty ticks the day before and she may have been slightly fevered. They were a small tick. Once they took a fill of blood most fell off and it was possibly better to let them do that. The ones I pulled off left a puncture in the skin which became more irritable than the ticks left alone.

The plan today was to skirt around to the east of the valley and work back to the creek where it disappeared into a deep gorge. Jack led the two boys up the valley to this gorge when out of desperation he tried to set off for Mount Hart.

I had hoped a wide belt of open woodland country would provide better walking, but it was covered in gibber rock, much of it loose. Pat had a nasty stumble and almost fainted when her knee struck one of the gibber rocks. We waited for a while, me thinking we must return to the camp. But Pat doesn't give in to pain. We pressed on and very soon we were in the blue grass again. There was no way round it short of climbing into the range. Within minutes the ticks were crawling over sleeves and trousers. Pat wore shorts. Also her knee was swelling rapidly. She finally announced she was going back to the camp. A passionate naturalist, I knew the decision was hard for her. The opportunity to tread some of the most virginal country on earth comes by less often than you can count on one hand. To return with her would have mortified her.

The entrance to the gorge was clothed in jungle. I had

ticks crawling over me like hundreds of tiny spiders. With ankle boots and gaiters, dressed as though I was ready for combat, I didn't expect many to reach my skin, but Pat would have been covered like a grape vine if she hadn't turned back. I didn't like the place much. It was brackish with most of the sunlight shut out. A bull crocodile uttered a deep-throated sound from well within the gorge. It's more of a rumble than anything else.

The gorge was about sixty metres deep and magnificently walled in by vertical red rock. The creek here was one continuous waterhole, more like a small river. Blue grass grew between the jungle strip and the rock wall. When cattle roamed this country unchecked, a gorge like this would have been eaten out and the jungle destroyed. This was probably the gorge Jack and the boys rode into one day.

It was only our third day, yet a routine had already developed. Nelson was back in Wally's shelter and Pat was sitting under the paperbark reading, her knee bandaged. She looked up brightly when I emerged from the blue grass and said she had discovered a python about thirty metres from the camp. A steep, boulder-packed escarpment rose from the eastern side of the pools. Hobbling a little, Pat took me over. She had seen him about an hour ago and he hadn't moved much. About two metres of the reptile protruded from the rocks at the tail end, and another two metres higher up, a lot more of it appeared before I finally saw its head. Looking for something, he was unperturbed at our presence and went on smelling into the cracks and crevices, moving very slowly forward. It was difficult to estimate length. I said five metres and Pat didn't disagree. She said he was an olive python so we named him Olly and the waterhole after him. It was obviously his home. We didn't know the gender. There were a few scars towards his tail and thought male was appropriate – perhaps an old warrior. The common prey is the small scrub wallaby, seized when they come in for water. He seemed such a quiet boy with Pat stroking his midriff. The same wildlife expert who told me all about king browns informed me that the python's speed is faster than sight and their bite vicious and loaded with toxic germs. He would wait in ambush for a wallaby to come in for a drink, most likely on one of the rock shelves above the game pad between the rock and the water. The hapless wallaby finds itself in a coil, doomed. After the conversation I thought of Pat for a while – she wasn't a lot bigger than those wallabies. She laughed when I told her and didn't believe she'd been in any danger. I think Olly was Pat's highlight in the few days we had there.

A quart pot in the flames for tea and one of Paddy Pallin's gourmet dried food packages softened the tick pulling. I picked up another twenty-odd during the morning and Pat took on many more than that. We were not going to be able to do much more bush trekking. Both of us were taking antihistamine and it had its side effects as well.

Nelson walked over from the rock bar and reminded us the tide was nearing its full moon or spring tide peak. In the hot sun, with nowhere to take cover, we ate the instant meal from tin plates in about two minutes and carried our tea mugs to the croc hole.

The highest tide of all, due in twelve hours, wasn't going

to push water up over the bar. But we were staggered at the floating logs and debris; it was clearly the highest tide for months. Having witnessed a crocodile attack, I knew not to walk close to the edge. They are lightning-fast – snatching birds off low-hanging branches over the water is not uncommon. Much to Pat's concern, I had been into the mangroves the day before and found the lie-up hole. I didn't loiter. Took a good look at it and left.

I found an old pandanus palm and threw it in, deliberately making a splash. He was too cunning to show himself. A burst of big bubbles broke the surface, right next to the edge of the rock about two metres from where I stood.

'That's im,' Nelson burst. 'You watch out. He can see.'

Pat took a step forward and Nelson flung up his arm. She stepped back.

It was ten or fifteen minutes before the next lot of bubbles broke the surface. This time it was opposite Pat. The croc wasn't going to show himself and it was too hot to stand around any longer. Back at the camp we checked the tide chart and given it would be after midnight when the ultimate full tide surged into Walcott, the croc might seize the opportunity. I decided to try and eliminate the danger by feeding the bastard. Better black bream than one of us.

The big Kimberley tides drop quickly. Two metres deep at the top end, the croc hole emptied as though a plug had been pulled. It was like watching a bathtub of dirty water go down the drain. The entrance was a sinister looking mud channel, about three metres wide. While the tide was on the run I caught two black breams from the pandanus pool and lit a fire in the croc hole on a slab of rock. Exposed to the sun once again, the thin layer of black silt dried within minutes and in no time a fishy odour was drifting down to the croc's permanent hole in the mangroves. The return tide wouldn't push up the channel again until midnight. Nelson and Pat didn't approve of the plan, thinking the croc might have chosen to lie-up in the tall reeds and not cruise down the channel with the tide. Well, he had to cover fifteen metres over soft mud and I had to scale two metres onto the shelf. It was a split second my way. A racehorse at full gallop covers sixteen metres in a second, a croc at full charge perhaps twelve. You have to enjoy weighing the odds to take such risks.

The bait worked. A bit groggy from the antihistamine I fell asleep soon after dark and woke a couple of hours before the final thrust of the tide. I walked over with a torch and sure enough the croc's tracks were gouged into the mud and the fish were gone. We never saw him once and believe it or not we were disappointed, as any sense of danger diminishes with familiarity.

Next morning Pat looked like she had chicken pox with some angry sores double the normal size. My tick sores were innocuous to begin with, a delayed reaction. As each day passed, the itchiness intensified. Nelson avoided the blue grass and the ticks, but was hit with mosquitoes at night. It may have been because he hadn't swum. With one lung and some-times coughing convulsively, he couldn't risk it. He was our wood man. It was a huge effort for him, but I knew he wanted to make a contribution to the camp and never suggested he shouldn't. It was during one of his wood forays he found the gooseberry bushes. Peter Wann and Peter Camp collected the berries every day; it kept them and Jack Camp alive. Pat and I hadn't been able to find them. It had been an essential part of the survival story that wouldn't fall into place, like a missing piece of jigsaw. We saw wild passionfruit everywhere, also a small pleasantly flavoured fruit, but it contains hydro-cyanic acid and should be avoided.

We were nearly out of food and glad the helicopter was returning next day. It was to be six days, but on the way in I instructed the pilot to land at the mouth of the Isdell River so I could take some photos. The original plan was to walk over the salt plains from our camp. Landing there saved a day and it was just as well. I hadn't anticipated the extraordinary heat in August.

It was hard to sit in the heat of the sun and do nothing. You can only sit in the water for so long, submerged to the chin with a hat on. Also there was a mystery tantalising me. About every two hours a flock of brolgas circled overhead and vehemently voiced their disapproval of our occupation of the rock bar pools. Upstream about a kilometre, there was a waterhole ten times the size of these two pools with abundant rock surface for large birds. Why didn't they settle there while we occupied this one? In addition, Pat was concerned we were taking too may fish from the pandanus hole, so we decided to secure the evening catch at the big hole and try and find out what was inhibiting the brolgas. Although a vast sheet of water for this time of the year, it didn't look suitable for a saltwater crocodile.

It meant taking on more ticks, going up there. I didn't

think a few more would make much difference. Pat felt the same way. Perhaps tick fever was affecting our brains. Anyway we set off into the head high blue grass.

It was a long walk in the heat. Lateral watercourses were defined by narrow quartz outcrops. Elephant ear wattle pushed up through the cracks in the sandstone and sometimes the contrasts were irresistible and we would linger on the stone surface taking photographs. Most striking was the Kimberley heather with its pink–mauve flowers. Sometimes boabs, rock figs and Kimberley heather all grew in a bunch.

Down in the blue grass I had difficulty finding the waterhole. Much shorter than me, Pat was buried in the grass and soberly I thought about the ticks loading onto her. Suddenly we stepped out of the wall of grass onto the smooth sandstone. Right in front a freshwater crocodile was sun baking. I reached for the camera, but too late. Out of view another loud splash. I had developed an enormous respect for wildlife photographers. At every opportunity I was a half-second too slow.

Pat sat under a paperbark and I prepared to cast out. I glanced down into the water and couldn't believe how stealthy it was. A little freshwater croc was a metre away. He must have been staring up into my eyes, for the moment I saw him he flipped and deliberately made a loud splash. I cast out and as always the strike was in three to five seconds. The line had a low breaking strain and I always had to let the fish run. The bream tired quickly and as I drew the fish in the freshie followed it. He made no attempt to take it. At my feet he enacted the big splash again.

It was his waterhole and his fish. I felt even more guilty

when he hovered two metres out, the little eye hoods protruding above the water. Considering the size difference between us, he was very brave and almost heroic in defence of his hole. 'Can I have one more?' I said to him. 'I need three.' No reaction, just a furious little croc. The next cast was exciting. Never in my life have I caught a barramundi. It took off like a rocket and I desperately paid out the line. I had no hope of landing it. If I took the weight the line would break and the fish have a cruel hook stuck in its mouth. I've known many adrenalin charges in my life, but this was a new experience. The big long fish torpedoed along the surface, whipped back and flew right out of the water, the sun catching the underbelly. 'Throw the hook,' I hissed. 'I can't land you!' It lasted perhaps a minute and it did throw the hook. The next cast secured the one kilogram bream, I thanked the little croc and we left, the mystery solved. Brolgas need plenty of fresh water and in the height of the dry season there's very little of it. The freshwater crocs had no intention of sharing this hole with them.

Nelson's eyes lit up when we got back. He wasn't a gourmet tucker man and lived on the fish. The heat had exhausted us again and we sat on our reedy beds as the sun dipped and the moon rose. In Broome the tourists would be watching the 'Stairway to the sky,' when the iridescence of the full moon on the still waters of Roebuck Bay gave a spectacular display. Compared to here, Broome might have been another planet, though bathed by the same moon, for only Gina was moved by it. She seemed to be in quite a state, having found no mate. I'd hear her one side of the camp, then the other. Pat had no problem with it. A king brown had curled up in her bed once and bit her when she moved. 'Oh it was just a graze,' she said, 'a warning bite you might say. A shot of the wrong antivenin made me feel worse. Just don't move.'

We slept fitfully, disturbed by the night noises and the mosquitoes. When I woke I lay still. Was Gina there? Could I feel a weight that wasn't there when I drifted off?

The nights seemed to go on and on. Nelson's little fire at dawn prompted a sigh of relief every morning. 'Good morning Pat, did you sleep?'

'Not much, but I'm fine.' 'Not much' in her language was none at all. Pat didn't like fuss. Yesterday she looked like someone with chicken pox. Now she looked like a leopard. Some people can endure extreme discomfort and never utter a word.

Gum leaves in the quart pot for tea, one piece of toast each and we packed up. The helipad was to be the same place, Morgan instructed. We walked down through the mangroves and waited. The bowerbirds were busy and resented our appearance. It might have been mating time for them as well. They squawked at us, making it difficult to listen for the chopper. We could hear a vibration from far away and more than once stood up to look for the chopper. Then we realised what it was – the Kimberley tide. If you strained to listen you could hear a constant throb. It was as though the country had a vibrancy; a living phenomenon. With the run of the great tides, in or out every six hours, the land had its own pulse.

Long after the agreed time Pat tried to call the helicopter

base with her satellite phone but the battery was flat. In Derby everyone talked about the problem with satellite phones. You entered the bush with a freshly charged battery and a few days later the phone was flat. A solar energy booster is almost essential. She couldn't get a call out, so we waited another hour. After that it was too hot. Something had happened. A breakdown, pilot illness, a multitude of possibilities. We returned to Olly's waterhole.

Back at the camp I began to appreciate the hopelessness of Peter Wann's situation in 1971. In March and April the heat never wanes, day or night. They had nothing of any substance to eat and no hope of rescue. In comparison, our situation was nothing more than a minor annoyance. Still, it was time to get out. The punctures left by the ticks on Pat and me were becoming more and more irritated and if some became septic, itchiness would be the least of our problems. The dogs, too, were becoming bolder. On the morning we were due to leave a whole pack howled a stone throw from the camp. Any I saw didn't look like dingoes in the familiar form of the species. That they had a high infusion of native dingo was beyond doubt, but they were more like wild cattle dogs. When Munja was abandoned, it's rumoured, a few multi-breed dogs were left to fend for themselves.

An hour after dawn next morning we heard a chopper. It was a long way off, out towards the Harding Range. A tourist flight from Derby, we thought dispiritedly. The noise faded and we began to pack up again. All we could do was be at the helipad on time, 8 am, and hope. Nelson set off first and Pat about ten minutes later. I knew by the way she walked she didn't feel great, unaware that her languid movements may have alerted a large dog. I was washing a plate in the sandstone pool and he either hadn't seen me or I was of no interest, until I stood up quickly. He was between Olly's boulder escarpment and the water, twenty metres behind Pat. When I moved he spun around, jumped forward on straight front legs and snarled, an ugly snarl with bared yellow and black teeth. It was flat-eared with a deep chest and in colour a reddish brindle. It lost interest in Pat and jumped onto a boulder. It may have had no interest in Pat from the beginning, merely coming in for water but you have to be forever vigilant where animals have never seen man before, reducing us to a common level: another mammal, another source of food. The dog left, reluctantly, turning to look at me after each bound up the slope.

We carried our gear to the helipad and heard the chopper again, this time much closer, over towards the Munja ruins. It wasn't a tourist flight, much too long. There was no one else to be collected either. We were planted in one of the world's most uninhabited wildernesses. That chopper had come out to collect us and we couldn't image why it was so off course. Morgan wasn't the pilot – that much we could be sure of.

Covering the ground as quickly as I could, I went back to the camp to re-light the fire. Nelson told me to drop some spinifex on the flames; it was the best for dark smoke.

The smoke from the fire was exasperating, drifting straight into the paperbarks. It was only a gentle breeze, just enough to carry the smoke. The pilot wouldn't see it from any distance. I climbed up Olly's escarpment and from the highest boulder tried catching the sun on a tin plate Pat had given me. The reflection was too dull and would only catch someone's eye at short range. The smoke was our only chance. I broke off a couple of paperbark branches, gathered an armful of cane grass and tossed it all onto the flame, nearly smothering it all. A mass of smoke belched from the pile of charcoal and when flames burst through the brittle dry cane grass a cloud of whitish-grey smoke rose into the paperbarks. A useless colour, I thought, for trying to attract a pilot. But minutes later the chopper came straight in. The pilot circled the camp once and landed on the rock shelf between the rock bar and the sandstone. His name was Pat. He said he saw what looked liked valley mist and knew there's no such thing on a dry day in the King Leopolds. It had to be smoke! He was down to his last five minutes of fuel before he would have been forced to return to Derby and declare us missing.

With the satellite phone flat, the helicopter company couldn't call us to explain the situation. Morgan had been injured in a maintenance accident and sent to Perth. Only he knew where we were. The coincidences of life never cease to amaze me. According to Peter Wann, when they were stranded at Walcott Inlet, only one person knew where they were.

I put the fire out and we flew back to Derby and spent the next three weeks recovering from the ticks. For the first week, sleep was not possible until thoroughly exhausted. Perhaps the ticks will protect one of the last pristine regions left on earth. It wasn't a one-off experience. A group trekking in the Prince Regent area in 2003 was exposed to them for two weeks and some walkers became so ill they had to be rescued.

Peter Wann couldn't recall a problem with grass ticks in 1971. Only the larger kangaroo ticks, which remain on the ground. It appears heavy infestation of the blue grass is a seasonal condition and the presence of large numbers of cattle may have considerably altered the ecology of the region from the 1920s until about 1980.

APPENDIX I

ALEXANDER FORREST NEAR WALCOTT INLET, 1879

THE FIRST WHITE explorer to enter the country west of the Victoria River in the Northern Territory and east of King Sound in Western Australia was Alexander Forrest. His lavish and effective report to the Western Australian government resulted in rapid white occupation of the Ord and Fitzroy river basins in the 1880s. The Durack family, based near Goulburn in New South Wales, in particular, were quick to respond to the widely circulated report of unclaimed savanna grasslands far superior to the settled regions of southern Western Australia. Unfortunately Forrest had only observed the country in a very rare 'fresh' spring season, when rain fell throughout the normally dry months.

There is an interesting twist to the Forrest expedition. His self-imposed mission was to cross the King Leopold Range, find the Glenelg River which George Grey had discovered in 1838, proceed north to the Prince Regent River and from there trek east across more than 300 miles of unexplored territory to the Victoria River in the Northern Territory. In

1855, explorer Augustus Gregory had disembarked on the eastern shore of the Victoria and explored the northern savanna country all the way to the Great Divide of Queensland. So if you think of the map of Australia as a giant jigsaw puzzle, the country between King Sound in Western Australia and the Victoria River in the Northern Territory was the sole missing piece in 1879.

Forrest failed to cross the King Leopolds, losing a third of his horses in the struggle. When he retreated from the range and trekked east, he was driven by nothing more than survival. His desperate dash, often hampered by sick and half-starved men, landed the expedition in the Ord River country which eighty years later was dammed and converted into the most significant irrigation region in northern Australia. Had Forrest crossed the King Leopolds he would have reached Cambridge Gulf, and probably hugged the coast all the way to Darwin, missing out on discovering the most fertile river country in Western Australia.

The following is an account of Forrest's struggle to try and cross the King Leopolds between Yule Entrance, where the range terminates abruptly into the sea, and the Isdell River: exactly the same location where Jack Camp crossed the Leopolds. It all began with a letter to the Commissioner of Crown Lands for Western Australia, dated 8 April 1878 (reproduced p. 246).

SIR,   Perth, 8th April, 1878

As directed by His Excellency the Governor, I beg to submit for his consideration the following outline of the proposed expedition to the North portion of the Colony, which I am anxious to undertake after finishing the survey at the North-West.

1st. The expedition to start at the De Grey River, on or about 1st February, 1879, to explore the whole of the country seaward of the watershed of rivers running into the North Coast, as far as the Victoria River, and thence onto Port Darwin.

2nd. The party should consist of six whites and two native assistants, well armed and fully equipped for six months. The horses and provisions could, I believe, be procured from the settlers, whilst if the equipments of the present survey party were placed at my disposal, the cost would be very much lessened.

3rd. The party should have the services of a Geologist and Botanist, and I believe the latter would readily be supplied by Baron Von Mueller without cost. It is well known that gold is found all along the North Coast of Australia.

4th. The total cost of the expedition proposed will not I believe exceed £800, and such a small sum would be as nothing compared to the information that would be obtained; as, for instance, the examination of the Fitzroy and other large rivers on the North Coast, which would speedily lead to their occupation, whilst the magnificent timber said to exist would be quickly utilized, not mentioning the founding of a settlement for the culture of tropical plants, fruits &c.

5th. If entrusted with the command, you may rest assured that I will do all I can to successfully carry out the service. Thanking you for your interest and support towards the proposed exploration,

                                        I have, &c.

                                        ALEX. FORREST.

The Honorable M. Fraser, Commissioner of Crown Lands, &c., &c., Perth.

Disembarking from the schooner *Amy* at the little pearling village of Cossack, Alexander Forrest and his colleagues proceeded to the De Grey Station after collecting a number of horses made available by pastoralists who lived inland from Cossack. Forrest had acquired the horses by correspondence before leaving Fremantle. He had also arranged for supplies and equipment to be offloaded from the *Amy* at Condon, the sea port for De Grey.

On 25 February Forrest left for Beagle Bay, nearly 500 miles to the northeast in a direct line. Apart from Roebuck Bay Station, Forrest knew there were no settlements beyond the De Grey district. After riding for 375 miles he was appalled to find Roebuck Bay abandoned and burnt to the ground. They hastened on to the pearling port of Beagle Bay and there were overwhelmed by the Aboriginal hospitality. The coastal tribes in the Cape Leveque area had become accustomed to the pearling fleets and the white captains of the various vessels shrewdly respected the indigenous people. It was long before blackbirding began in this region. The expedition members were presented with more fish than they could eat and at night were entertained with corroborees. When the expedition departed, several warriors elected to be guides as far as the Fitzroy River.

Forrest's immediate mission was to follow the Fitzroy to its source and ride north to the Glenelg River. The west Kimberley was unexplored territory. Mariners by this time had sighted a mystery entrance, but no charts had been drawn and officially the Perth colony was unaware of the existence of Walcott Inlet and the rivers which flowed into it. The lack of specific intelligence on this section of the Western Australian coast was to prove most unfortunate for Forrest. The Glenelg is a minor river, shorter in length than some creeks marked on the map and today is of little significance.

Forrest proceeded along the Fitzroy on the tail of a very wet season. He recorded in his diary that the river plains would carry more cattle and sheep than the rest of the colony put together. At Geikie Gorge he was forced to leave the security of the river and trek in northwesterly direction, towards what he expected to be the Glenelg River. On the way he named the Oscar Range, after the King of Sweden who took a great interest in British exploration, then on 6 June the expedition came up against an imposing and impenetrable range which Forrest named the King Leopolds, after the King of Belgium who was also interested in exploration. The kings of Europe received considerable acknowledgement as Alexander Forrest advanced into unexplored country.

Trekking through the rugged foothills of the King Leopolds, the explorers encountered a land very different from anything they had seen since De Grey. The country was stony, jagged and hard. Numerous fast-flowing streams constantly impeded their progress. The horses rapidly tired and the stones sprung their shoes. One had to be shot and another left behind. Some of the men, too, were ill, one from malaria and another plagued by unremitting headaches, probably sunstroke. Forrest suffered from an eye condition known as sandy blight and sometimes the glare off the rock was so intense he was forced to call a halt.

After losing another horse near the present day Mount

Hart, the party approached the slopes of Mount Humbert, which Forrest named after the King of Italy, on 14 June. From the summit he observed a significant watershed and assumed it was the Glenelg. It was in fact the Isdell.

The next day the expedition camped about four miles upstream from Jack Camp's Humbert Creek camp. Forrest recorded that the country was covered in loose stone and they had difficulty finding a suitable place to hobble out the horses and set up camp. He climbed a prominent peak nearby, high enough to scan the country to the northwest, and saw an expansive spread of water which he thought must be an inland sea. It was Secure Bay, which from the air looks just as Forrest described it: an inland sea.

Pushing west, Forrest drove the horses through the coastal mangroves to a point where the cliffs extended out into a bay. Unable to continue, he climbed to the summit of a range with his Aboriginal guide Tommy Pierre. He recorded a magnificent view in every direction, observing Collier Bay to the north and his binoculars brought up a deep gorge not far to the northwest which he thought was a passage through the main range to the northern Kimberley.

The men rested for a couple of days close to a waterfall, catching fish out of the freshwater creeks, and those stricken with fever or sandy blight had some respite. When Forrest marshalled them again for action he attempted to put the horses through several tight gorges, resulting in the first serious blunder of the expedition. Instead of appreciating the impossibility of trying to cross a range carved like a fortress out of dolomite sandstone with footsore horses, he ordered the party to ascend a long steep pitch to a high, mesa-like plateau. Two more horses were abandoned, a grim decision for any nineteenth century land expedition with no base camp to fall back on. Without horses to carry vital rations, expeditions faced perilous consequences.

Upon reaching the comparatively level terrain of the plateau, Forrest doggedly searched for a route to the beckoning gap in the range. The plateau was bisected by gorges dropping away vertically from the top and refusing to yield he directed a dangerous descent to the northern shore of Secure Bay. He was elated at having reached the shores of the 'inland sea' and remarked on the splendid waterfalls coming off the range. The men caught more fish, this time directly from the tidal waters of the bay, and the camp that night was the best since the Fitzroy River. Forrest was in a jubilant mood, firing off a volley of shots. He firmly believed the gap in the range, now only a few miles away, was the key to the Glenelg River and beyond.

The euphoria didn't last long. Cliffs plunging into the bay blocked the way. Abandoning his quest for a northwest passage to the unexplored northern Kimberley, Forrest put the horses to another steep climb back to the plateau.

The situation was now quite serious. One man was down with high fever and Forrest's brother was delirious. The horses were exhausted and becoming emaciated. Forrest called a meeting to discuss the party's predicament and it was jointly decided to try and work across the rocky surface of the plateau in an easterly direction, following the summit of the main range. Down five horses, they buried packsaddles, saddlebags, water drums and any inessential gear. At this point Forrest took a reading from his sextant and upon checking George Grey's sextant reading made in 1838 he discovered he was forty miles south of the Glenelg. Examination of current maps demonstrates absolute accuracy of the two explorers, which is remarkable considering the privations and ordeals both endured.

Forced to negotiate numerous streams, most of which were carved into the plateau with vertical edges; the horses were soon too exhausted to travel. One horse had begun to walk in circles, colliding with trees and boulders. It soon disappeared over a cliff. It may have been the first horse to die from eating the poisonous walkabout plant, which only grows in the Kimberley tablelands and nearby coastal plains.

The expedition's plight worsened when fifty Aboriginal warriors appeared, each carrying bundles of spears: The white men quickly armed themselves. By the 1870s, indigenous people in every pocket of the country knew about firearms. If they hadn't actually seen them, they'd heard the rumours spread from other tribes. They backed off in this instance, prompted by Forrest firing his revolver at a tree. But until the expedition left the area they stayed close by, unnerving Forrest and his men. Forrest recorded the country could not have been more alien to European occupation, yet the natives had adapted to the harsh environment and were in considerable numbers.

Forrest found himself trapped on a high plateau in the heart of the King Leopold Range. Cliffs blocked a retreat to the south into the Humbert Creek valley and the horses were too weak to return to Secure Bay, back through a tangle of shallow gorges and steep cuttings in the hard sandstone surface. Another horse had been lost in the struggle to reach the high crest of the plateau.

In his diary, Forrest records his concern about the constant presence of the Aboriginal warriors, who were becoming bolder by the day. He knew he had to get out of their country as quickly as possible and, after three days of trekking into dead-ends, he set off on foot with Tommy Pierre to try and find a route off the plateau. The remainder of the party took up a defensive position and waited. Taking one horse at a time, they were able to water the horses in a deep defile. The sick men were no better, exacerbating the situation.

No route was found and at daylight next day Forrest set off again with Arthur Hicks, heading for a high point in the range which he named Mount Hopeless, abandoning the European monarchs. They scrambled over rocks and climbed in and out of steep gullies for fourteen miles, running into vertical drop-offs in every direction. Faced with exhaustion, lack of water and the grim possibility of an overwhelming Aboriginal attack, Forrest realised he had to force his way down to the low country. The following day, with all hands that were able, he made a track down a very steep washout. It took most of the day to get the horses down, but there were no losses.

Back on the Humbert Creek plains, Forrest conceded defeat and recorded his bitter disappointment. He said he had never exerted himself so much in his whole life and the same could be said for his men. According to his post-expedition map, Forrest never saw Walcott Inlet.

Forrest estimated his supplies would last until Beagle Bay, where he knew he could count on fish from the local people. The problem was the 560 miles south from Beagle Bay to De Grey. To undertake that trek with worn-out horses and try to live off the land was suicide. He chose instead to push east to the new telegraph line between Darwin and Alice Springs, knowing there were frontier outposts staged along the line.

Having undertaken some relatively short packhorse treks, but of sufficient duration to know what horses can tolerate, I would have opted for Beagle Bay and waited for a pearling lugger, hopefully securing one of two options: either buy supplies from the pearlers or negotiate a passage to the port of Cossack. Forrest didn't know what lay ahead between the Fitzroy River watershed and the telegraph line, a distance of several hundred miles. He took a huge gamble and what happened is yet another story of one of the most determined and daring explorers in Australian history.

APPENDIX II

'JAPANESE INVASION', MUNJA, 1942

Based on a file held by British and United States Intelligence on the South West Pacific Region

IN THE DRY season of 1942, the Munja Government Aboriginal Station had a population of 700. Bush tucker is always scarce in the spring, leading up to the first monsoonal rains. During the wet months the Aborigines would go walkabout, enjoying the variety of bush fruits that matured as the season progressed. For the various clans throughout this region, Munja became a base camp.

The government supervising officer was Harold Reid, an ex-station overseer. Reid organised all the station activities, from growing peanuts to the slaughtering of cattle for meat. The peanuts were shipped out on the mission lugger from Port George to Derby, then loaded onto a freighter to Perth. The whole purpose of the new settlement was to encourage the surrounding tribes to enter the commercial world and become independent. The peanut plantations flourished at Munja and funds acquired from the trading were used to purchase provisions and materials not provided by the government. A capable manager and greatly respected by the clans,

Reid made the settlement almost self-sufficient with a large area under cultivation for tropical vegetables, irrigated from a nearby wetland. If it had not been for the pernicious advance of leprosy, which aroused so much fear among the clans and led to rapid family disintegration, Munja on the eastern tip of Walcott Inlet might have become a model of successful Aboriginal enterprise on their traditional lands.

In October 1942 Harold Reid found himself almost alone with his wife and young family, a nursing sister, a school teacher and a handful of faithful Aboriginal assistants. Everyone else had fled to the hills. It appeared that foreigners had landed on the coast at Doubtful Bay, a little more than twenty-five miles away. Japanese aircraft had flown over the settlement in recent weeks and Reid suspected an enemy landing. He didn't have a pedal radio transmitter and dispatched an Aboriginal runner to Mount House, ninety-four miles south-east of Munja. In a letter to the manager, Reid reported strange rumblings coming from Doubtful Bay, indicating the use of heavy machinery. He explained he was in no position to undertake a reconnaissance himself, with nothing more than an old Lee-Einfield rifle to counter any attack. In addition, those left at Munja were totally dependent on him. The Mount House manager radioed Army Headquarters in Darwin and waited for a reply before sending the runner back to Munja.

The situation in northern Australia was extremely tense. An invasion was considered imminent and the Operational Base Unit (OBU) had just been hastily formed in Darwin to mount a counteroffensive. Only a few weeks before Reid's message was sent on to Darwin, the OBU had instructed the Kalumburu mission to prepare for evacuation at short notice. The mission was only 187 miles north-east of Munja. If the Japanese landed, the mission people were to trek south along a bridle trail to Gibb River Station, which in the 1940s was the last settlement of any significance north of Mount House.

For Australia, 1942 was the lowest period of World War II. The Japanese had bombed Darwin and Broome and forced the withdrawal of most Australian units from Timor. From bases there, the Japanese had established air supremacy over the Kimberley region. However, following their defeat at the Coral Sea Battle in May 1942, their frontline was over-extended and, provided they didn't establish a base on the mainland, the Australian generals were confident the Japanese advance could be halted.

By radio transmitter, Mount House received a return message that a ground force would be mounted as soon as possible. There were no soldiers to spare in Darwin; the troops for the operation would proceed north from Perth. They would be men with minimal training, though under experienced officers. The Aboriginal runner returned to Munja with a letter for Harold Reid.

Major G. D. Mitchell was given command of the Munja fighting patrol, which comprised five officers, thirty soldiers and two Aboriginal guides from Mount House. Travelling in two light trucks from Perth, the patrol arrived at Mount House on 1 November. The next two weeks were spent breaking in wild bush donkeys to harness, which were cajoled into trap yards by the stockmen. The donkeys quickly settled down and Lieutenant Bayliss and five hand-picked men set off with the team towards Munja. The plan was for the donkeys to get used to walking in harness before the packs were loaded. Major Mitchell gave Bayliss five days to reach Old Beverley Springs before following in the trucks. Beyond the rendezvous stretched some of the most rugged country in Australia.

At Old Beverley Springs the donkeys were packed up and the unit trekked north-east towards the Synott Range, named by explorer Frank Hann nearly half a century before. The donkeys lugged the ammunition, cooking utensils, packs of bulk food and medical supplies. Each man carried twenty-pounds, including everything from a mosquito net to a hundred rounds of ammunition.

It was the hottest time of the year with the sun directly overhead. From midday onwards, storms rumbled across the ranges and at night lightning made sleep difficult. The first rain squalls from the impending wet had not arrived and surface water from the long dry season had contracted to stagnant pools. The unit bivouacked by a lagoon on the second night and the men drank the water without boiling it, resulting in every man going down with dysentery.

Some days later and considerably weakened by the illness, the men pressed on into a tangle of gorges and cliff lined escarpments. The early wet storms began to burst over the ranges, adding to their misery. The country had been burnt out during the dry and game was scarce. Towards evening the unit would split into small hunting patrols to secure kangaroo meat. The terrain was so broken and unpredictable a special drill was enforced upon each patrol, whether hunting or on reconnaissance. Each man was to carry extra water, take a compass, keep checking landmarks, rest up in the heat of the day and light signal fires at night if they became lost. During the six-day trek the men complained of scorpion bites, snakes curling up at night for the warmth and chronic fatigue from sleeplessness caused by the coruscating lightning at night.

On 28 November the officers led the way to the summit of the Edkins Range, overlooking Walcott Inlet. Coaxing the donkeys down 2000 feet to sea level was demanding enough, but nothing compared to the ordeal ahead. On the eastern shore of the inlet the chief Aboriginal guide sent a smoke signal for his counterparts at Munja. Almost immediately one of the Aborigines at Munja braved the crocodiles and swam over with a message from Harold Reid: 'Boat out of action. Cross on the first low tide after daylight. Crocs bad.'

The donkeys were hobbled out near a shady pandanus pool. Bayliss and the two guides from Mount House stayed behind to attend them. The rest of the men prepared themselves for the crossing. One soldier took a glance at the out running tide and declared a fire exchange with Japanese troops would be an anti-climax.

All the packs were fastened to a long rope, a few yards apart. By pulling on the rope, each man played a part in hauling the packs through the water. The packs were made from thick canvas and leather, and inside, everything was tightly wrapped in a waterproof ground sheet. They were buoyant in the water and all went well – until the tide turned. The Munja native swimmer, acting as guide over the main channel, shouted a warning and seconds later the first wave swamped the struggling men. They lost their footing and some men floundered, taking gulps of salt water. From the other side Reid saw the strife unfolding and, with four other men, plunged into the water to the rescue. Luckily the lead man on the rope had touched bottom and managed to hold on long enough for Reid and his men to seize the rope. Within seconds disaster was averted, all men struggling desperately in heat of 110°Fahrenheit.

Reid reported to Major Mitchell that the noise coming from Doubtful Bay had ceased the moment the fighting patrol appeared on the far shore of Walcott Inlet, which suggested that the settlement was under constant surveillance. Why it hadn't already been attacked was a mystery. He also reported food supplies were very low as the mission lugger from Port George having not appeared for some months. Prompted by the bleak news, Mitchell ordered his officers to immediately organise fishing excursions, including the collection of mud crabs. The bush tucker in the immediate area had already been depleted. The food in the packs was to be saved for the search and destroy patrols, when there would be no time to go fishing. Mitchell also wanted his troops to rest as much as possible for two days. He feared the worst. When the patrols filtered out towards Doubtful Bay he expected action against the enemy in appalling heat.

The next two days provided great experience for the men. Armed and always on alert, they followed the Aboriginal men to catch barramundi and turtles, collect yams and raid crocodile nests. All put together it was a bush tucker feast.

On the third day the unit was split into three fighting patrols and left Munja on foot for Doubtful Bay. There were no good maps available and each patrol set a different compass bearing in order to comb the whole area and search for enemy activity. Further north at Kalumbura enemy aircraft was being sighted most days, but Major Mitchell had no way of getting news. Had he known of this aircraft activity, he would have realised that the Japanese were more likely to stage a landing somewhere along the north Kimberley coast. While the patrols were away, the mission lugger arrived with two new pedal wirelesses, dispatched from Derby. Unfortunately when they were assembled, Reid discovered that vital parts were missing and both sets were inoperable.

In blistering heat, which was often followed by tropical downpours, the patrols spent a week combing the coastal ravines for a trace of enemy activity. Lieutenant Thomson discovered an ominous signal on the Walcott Inlet side, not far from Yule entrance. Black rocks had been stacked on a white saltpan. Thomson reported that only one king tide had been over the landmark, suggesting the construction was recent. The spot was perfect for a landing.

With no enemy sighted, Mitchell had to withdraw. An invasion somewhere along the coast was expected and fighting men needed to be based where they could be promptly moved to the frontline if an invasion occurred.

Mitchell was most impressed with Harold Reid. He left him 3000 rounds and several rifles for use in the event of an attack. He also gave Reid an army Luger and told him he would recommend a commission and the deployment of an infantry patrol, based at Munja. Mitchell proposed that Reid's command would include Kunmunja and Port George missions.

A mechanic among the troops managed to repair the engine of the small boat kept at Munja. It was used to meet the mission lugger, which was forced to anchor more than six miles from Munja except on the rare king tides when the lugger was able to sail to the settlement. With the boat operational Reid arranged for the unit to be ferried to the eastern side, where the donkeys were loaded again with much lighter packs.

On the climb from sea level the donkeys struggled under their modest loads and after each jump up they had to be given long spells to recover. It took two days to cross the Edkins Range in the searing heat, then, just as the unit entered the gorge country, a storm struck. Minor streams erupted into raging torrents. Donkeys were swept from their feet and sent spinning into backwaters. On several occasions the troops were forced to unload the packs in the water to save the donkeys. Much of the already depleted food supplies were lost in the torrid conditions and hunting for meat became impossible. Food was limited to survival rations only, but the men remained in good spirits, often remarking on the extraordinary beauty of the country. The unit finally plodded into Old Beverley Springs on 16 December, where the trucks had been left. They had trekked 300 miles of some of the most rugged terrain in Australia.

Back at Munja nothing had changed. Two days after the unit departed, the strange rumbling sounds from the direction of Doubtful Bay returned to haunt the little outpost. The Aboriginal clans remained in the hills and the trackers who ventured in from time to time, seeking tobacco and any flour Reid could spare, refused to go anywhere near the bay. Reid wanted to investigate himself now that he was adequately armed, but the women resisted vigorously, declaring they could not be left to defend the settlement.

Despite the fact that aggressive enemy activity was confined to the Kimberley north coast in December 1942, Mitchell reported to the OBU that a Japanese invasion at Walcott Inlet was imminent. He stated that the central channel of the inlet was deep enough to facilitate a battle fleet. In addition, it was the most protected waterway in north-western Australia with a full encirclement of steep hills and mountains. Upon the installment of anti-aircraft guns it would be an easy site to defend. The inlet could even accommodate a seaplane fleet. Under duress the local Aborigines might be forced to act as guides for an invasion force. The Japanese would have a secure base and be able to penetrate inland where Allied deployments were non-existent.

Mitchell's report was referred to the Allied General Headquarters for the South-west Pacific area. An extract from a letter written by the chief military liaison officer to Colonel N. F. Wellington on 4 March 1943 appears to discount the possibility of a Japanese landing at Walcott Inlet. Due to lack of communication, no one knew the alien activity in the Doubtful Bay area had resumed.

Those readers who do not know the area, the Kimberley, situated in the north-west of Western Australia, comprise some of our toughest country. As indicated in the report, sun and shade temperatures are high, add a high humidity range, and the resultant conditions are very bad. From Munja to Doubtful Bay, only the nomadic Aborigines know the gaps in the mountain ranges, as few white men have been there.

Clearly, the Australian military command didn't anticipate a Japanese landing at Walcott Inlet on the grounds of climate and terrain extremes. Troops reared in a cool to cold climate in the northern hemisphere would probably buckle like flies hit with insecticide at Munja, and contrary to Major Mitchell's claim, the enemy would never have sighted a single Aborigine. Under duress, Mitchell argued, the Aborigines would be forced to act as guides. It was a case of not understanding Aboriginal people in general and the loyalty and great respect for Harold Reid of the Munja community.

The mysterious activities on the shores of Doubtful Bay needed explanation and nearly twenty years passed before the true story emerged. According to Robert Dowling, whose father owned Panter Downs for about twelve years, there was an Aboriginal elder called Old Johnnie who not only claimed to know the whole story, but actually provided fish and native foods to an outfit of Chinese miners who took advantage of the war situation to land on the Australian coast at Doubtful Bay. With gifts, such as axes and knives, the miners secured the favour of at least one clan of the Worrorra or Yawijibaya people.

In that part of the Kimberley, between Walcott Inlet and the Prince Regent River, the existence of silver was no secret. Station owner Frank Lacey found a whole nugget near what is called the 'jumpup' and traces of the precious metal were frequently spotted along creek beds. The Chinese evidently located a silver vein between the high and low tide mark somewhere along the shore of Doubtful Bay. To access the ore they regularly blasted the shelf. In Old Johnnie's own words 'Bang bangs' and he was known to become quite animated when talking about them, like a boy might when relating a fire-cracker story.

At that time there was no shipping in the area so the miners clearly felt they could operate with impunity. To handle the fickle tides and keep their lugger stable, the Chinese entered Walcott Inlet with tons of rice acting as ballast. When the ore was ready to load, the rice was dumped.

Evidently caught in a tide rip, a lugger was wrecked on a shallow reef in Doubtful Bay soon after the war. The fate of the crew is unknown. To the astonishment of those who discovered the wreck, the remains of the ballast contained shattered rock impregnated with silver fragments. The exact location of the Chinese mine remains a mystery to the present day.

In the event, Major Mitchell and Harold Reid's conclusions proved to be anything but fanciful. On 27 September 1943, twenty-two Japanese fighter planes bombed and wiped out Drysdale Mission Station, killing a Roman Catholic priest and five Aboriginal children. The mission was only 160 miles from Munja. However, Drysdale Mission was close to a strategic aerodrome that the Allies had begun to use in earnest by April 1943, knowing the Japanese had four divisions poised for an invasion. Flight Lieutenant F. L. Bragg inspected the bush airstrip from horseback in mid-March and by early April Allied bombers were taking off to attack Japanese positions in Timor. Why the Japanese pilots didn't destroy the airport and the fuel dump, instead of a defenceless mission, is not clear. Perhaps instilling fear was the prime objective.

APPENDIX III

A SHORT NOTE ABOUT CROCODILES

WHILE RESEARCHING THIS story it became clear that crocodiles were not facing extinction in the Kimberley in the 1960s and '70s. At the age of eight, Robert Dowling, whose father owned Panter Downs in the 1950s and '60s, witnessed an extraordinary and frightening scene on the Sale River in the early 1960s. His father Bob had set up a permanent camp on the north side and had a generator to power a deep freeze. They needed meat and a mob of cattle were spotted on the opposite bank. Launching a twelve-foot rowing boat, the men crossed the river and shot one. Robert was allowed to go for the ride and he recalled that the whole beast was quartered and loaded onto the boat. The oarsmen hadn't gone forty yards when the first croc surfaced. The boat was so low in the stern that to avert the danger, one of the men threw the croc a chunk of meat, thinking that might satisfy it, but next thing there were five, then ten, then God knows how many. The men panicked, and by the time they reached the shore there was only enough meat for dinner. Disgusted, Bob Dowling shut down the generator.

In 1964 Robert was again camped with his father, this time at Munja. The homestead burnt down in 1957 so Bob Dowling had erected a large ex-army tent. They were mustering cattle at the time. Bob had a cattle dog and one night it barked so furiously he got up to discover a huge crocodile approaching the makeshift kennel. He let the dog off the chain, hunted the croc back into the water and went back to bed. An hour later the dog's barking wildly, backing into the tent. By the time Bob found his rifle the croc's head was through the tent entrance.

'You know,' Robert said, telling me the story. 'Those crocs love dogs. Sooner eat a dog than anything.'

Bob Dowling shot it with its head in the tent. It measured nineteen feet (six metres) and the vehicle they had couldn't pull the carcass. They had to pack up and shift camp instead.

'Next time the bastard can have the dog,' growled Bob Dowling. 'In fact, the crocs can have Munja.'

Well may he say it, for today there is nothing at Munja but monster crocs.

ACKNOWLEDGEMENTS

Katie Stackhouse: I want to thank my publisher for her encouragement and support to undertake this difficult project. Katie is an astute editor, always ready to offer a suggestion.

Peter Wann: without Peter's contribution this book could not have been written. Peter spent hours with me going over the details, day after day. In February 2005 he flew out to Walcott Inlet with me in a helicopter and found the campsite. It was a most exciting day.

Pat Lowe: a special thanks to Pat for helping me track down people who retained a few memories from the early 1970s in the west Kimberley. In a story like this some of the detail has to be almost chiselled out of the recalcitrant landscape. Pat also provided valuable ecological knowledge.

Sam Lovell: provided me with an overview of the country. The rivers, the mountains, where the wild cattle once ran and where the crocs lurked. An incredibly modest man, Sam would not agree, but it's likely no one alive knows the Walcott Inlet region as well as Sam.

Malcolm Douglas: a visit to Broome is incomplete without a tour of Malcolm's Broome Crocodile Park. Despite a few close encounters with crocs, I know little about the reptile and I am grateful to Malcolm for taking the time to discuss some of the characteristics of these magnificent creatures.

Robert Dowling: worked on Panter downs in the late 1960s when his father still owned it. His observation of station life during that era provided a clear picture of the culture at the time and the problems and frustrations owners had to contend with.

Sylvia Wann: serves the best cup of tea in Derby. I am not sure whether it's her stories from the old days in the Kimberley or the tea, but I can't wait to get back to Derby for another cuppa with Sylvia. Sylvia was the wife of Allan Wann – Peter's uncle.

Anthea Henwood: was always able to provide a helicopter when I needed it and for anyone who wishes to travel that way, no one knows the country from the air better than Anthea.

Tony Gavranich: provided local knowledge on the Walcott Inlet region. Few have actually fought off a crocodile to save another man and, true to the nature of most outback bushman, Tony would scoff at the suggestion he is in anyway a bush hero. The richness of Derby as a town is characters like Tony.

Kingsley Miller: district wildlife officer, was always helpful when I wanted details about mammals or reptiles. Those olive pythons look sleepy enough, he said to me one day, but just remember, they kill and swallow wallabies.

The staff at the Macquarie Library Dubbo were fantastic in procuring rare diaries and books.

A special thanks to Jennifer Ninyette, project officer re Kimberley Region Land Asset Management Services, for helping me clear up the title issues on land adjacent to Walcott Inlet. Without such clarification, this story would not have a solid and indisputable foundation.

A considerable effort was made by Senior Archivist David Whiteford, from the JS Battye library in Perth, to provide old articles on Cyclone Mavis. Once again, thank you.

Special acknowledgement: as has been the case in previous publications, my wife, Sal, provided tremendous help with her typing skills, receiving and responding to emails and always enthusiastic about our next adventure. Fiction is a story in someone's mind. Non-fiction is real, historic and unforgiving. It's a difficult job to undertake without a lot of support.

Other books by Mike Keenan

THE HORSES TOO ARE GONE

The drought had reached crisis point. Cattle farmer Mike Keenan decided there was only one solution: he would have to get his starving cattle – and his beloved horses – to greener pastures north of the border. But when he finally got there he found his troubles had only just begun. South-west Queensland seemed like a modern-day Wild West and, as Keenan moved his cattle along the traditional droving routes in search of long-term pasture, he had to match wits with a host of characters – as well as Nature herself.

The Horses Too Are Gone is the true story of Keenan's struggle to survive against mounting odds, and it's an action-packed adventure that rivals any fiction. A fresh voice from the Bush, Mike Keenan writes with a deep passion and knowledge of Australian life on the land, tinged with a sadness and nostalgia for a way of life that is under threat. *The Horses Too Are Gone* will strike a chord with all Australians.

ISBN 1 86325 167 6

WILD HORSES DON'T SWIM

Australian farmer Mike Keenan's first book, a true story of battling drought to save his cattle and his farm, touched the hearts and minds of readers all over Australia. Now Mike takes us into the magnificent wilderness of the west Kimberley in a personal quest to highlight the problems of this beautiful but troubled region.

The Fitzroy River – one of the last great rivers still flowing freely to the sea – is the lifeblood of the region, so when Mike learned of plans to dam it to allow cotton-growing, he was horrified. A dam could cause an environmental disaster on a horrific scale.

With the help of the local Bunuba people, fierce opponents of the dam which threatened their homeland and sacred sites, Mike organised a horseback trek to explore the area and discover what was at stake. What he found was a paradise of unique plants, pristine rivers and dramatic gorges.

In *Wild Horses Don't Swim*, we join Mike, his intrepid wife, Sal, and their Bunuba friends in an action-packed adventure as they dodge wild bulls, ford raging torrents, brave bushfires and climb sheer cliffs – searching for the legendary rock art that might be lost forever.

'A stunning account of a noble quest to save a unique part of Australia from those with small minds but large chequebooks.'
The Gold Coast Bulletin

ISBN 1 86325 183 9

IN SEARCH OF A WILD BRUMBY

'I think it was one of the scariest half-minutes of my life . . . In *The Man from Snowy River*, one rider gallops headlong down a mountainside to turn the wild herd. All my life I'd thought it was poetic licence – until now.'

When Mike Keenan decided to search for a brumby to add to his dwindling stock of farm horses, he never dreamed he'd find himself crashing down a mountain in classic *Man from Snowy River* style. But he lived to tell the tale – and the result is both an adventure story and a compelling portrait of the life and troubled times of the Australian brumby, and of the mountain people who live alongside them.

Brumbies hold a special place in the hearts of many Australians, reared on Banjo Paterson's epic poem and Elyne Mitchell's *Silver Brumby* novels, and the news of the slaughter of more than 500 in Guy Fawkes National Park caused public outrage. But what does the future hold for the brumbies that have roamed the Snowy Mountains and other wilderness areas for more than 150 years? Are they part of our unique heritage, or merely feral creatures threatening delicate ecosystems?

As his quest for a brumby of his own is overtaken by his growing interest in their plight, Mike shares campfires and rollicking yarns with a host of bush characters who could have stepped straight out of Banjo's poem – and pursues the elusive wild horses through the snows, mists and treacherous bogs of the spectacular Snowy Mountains landscape.

ISBN 1 86325 319 X

ABOUT THE AUTHOR

There's little Mike Keenan hasn't experienced when it comes to writing with authority about outback Australia. A fifth-generation farmer born during WWII and reared on a western NSW sheep station, he has lived among the people of the Australian bush for more than fifty years. He has observed the despair, the starkness, the humour and the brief glimmers of hope, all set against the backdrop of a harsh landscape. With his true stories from the bush, Keenan always aspires to awaken a consciousness of identity and the realisation that Australia is a land which doesn't fit well with the fast pace, indifference to the environment and heedless consumerism of modern urban life.

Last Horse Standing is Mike Keenan's fourth book. His first, *The Horses Too Are Gone*, the true story of his fight to save his cattle and his property, Myall Plains, from drought, struck a chord with readers all over Australia and has sold over 36,000 copies since it was first published.

Now living in Blackheath in the Blue Mountains of NSW, Mike is working on another book about his life at Myall Plains.

Visit Mike's website for more information about Mike Keenan and his books: www.michaelkeenan.com.au